When Tomorrow Comes

Julie Ellis titles available from
Severn House Large Print

Another Eden
The Hampton Passion
Single Mother
A Town Named Paradise

When Tomorrow Comes

Julie Ellis

Severn House Large Print
London & New York

8152083

This first large print edition published in Great Britain 2003 by
SEVERN HOUSE LARGE PRINT BOOKS LTD of
9-15, High Street, Sutton, Surrey, SM1 1DF.
First world regular print edition published 2003 by
Severn House Publishers, London and New York.
This first large print edition published in the USA 2004 by
SEVERN HOUSE PUBLISHERS INC., of
595 Madison Avenue, New York, NY 10022.

British Library Cataloguing in Publication Data

Ellis, Julie, 1933 -
    When tomorrow comes - Large print ed.
    1.   Displaced homemakers - New York (State) - New York - Fiction
    2.   Large type books
    I.   Title
    813.5'4 [F]

    ISBN 0-7278-7320-2

Except where actual historical events and characters are being described for the storyline of this novel, all situations in this publication are fictitious and any resemblance to living persons is purely coincidental.

Printed and bound in Great Britain by
MPG Books Ltd, Bodmin, Cornwall.

For Joan Paul,
a very special lady—with love

One

Still a pretty woman despite the twenty pounds she'd added to her small frame through the years and the streaks of grey that dulled her honey-colored hair, Helen Avery completed her four-hour stint as a volunteer at the Friends of the Library thrift shop and headed for her SUV, parked in the area behind the shop. Tonight, she promised herself, she'd sit down and focus on the guest list for their dinner party at the end of the month. Paul was showing little interest in the party, she remembered. Unusual for him. But he preferred their guest list to consist of what he called "good business contacts." The guest list of their silver wedding anniversary party should consist of long-time friends—not business associates.

The last Sunday of October 1999 would be their twenty-fifth wedding anniversary. Each time she remembered this, she marveled at the passage of time. She'd call Gerry—her closest friend of over twenty years, though they didn't see each other as often as they'd like—and invite her up for the weekend. She'd like to have Deedee and Zach up from New York—but they were both so involved in their lives down there.

Paul had seemed shocked when she'd reminded him last week that their anniversary was coming up. At moments she was astonished to realize she was forty-six, Paul a year older. They'd married straight out of college. His mother had been horrified until they assured her he meant to go on to law school. His mother paid his tuition at NYU Law. She went to work to support them.

Paul had been so ambitious. He still was—always looking for something better. In jobs, houses, vacations. Right now she was uneasy about his insisting that this winter they buy a house out in the Hamptons. This was not the time, instinct told her, when prices were spiraling to astonishing heights.

Once—shortly before she died—Paul's mother had said, grudgingly: "You know, Helen, you have a much sharper business mind than Paul. He lives up in the clouds too often."

But they'd done well, she congratulated herself. Two great kids, a beautiful house—that seemed strangely empty with Deedee out of college and working as an analyst at a top investment banking firm, and Zachary starting his sophomore year at Columbia.

Approaching their colonial cape that sat elegantly above a terraced acre, Helen was surprised to see Paul's BMW parked in the driveway. He never arrived home before eight—often later. Fighting unease, she parked beside the BMW, hurried into the house. She heard the den TV blaring as she opened the door. Of course, he'd be surfing the TV in search of baseball news. Even in the direst circumstances he'd be following the baseball season.

"Paul?" she called from the foyer. Instantly the TV was turned off.

"Helen, come into the den," he yelled back. A strained quality in his voice warned her of a problem. He wasn't leaving Edmund & Jackson, was he? This was his fourth law firm in the past twenty-two years. It was time to stay put.

"You're home early." She tried to sound casual.

Paul was staring out on the terrace. He swung about to face her. He looked younger than his age, she thought in a corner of her mind. He rarely missed a day at his health club down in the city, watched his weight. Not a touch of gray in his dark hair.

"We need to talk," he said brusquely.

"All right—" She lowered herself in a lounge chair. At intervals Paul made this brief statement. Usually it meant he was about to make a job move. She would be nervous—but Paul had a way, her late mother-in-law used to say, of landing on velvet.

He swung around to face her. "We have to sell the house."

"Paul, it's a beautiful house," she protested. They'd been here almost six years—longer than in any house. "Why should we sell? We—"

"You don't understand," he broke in impatiently. "I'm in deep trouble. The damn stock market!"

Helen was bewildered. Her knowledge of the stock market was limited, but Paul always boasted about their portfolio. "Solid, blue chip stocks."

"What about the stock market?" She tried for calm. "The economy's great—better than it's been in many years."

"You don't understand—I've had margin calls like crazy. I—"

"I thought buying on margin was illegal." She was unnerved. "Ever since the 1929 crash—"

"Forget that," he said impatiently. "Today you borrow from your broker—and when the stocks drop too low, they call for cover. I tried to save our portfolio—I got into deep shit with the loan sharks."

"You borrowed from loan sharks?" She gaped at him in disbelief. Only desperate people on the fringe did that—she'd thought.

"Oh God, Helen! You've always been so

penny ante. I looked around and saw all these kids— Deedee's age—making millions almost overnight. I wanted to do what was best for us—I know this is the age of technology. I—" He gestured despairingly.

Helen was all at once cold. "You sold our blue chip stocks and put the money into IPOs?" She had a vague knowledge of this latest phenomenon from remarks of Paul's in the past year.

"They all sounded so great! My damn broker!" He pounced on a scapegoat. "He had tips that made them appear sure winners. We should be multimillionaires within two years."

"On paper," she emphasized. *But what does he mean—"we have to sell the house?"*

"It looked great. I borrowed on our charge plates, maxed out. Then to save our hides— I thought—I took out a second mortgage on the house. From a loan shark group. They're demanding payment now—"

"I didn't sign any second mortgage papers." She stared at him in disbelief.

"I—I signed for you. I didn't want you to worry. I was sure everything would work out. I didn't expect these companies to fold!" He took a deep, anguished breath. "We have to sell the house to pay off the loan sharks. With the real estate market so healthy, we'll end up with a few thousand each to start up again."

11

What does he mean—a few thousand each?
"Paul, how could you sign for me?" She was dizzy with shock. "That isn't legal!"

"Don't give me that crap! You're going to throw me into jail, disgrace the kids?" he demanded. "I made a mistake. I thought we were going to have millions."

"What about asking for a loan from the firm?" she asked unsteadily. "That would—"

"I've left the firm," he told her. "I have something lined up in Silicon Valley."

"When did you leave the firm?"

"Today." *Did he leave or was he fired?* "I was getting nowhere. They showed no appreciation for all the business I brought in. It was time to move on. So it'll be like starting all over again."

"But Silicon Valley?" Her head was reeling.

"I'm fucking tired of this rat-race. The need for the big house, the fancy cars, Ivy League colleges for the kids." *All the things he had wanted.* "I want a fresh start." He paused, his eyes suddenly opaque. "Alone."

Helen tried to assimilate what he was saying. "What do you mean?"

"Look, let's be honest. Our marriage has been dead for years. Let's make this a clean break. I'll talk to Jeff Madison," the family lawyer, "—he'll arrange a civilized divorce. Low keyed, inexpensive. Whatever's left

12

when we pay off the two mortgages, we'll split down the middle. You go your way—I'll go mine."

Helen stared into space. Her face drained of color. *This isn't happening. It's unreal. Divorce happens to other women—I never expected it to happen to me. But I mustn't fall apart.*

"What about Zach's college?" She contrived to keep her voice even. "Will you be able to handle that with your new job?" The job he'd never bothered even to mention to her. *Does he have a new job—or is he grandstanding?*

"I'll have a lot of expenses settling in out there." He was evasive. "Zach may have to switch to a state college, go out for college loans. Hell, other kids do it."

"He'll be so upset—"

"How do you think I feel?" Paul flared. "Such bitchy luck!" He turned to stare out onto the terrace again. "At least, the real estate market is strong—we'll be able to sell fast. At a profit. But we can't turn down any reasonable offer," he warned. "Get on the phone with the brokers first thing tomorrow morning. I want the closing to go through before I head west. The new firm will wait a few weeks for me—but no longer than that."

"I'll call the brokers first thing in the morning," Helen said. *Will I wake up later and discover this is an awful nightmare?*

13

Paul glanced at his watch. "I spoke with Jeff earlier. I have to meet him in twenty minutes. We'll grab dinner somewhere in his neighborhood." Jeff lived two communities away. "I'd better run." He cleared his throat —a gesture that revealed his unease. "I'll ask Jeff to recommend a real estate lawyer. The guy we used when we closed on this house moved to Texas three years ago."

Helen sat motionless in her chair. She heard the front door open and close, then moments later the engine of the BMW starting up. Paul was on his way to discuss their divorce. Her silver-wedding anniversary gift.

Dinner preparations forgotten, she left the den, went upstairs to the master bedroom. Paul's voice echoing in her mind. *"I'm fucking tired of this rat race. I want a fresh start. Alone."* Would he be alone? Gerry said when a husband asked for a divorce after a lot of years of marriage there was almost always some young replacement in the wings. Had Paul been carrying on an affair she never knew about?

No, she thrust this aside. He was panicking over the financial situation. How could he have been so stupid? But it had been that obsessive passion of his for money. Lots of it.

His voice ricocheted in her mind again: *"Look, let's be honest. Our marriage has been dead for years.* " She'd thought this was the way it was after a lot of years together—and she remembered the early passionate years with wistful longing.

Sometimes she'd told herself there was no time for them because of their frantic lifestyle. Paul coming home so late from the office, tired after the long commute. The endless socializing that was important for business. When they did make love, it was almost mechanical.

All at once she felt suffused with rage. She strode to his chest of drawers, pulled the top drawer wide, dumped its contents on the floor. When all five hung empty, she reached down to clutch their contents and carried them with frenzied haste into the guest room. She emptied Paul's closet, transferred his expensive suits and shoes to the guest room, removed his toothbrush, toothpaste, toilet articles to the guest bathroom.

Breathless from exertion, she returned to the master bedroom, closed the door. Paul would never set foot in this room again. Her heart pounding, she crossed to the mirrored closet wall, inspected her reflection. She flinched at the sight of the extra pounds, her graying hair. But her hair began to turn gray before she was twenty-five. In those days it had seemed amusing. Paul had joked about it. She lived in gray and beige pantsuits and "little black dresses" because that was what

15

Paul liked her to wear. So she wasn't twenty-three and slim and beautiful. Was that a reason to discard her?

Exhausted, she sat in the small lounge chair by the window. The kids would be so shocked. They'd be furious with Paul. And how was she to manage Zach's college expenses? How much did Paul owe? Would there be enough left over when they sold the house to see Zach through this year? Instinct warned her that Paul would offer no help on Zach's last two years of college.

How will I live? No point in trying for alimony. How could I ever catch up with Paul when he'll be on the other side of the country?

Her mind recoiled from fighting for alimony. She'd have to find a job. The newspapers kept talking about the great job market. But the prospect was terrifying. She'd held no regular job since two months before Deedee was born. She'd had to work—of course—because Paul was in law school. She'd worked out of the apartment —freelance proofreading, editing, writing book jacket blurbs—anything that she could do at home.

She'd worked freelance until Zach was born. By then Paul was making decent money. They'd left the Manhattan apartment, bought the first house when Zach was only a few months old. Two years later— with Paul in a better paying job—they'd

16

bought a bigger house. "Helen, you have to look like a success," he ranted regularly. He insisted she play the corporate wife scene. Entertain regularly, volunteer for popular local causes. Create the image of the wife of a man on the way up. But what value would this have on a job resumé?

I'm forty-six years old and with few skills. How will I survive in the job market?

Two

Paul leaned back in the comfortable armchair the restaurant provided for its high-income diners, managed a wry smile as he concluded a lengthy monologue to Jeff Madison.

"That's about it," he said. He'd given Jeff the whole story. Let him understand this wasn't a half-of-Fort Knox case.

"I'm sorry, old boy." Jeff had been through two divorces himself. "Be glad the kids are grown. You won't be stuck with child support payments forever." Jeff's own problem, Paul recalled. Two kids from his first wife, three from the second. His current wife was an attorney, in practice with him.

"I still have one in college—and you know

how Ivy League tuition keeps growing every year." Paul glanced at his watch. "I should make a call about now—"

"Go ahead," Jeff said indulgently.

"My cell phone's in the car," Paul said with an air of sudden realization.

"Mine, too," Jeff conceded. "I guess it's back to the old pay phone," he chuckled.

"This will only take a minute," Paul apologized, rising from his seat.

At the public phone in the men's room Paul punched in the familiar number.

"Hello—" An almost childish feminine voice greeted him.

"Everything's going on schedule, Iris," he said, grateful that this early in the evening few patrons had arrived. "Happy days are coming." No doubt in his mind that the Silicon Valley deal would go through.

"She won't be yelling for a lot of alimony?" Iris asked.

"It never came up. I guess she was in shock," Paul admitted. He stopped himself from mentioning their imminent silver anniversary. Iris thought he was thirty-nine. That the kids were still in high school. "I'll be clearing out of the house tomorrow night."

"I'll make room for you in the closet," Iris purred. "Honey, I can't wait to have you all to myself."

"I'm having dinner with the lawyer. I'd

better get back."

He hadn't mentioned Iris to Helen—but she'd probably guess there was another woman in the picture. The day Iris joined the firm as a paralegal, he knew this was what he needed in his life. Twenty-four and sexy as hell. Just sitting next to her set his teeth on edge. Her hand on him was like a double dose of Viagra.

They couldn't get married for a year, until the divorce was final—but people were broadminded these days. They'd live together out in Silicon Valley. Iris was sharp. She'd be a real asset career-wise. But let the house move fast, he thought in a surge of anxiety. He couldn't keep the firm out there waiting until the end of the year.

Helen went downstairs, made coffee for herself. The thought of food made her queasy. She sat in her perfect kitchen and sipped at the strong black coffee—her mind in chaos. In a matter of minutes her whole life had been turned upside down. For the first time in her life she'd be alone. That was scary.

How was she going to tell the kids? They'd be so upset. She glanced at the kitchen phone. With Deedee's insane work schedule she'd still be at the office. How could she leave a message on the answering machine: *"Guess what? Dad's in terrible financial trouble, and we have to sell the house. And oh yes, he's divorcing me."*

Call Gerry, she ordered herself. In every moment of crisis she and Gerry had been there for each other. She remembered Gerry's sordid divorce. Even now—eight years later— Gerry talked occasionally about "Al and his whore." She'd suspected for years that Gerry didn't like Paul, attributed this to her bitterness towards men in general.

Cold and trembling, she reached for the phone. She hadn't spoken with Gerry in almost two months, hadn't seen her since the weekend Gerry came out to their Hampton's rental in July. With a sudden need to talk with Gerry, she punched in her phone number.

"Hello—" A charming—strange—voice responded.

"Oh, I'm sorry. I must have dialed the wrong number," Helen apologized.

"What number are you calling?"

Helen told her. The woman at the other end assured her she had the right number.

"Are you calling Gerry?"

"Yes—" Gerry had guests, Helen gathered. All right, she wouldn't talk long.

In a moment Gerry was on the phone with her.

"If you have guests, I won't hold you up," Helen told her. "I'll buzz you tomorrow."

"No guests." Gerry sounded stressed. "Sheila's my new apartment-mate. I'm sorry—I didn't get around to telling you. It's been such a hectic time at work." Gerry managed the office of a highly successful publicist.

"I wanted you to be the first to know," Helen said with an effort at black humor. "Paul's lost all our money on the stock market, we have to sell the house to bail him out from the loan sharks, and he's asked for a divorce."

"The son-of-a-bitch!" Gerry's voice was shrill with rage. "He found himself a whore half his age!"

"I don't know. It could be," Helen conceded. "All I know is that he's heading for Silicon Valley for some new job. And we'll split whatever funds exist after we pay off two mortgages." In a corner of her mind she put to rest the simmering thought of moving in—temporarily—with Gerry. Deedee had a tiny one-bedroom apartment—that once had been a studio until the landlord divided it up. No room for her there, either. "I have to call a real estate broker in the morning. And once the house is sold, I'll be heading for Manhattan—and a job."

"Come into the city and let's have lunch." Gerry was upset.

"As soon as I have everything here under control," Helen promised.

"You're the most disciplined woman I've ever known," Gerry said gently, astonishing Helen—she'd never thought of herself as disciplined. "You'll survive."

Off the phone, Helen left the kitchen, went up to the master bedroom, closed the door. She didn't want to see Paul when he returned to the house. She'd made a point of leaving the guest bedroom door open. He'd get the message. He'd be relieved. In the morning, she'd stay in her room until he was gone.

After a night of little sleep Helen became aware of sounds down the hall. Paul was preparing to leave for the day. Yesterday morning, she taunted herself, she awakened to a normal life. Today she didn't know what tomorrow would bring. But she wouldn't fall apart. She had too much pride for that. And she had the children to consider.

Somehow, she must force Paul to help in seeing Zach through college. He had a way of landing on his feet job-wise. She wasn't asking anything for herself—and in today's world divorced women usually came out for the worse financially. So she'd have to adjust her scale of living. But Paul had a responsibility to help Zach through college.

She stiffened to attention. Paul was going downstairs. She glanced at the clock. Right on schedule. He'd probably given the firm two or three weeks' notice. Or was this one of those "you're fired—clear out your desk by 5 p.m."? Was Gerry right? Had he gone berserk over some young slut, gambled away their assets trying to make himself rich for her? Would she ever know?

As soon as she heard the BMW rolling down the driveway, she rose from the bed. She was conscious of faint hunger, remembered she'd had no dinner last night. All right, shower, dress, have breakfast—and call the broker who had sold them the house six years ago. Amelia Blair was a smart woman. Give her a one-month exclusive. It would be a hefty commission—she'd work her butt off to make a fast sale.

In beige slacks and matching cotton turtleneck—what Paul good-humoredly derided as her "soccer mom" uniform—Helen went downstairs. In the kitchen—propped against thc coffee maker—she found a note from Paul.

> Jeff won't take us to the cleaners on the
> divorce. He understands the situation.
> He'll be calling you some time today to
> set up a meeting. Just the routine deal.
> Paul.

She put up coffee, slid two slices of whole-wheat bread into the toaster—hungry yet recoiling from food. Later she'd phone to cancel the day's appointments—after she'd called Amelia Blair. She glanced about the kitchen with the sense of being in a strange house. Very soon it wouldn't be hers anymore.

After she spoke with the broker, she'd drive into the village and pick up a copy of the *New York Times*. She'd have to start reading the "Apts For Rent" columns. She'd need a place to live once the house was sold. She'd never lived alone. The prospect was intimidating.

She'd look for a one-bedroom, take the convertible sofa from the den for her living room so there'd be a place for Zach to sleep during school holidays. Oh God, he would hate that! But everybody said rents had gone berserk in the city.

At 9:30 sharp—because she knew Amelia Blair made a point of being in her office early—she phoned the real estate office.

"With Deedee in her own apartment and Zach in college this is just too much house for us," she told Amelia.

"Would you be interested in something much smaller? I have a perfect two bedroom that's just come onto the market—"

"No, we'll probably be moving into Manhattan," Helen interrupted. *I'll be moving into Manhattan.* "But you're familiar with the 'empty nest' syndrome." She struggled to sound indulgent. *Who am I kidding? In a matter of days it will be all over the community that Paul and I are divorcing. God knows, it's a familiar story.* "This isn't a distress sale," she emphasized, lest Amelia expect her to take the first offer that came in. "But we would like a fast sale."

"May I come over and see the house?" Amelia asked. "I know I sold it to you—but you've made improvements," she added diplomatically. "And prices have soared since then."

"Come right now if you like," Helen said.

"I'll be there in thirty minutes," Amelia said.

Helen remembered a neighbor saying the brokers were crying that there were so few houses for sale in their area. It was important to squeeze out every possible dollar. Only now did she realize she had no figures in mind. All right, she'd have to sit down with Paul and see just where they stood. And when it came to a closing, she thought with a new wariness, she'd make sure the money due to Paul and herself was made out in two checks. One to each of them.

On schedule Amelia Blair arrived.

"I've always loved this house," she said. "And your additions—enlarging the rear terrace, the sauna, the bay windows—add to the value."

"I know the market is soaring—" Playing the role now, Helen smiled in approval.

"But what would you consider the right asking price?"

Helen tried to conceal her astonishment at Amelia's reply. That much? But how much would be left after the two mortgages were paid off? Tonight she must sit down with Paul and have a realistic talk with him. He'd handled all their financial affairs other than the expenses of running the household.

Amelia herself brought up the question of her having an exclusive listing. They fenced for a few moments, settled for a thirty-day exclusive. Lots of houses sold within that time, Amelia told Helen.

Clearly pleased at having acquired the property, Amelia left with a promise of going through her prospective buyer list immediately. Alone again, Helen felt herself adrift. It was as though she was two women—one who stood in the shadows and watched the other in an unreal performance.

Tomorrow her cleaning woman would be here. The house would be in perfect condition for showing. There had never been full-time help. "When I'm getting million dollar bonuses," Paul had said. The million dollar bonuses that never materialized, to Paul's anger and frustration.

So much to do, Helen thought tensely—yet there was little she could do until the house was sold.

Later in the morning Jeff Madison called.

"Helen, I'm so sorry things haven't worked out for you and Paul," he commiserated. "But I'll try to handle things as unobtrusively as possible."

Helen made an appointment to see him at the house that evening, when he returned from his Manhattan office. Not until she was off the phone did she wonder if he expected to meet with Paul and her together. What happened at his meeting with Paul last evening?

The hours ahead would be dismal, she thought. She wasn't accustomed to idle time. But she was no longer to be part of the local volunteer world. She had not yet joined the league of divorced women living in the city. She was in limbo.

Paul glanced at his watch. It was almost five—call Helen and tell her he wouldn't be at the house tonight. He was annoyed that his resigning from the firm seemed to be welcomed. He grandly offered to remain for another three weeks because he needed the salary checks. For a tense moment he thought the old man was going to tell him to clear out right away.

Gearing himself for a cold reception, he called the house.

"I'll be stuck in the city tonight," he said when Helen picked up the phone. That happened at intervals—she knew that was part of the job. "Don't worry about the car being at the station—I drove in this morning." Which he always did when he planned on staying over. Helen figured he stayed at the firm's condo on those occasions. He cleared his throat. "Did you hear from Jeff?"

"He'll be over at eight." Helen was unfamiliarly impersonal. "Amelia Blair came over to the house."

"What's she asking?" Paul demanded. Flinching at the figures to be paid off that popped up in his mind.

Helen told him. He hedged when she tried to pin him down on outstanding payments that must come out of the selling price. Damn, she could be so irritating at times like this!

"Helen, I have to go to a meeting," he said brusquely.

Off the phone, he debated for a moment. Hell, why stay any longer? He dialed Iris's extension.

"Iris Grant—" Her familiar voice came to him.

"I'm leaving now. Will you be stuck late?"

"I should be out in an hour." Her voice guarded now. They felt confident the others in the firm were unaware of their affair. "I'll pick up dinner on the way home."

"See you there." Already Paul felt a flicker of arousal. Iris made him feel young. She was so unpredictable—you never knew what she'd want next. She made him feel he was a thirty-year-old hunk.

The deal out in Silicon Valley sounded great—though he heard horrendous stories about the prices of houses. Okay, so he couldn't afford to buy at this time. Everybody out there thought big. Out there he could end up with a million dollar bonus. Okay, not this year, but the next.

He'd left the BMW in a garage near Iris's Upper West Side apartment. She'd been lucky—last year she inherited the one-bedroom apartment she'd been sharing for two years. For the past six months he'd been paying half the rent. It was cheaper than going to a hotel every time they wanted to play.

Out in the Indian summer late afternoon he tried to flag down a cab. He'd forgot—at this hour they were changing shifts. After a fifteen-minute wait he snared a cab, headed for 75th Street and West End. The doorman at Iris's building knew him, knew he had a key. Probably envious as hell of him, he thought smugly.

Inside Iris's apartment he went to the air-conditioner. She had central air conditioning. It wasn't off for the season yet, was it? He pressed the button. Cool air emerged. He took off his jacket, his tie, kicked off his shoes and stretched out on the spaciously

29

designed sofa. In moments he'd drifted off.

He came awake to the sound of hard rock. The moment Iris came into the apartment, she turned on the radio. He opened his eyes, grinned.

"Hi, baby—"

She stood in the middle of the room. A tall, sexy blonde who might have been a garment center model except for the lushness of her breasts. She was thrusting her dress—at two inches above her knees acceptable under the unspoken office dress code—above her head.

"I'll heat up dinner later," she drawled invitingly while she tossed her dress to the floor, reached to unsnap her bra, kicked off her shoes. "Are you ready for the appetizer?"

"Honey, I'm raring to go!" He was on his feet, stripping already. Wow! After the longest day in the office, with her he was ready.

Three

Helen settled herself at the breakfast-room table, made a stab at eating an early dinner. She was conscious of every sound in the house. She felt almost an intruder. She dreaded the meeting with Jeff. What would they talk about? Would he have papers for her to sign? Could it happen that fast?

How did you begin a new life at forty-six? Was Gerry right in suspecting Paul was involved with another woman? Had she failed as a wife? Why hadn't she realized what was happening? Why was the wife always the last to know when the husband was playing around?

I don't know that Paul's having an affair. Gerry's just guessing. He's in a panic because of the money situation. Maybe once he's settled in another job, he'll revert to normal.

All at once it was urgent to know if Paul had been cheating on her. She pushed aside her dinner plate, left the breakfast room and headed upstairs, walked into the guest room. Paul hadn't bothered to make up his bed this morning. Had thrown his underwear, socks, pajamas, sports shirts into the guest room dresser drawers with no regard for order. She stared at the contents of first one drawer, then another. Not sure what she expected to find.

Guilt thrust aside by an urgency to know, she went to the closet where he'd hung up his custom-made shirts, expensive Italian suits, his L. L. Bean casual wear. His shoes and ties in flagrant disarray. With trembling hands she began to search the pockets of his ski jacket—bought, he said, for a weekend with a client at Stowe. She pulled out a lipstick-stained tissue, a tiny bottle of perfume.

Her heart pounding, she began a careful search of pockets. A bill from Saks for black satin panties and bra. Why hadn't he used his charge plate? Because she would see the bill, she guessed. She discovered a receipt from a posh Manhattan hotel—dated months ago.

Carefully she zipped up the pockets of his L. L. Bean jacket, hung away the other jackets. There'd be no reconciliation with Paul. He was out of her life forever. What a fool she'd been! Never once suspecting he was having an affair. The stereotypical stupid wife.

She should tell the kids what was happening. They had to know. She'd leave a message on Deedee's answering machine to call her. She'd wait a while to tell Zach.

The meeting with Jeff Madison was brief. Technically he was representing her as the one seeking the divorce. Alimony was glossed over, discarded with a few sentences. So quickly it had been arranged, she thought as she walked with Jeff to the door. Almost twenty-five years of marriage—and so simple to dismiss.

She settled herself in the cathedral-ceilinged living room, tried—futilely—to involve herself in watching television. Earlier she'd left a message on Deedee's answering machine: *Call me—no matter how late it is.* She knew that Deedee was putting in seventy and eighty-hour weeks on her job. It might be 3 a.m. before Deedee was home.

A few minutes before 10 p.m. Amelia Blair called. Helen was in her bedroom—in night clothes and struggling to focus on a mystery novel she'd brought home from the library a few days ago.

"I'm sorry to call so late," Amelia apologized. "Can we talk now?"

"Of course." Helen was instantly alert.

"I left a message earlier for a man down in the city who's house-hunting. He's been transferred from Denver. He called a few minutes ago. I told him about your house, and he'd like to drive up tomorrow morning to see it."

"Great." Helen struggled to sound enthusiastic. "Did he give you a time?"

"He figures he'll be driving against traffic, could be at my office by 10 a.m. He's very anxious. His wife refuses to leave Denver with their four children until they have a house. She won't hear of a rental."

"Oh, my cleaning woman comes tomorrow," Helen remembered in dismay. Elmira came in twice a week. She'd regret losing the job.

"Cancel it," Amelia urged. "Even if you have to pay her. This guy is panting to buy— and your house is just what he needs. And there'll be no problem about financing—he just sold his estate out in Denver for over a million."

"I'll call her early tomorrow morning," Helen told her.

Helen lay awake far into the night. Hearing all the strange sounds that she'd always ignored through the years. She simultaneously welcomed the prospect of an early sale and recoiled from it. No, the sooner the better, she told herself with a touch of defiance. She felt a stranger in her own house now. Let this man from Denver love the house, buy it. Promise him an early closing.

She started at the sound of the phone. Reaching for the receiver she glanced at the clock. It was 3 a.m.

"Hello—" Guessing the caller was Dee-dee.

"Mom, are you okay?" Deedee's voice was shrill with anxiety.

"I'm all right, Dad's all right." Helen struggled for calm. "It's just that something's come up." *How do I tell Deedee what's happened?*

"What's come up?" Fear lent a sharpness to Deedee's voice.

"Well, first of all—he's made some very foolish investments. We—we have to sell the house to bail him out."

"Oh, Mom!"

"There's more," she added grimly. "He wants a divorce. I—I think he's having an affair."

"After all these years?" Deedee shrieked. "I've been looking for presents for your silver-wedding anniversary."

"Don't bother. You might want to prepare yourself for a wedding present for him." Helen tried for sardonic humor.

"He'll never see a present from me!" Deedee hesitated. "Mom, do you think it's just a midlife crisis?"

"He wants to start over." Helen struggled to keep her voice even. "He's tired of the old rat race. He's moving to California."

"I don't believe this!"

"Believe it. A broker is bringing a prospective buyer tomorrow morning. Considering the market, she's sure she can move the house in a matter of weeks."

"Dad's lost his mind!" Deedee paused for a moment. "He has a job in California?"

"He says he has—"

"Then make damn sure you get decent alimony," Deedee urged.

"No alimony," Helen said tiredly. "What would be the point of insisting on that when he'll be on the other side of the country?"

"But how are you going to live?" Deedee was distraught.

"I'll have to find a job. I'll hopefully end up with enough to live on for a few months." She'd sell the SUV—a little money there after she paid off the car loan.

"What kind of a job?" Deedee sounded aghast at the prospect. "Where will you live?"

Helen was all at once defensive. Did Deedee think she was totally helpless? "I'll move back to the city, look for a job in some office. It's not as though I've never worked."

"Mom, that was twenty years ago!" Exasperation crept into Deedee's voice. "Dad ought to be horsewhipped."

"I'll manage to take care of myself." But she felt sick as she considered what lay ahead. "I'm not the only woman thrown out into the job market at forty-six. I have some marketable skills."

"I can't think clearly at this hour," Deedee

admitted. "I'll try to call you tomorrow from the office. But you're going to be all right, Mom," she soothed. "We'll work this out."

Preparing to leave for the office, Deedee decided to phone Zach. He'd be pissed at being awakened before 8 a.m. when he had no class today, she warned herself—but he had to know what was happening.

"Hello—" Zach sounded groggy. For some reason Thursday appeared to be a party night at Columbia.

"It's me," Deedee said tersely. "Something crazy's happened."

"You have to wake me before eight o'clock to tell me?" he demanded aggrievedly.

"Dad's lost all his money. He and Mom have to sell the house to pay off his debts. Mom—"

"Oh, shit!" Zach groaned. "Where does that leave me and school?"

"Where does it leave Mom?" Deedee shot back. "He asked for a divorce."

"At their age?" Zach was outraged.

"Mom thinks he's having an affair. She's letting him have the divorce." This was unreal. It happened in other families—not theirs.

"They ought to see a marriage counselor," Zach said. "Talk to them, Deedee."

"They're past that. Mom's already signed

the divorce papers—with no provision for alimony. Zach, she's going to have to get a job."

"What can she do?" Zach was stunned. "I mean, she can't even use a computer. She was all upset when I asked her to order me a jacket from L. L. Bean on the Internet. She insisted on using the telephone."

"People still do," Dee said impatiently.

"What about all our stuff at the house?" Fresh alarm in Zach's voice.

"We'll have to get it out as soon as the house is sold," Deedee said. *Where am I going to put it? I still have my Barbie dolls!* "Most of it can be junked."

"Should we go up to the house this weekend? Damn, I meant to cram for an exam."

"We don't have to go up this weekend." If she wasn't stuck at the office, she and Todd planned to run out to East Hampton for the weekend. She knew what was on Todd's mind—but she just wasn't sure she wanted to move in with him. "But call Mom. Let her know we're with her." Rage surged in Deedee. "I'll never talk to Dad again."

Once she'd phoned Elmira and told her not to come in today, that she would be paid anyway, Helen went out to the side of the house to cut several roses from the bush that was still in full glory. Since slightly past 6 a.m. she'd been housecleaning. Everything looked fine, she told herself. Put the flowers in a vase in the living room. She glanced at her watch. Amelia Blair and her prospective buyer ought to be here in about ten minutes.

They'd have to sell most of the furniture, have a big tag sale for odds and ends like linens and kitchen ware. According to the divorce papers—and community property law—all funds were to be equally divided. It was agreed that Paul would keep his BMW—she would keep the SUV, which she would sell right after the closing. What would she do with an SUV in New York?

Gerry was forever complaining about the price of a garage in New York. *"I pay for my garage space what my studio apartment cost me thirty years ago."*

With the roses displayed in a Waterford crystal vase on the oversized coffee table in the living room, Helen went out to the kitchen to put up coffee. The aroma of coffee filtering through the house lent a nice touch.

A few minutes past ten Helen heard a car turn into the driveway. Amelia Blair was here. From behind the screen door Helen watched while Amelia and a compact, well-dressed man emerged from the car. She was pointing out the beautiful landscaping of the terraces that led up to the house. She heard Amelia praise the charm of the exterior.

"Weathered shingles are great, you know—" Amelia's voice drifted up to Helen. "You'll never have to worry about painting."

With the requisite casual smile Helen pulled the front door wide. Amelia introduced her and the prospective buyer. Now Helen pretended to be busy with rearranging books on one of the bookcases. The past forty-eight hours still seemed unreal.

Amelia's sales pitch was good. Not too hard sell. This man was impatient to buy a house, Amelia said—but he was sharp enough to conceal that. Helen was conscious of a tenseness in her shoulders, a tightness in her throat as Amelia led her client up the stairs.

"In addition to the large den downstairs—which would be a beautiful master bedroom with its own full bath—there are four bedrooms upstairs," Amelia was explaining. She'd said he needed five bedrooms. "And the huge downstairs family room has a magnificent fireplace."

When Amelia left with her client thirty minutes later, Helen was alternately hopeful and pessimistic. She paced about the house for the next hour—waiting for some word from Amelia. When the phone rang, she leapt to respond.

"Hello—"

"He made an absurd offer," Amelia

reported. "But I think this was the opening round."

"He knows he can have a fast closing?" *How quickly can I find an apartment? Hotel rentals in the city are insane.*

"He knows," Amelia confirmed. "We'll have to play this by ear."

Moments after she was off the phone with Amelia, Zach called.

"Mom, you're going to be okay," he said urgently. "Dad's a real bastard!"

"Sssh," she said, startled by his rage, touched by his obvious concern. "He's still your father."

"Mom, he's—he's fooling around with another woman?"

"I'm fairly certain of that." Her face grew hot. How could she tell Zach she'd gone through Paul's pockets and found evidence? Yet she needed to know. She needed to realize this wasn't a mid-life crisis, that there was no chance he might come back to her.

"I can leave school, find a job," Zach blurted out.

"No!" Helen was shaken. "You'll stay in school." Somehow, she must handle that. "I'm not decrepit, darling—" She strived for lightness. "I'll get my act together, find myself a job."

"Mom, I love you." Like Deedee he sounded distraught. "Shall I come out to the house this weekend? I'm cramming for

41

an exam, but I can do it up there—"

"Stay at the dorm," she insisted. "We'll weather this storm. Stay cool."

Off the phone, Helen sat motionless, stared into space without seeing. Deedee and Zach must learn that she wasn't helpless, that she could survive on her own. Her mind darted back through the years. When her father died during her freshman year in college, her mother sold their house, made it clear there would be money to see her through school—but after college she would be on her own.

Even now—all these years later—she could hear her mother's voice: "Your father and I raised you. There's enough money to 'see me through,' but if I need help I expect you to remember your responsibilities as my daughter."

She'd gone to summer school to speed up being on her own. In truth, she had only the college dorm in which to live. Her mother moved to a hotel, took her meals in restaurants. There was no room in her life for a daughter.

Straight from college she'd married Paul. His mother had made it clear it was her duty to support herself and Paul while he attended law school. Never in her life, she thought defensively, had she shirked her duty. But Deedee and Zach were terrified at the thought of her having to support herself.

She must prove she was capable of standing on her own two feet.

But the prospect of living on her own, of going out into the job market at the rim of the twenty-first century, was unnerving.

Four

Helen dreaded the prospect of spending the weekend in the house with Paul. Even if she'd had a place to go, she reasoned, she should remain in the house in the event Amelia had some action on a sale. Every time the phone rang today she felt her heart begin to pound. Was it Amelia with another offer?

Would Paul want to go out for dinner tonight? He made a point of their dining out on Friday evenings. He liked being seen in the most expensive restaurant in town once a week. Why? she asked herself belatedly.

At a few moments to five the phone rang. Helen leapt to reply.

"Hello—" How low could she go on the house? Paul had been vague about the exact amount of his obligations.

"Helen, I'll drive out some time tomorrow to pack up a few things." She heard Paul clear his throat in that way that said he was uptight. "I think it would be better for both of us if I stay in town until I leave for California."

"Yes, that would be best." *How can I sound so matter-of-fact? So impersonal. I lived with this man for almost twenty-five years!*

"Did you—uh—" He paused. "Did you tell the kids?"

"Yes." But then—thinking back through the years—every time there was anything unpleasant the telling was assigned to her. When Paul's mother died. When her mother died. When Deedee had to have her tonsils out. When Zach couldn't go to his planned summer camp in Switzerland because what they'd thought was a 48-hour virus turned out to be pneumonia.

Off the phone, she focused on how to spend the evening. She'd go through the closets, decide what would be delegated to a tag sale. They'd accumulated so much through the years. Sometimes Paul had accused her of being a pack rat.

In the midst of her efforts, Gerry called.

"Why don't you come into the city tomorrow, spend the day with me," Gerry urged.

"We have a nibble on the house," Helen explained. "I should be here."

"Remember, the market's hot. Don't take the first offer that comes along unless it's great."

"I made that clear to the broker."

"I can't believe this is happening." Gerry exuded fresh rage.

"I just want the house to be sold and get out of here." How many times had she seen this happen to other women? Gerry was forty-two when Al announced eight years ago that he wanted a divorce. Why had she felt exempt from such a happening?

They talked for a few minutes, then Gerry explained she was calling from the office, working late.

"We'll talk over the weekend," Gerry promised.

The evening dragged painfully. Helen dreaded going to bed—knowing she'd battle insomnia. Close to dawn she fell asleep from exhaustion. At 8 a.m. her alarm clock was a raucous intrusion. She'd geared herself to dress and be ready to receive possible buyers who might appear at Amelia's office at some ungodly hour. On weekends, Amelia said, she was at the office 9 a.m. sharp.

In slacks and turtleneck she went down to the kitchen to prepare breakfast. She barely touched her scrambled eggs, focused on strong black coffee. Some women ate incessantly when they were upset, gained a shocking amount of weight. She found food repulsive at such times.

She was lingering over her third cup of

coffee when she heard a car pull up in the driveway. It couldn't be Amelia, she told herself—Amelia would call first. She hurried to the foyer. Paul was striding toward the door.

"Hi," he said evasively. "I thought I'd drive out early before traffic got heavy. Do you know where the luggage is?"

"Where it always is." Involuntarily she was cold. "In the basement storage room." She hesitated. "Would you like breakfast?"

"Thanks, no—I stopped on the way up." He seemed nervous. "Well, I'd better get cracking—" He made a move to head for the basement. "Jeff will keep us briefed—"

"Where can you be reached?" she asked. "I mean, I'll want to discuss any offer on the house with you before giving Amelia an okay—"

"Call me at the office," he said self-consciously. "I'll be there for the next two weeks."

"What about after hours?" she pursued. *Where will he be living? Not in the firm's condo when he's leaving.* "In case I need a fast answer." She couldn't accept an offer on the house without consulting him.

With an air of self-consciousness he reached into his pocket for a card and pen, scribbled on the back. "You can leave a message for me at this number—"

Helen retreated to the living room,

pretended to be involved in reading a magazine. She stared at the pages without seeing. Within thirty minutes Paul came downstairs with two Louis Vuitton valises.

"I'll be talking with you," he said, pausing at the entrance to the living room. He frowned in inner debate for a moment. "Look, you can't accept too low a figure. I've been doing some figuring on the calculator—"

Helen concealed her shock when he told her the amount of his indebtedness. If they were each to have even a small cache to start their new lives, then Amelia had to come up with top dollar.

Where was he staying? she asked herself while she watched him climb into his BMW for the drive back to Manhattan. *Why should it bother me? But it does. He was so cagey when he gave me the phone number where he could be reached after business hours.*

She fought a losing battle in her mind. She ought to be above such things, she reproached herself—but she took the card with the phone number out of her pocket and crossed to the phone. Dialed and waited for a voice. A tightness in her throat.

"Hello?" A querulous feminine voice—sounding as though just emerging from slumber—came to her. "Hello? Paul is that you?"

Slamming the phone down as though it

47

was super-hot, Helen was cold with shock. Paul was staying with this woman. This *girl*, who sounded younger than Deedee. How many were there before *her*? The nights through the years when he'd stayed in New York "on business."

Even if he changed his mind, wanted to come back, she'd have no part of him. She felt dirty. Used.

Would the woman at the other end tell Paul about a hang-up? Would he guess it was she? No, she insisted—he'd say, "it was probably a wrong number."

At a few minutes before ten, Amelia called. She'd be over around noon with a couple who'd been looking at houses in the area for weeks.

"They've had weird ideas about prices, but after all this time they may be seeing the light." Amelia was deliberately optimistic.

"If they've been looking for weeks, they should know." She hesitated. "I gather there's been no word from the Denver man?"

"No," Amelia conceded. "But then he won't want to appear too anxious."

"Maybe he just means to let us sweat a little." Helen tried for wry humor. "Well, he's doing that."

The morning was unseasonably cool. Deedee was pleased she'd worn a warm jacket, sipped at her still-hot coffee while Todd cursed at the slow-moving traffic on the Long Island Expressway.

"Hell, we should have gone out last night, straight from the office." He reached for her coffee container, took a swig, handed it back.

"At 4 a.m.? You'd have fallen asleep at the wheel." They'd managed four hours sleep before they left Todd's apartment to head for the garage to pick up his leased Mercedes. "I want to arrive in one piece."

"This is the perfect time to go to the Hamptons," he said complacently. "A good chunk of the summer crowd is gone. Though you wouldn't know it from this traffic—" Impatience crept into his voice again.

"When we get off the LIE, we can stop for a quickie breakfast at McDonald's," Deedee soothed.

"No," he brushed this aside. "We'll have breakfast at the Candy Kitchen in Bridgehampton," he decreed. Because entertainment field and publishing celebrities convened there, she thought in momentary annoyance. Sometimes—with his constant eagerness to make "the right contacts"—he reminded her of Dad.

"I feel guilty at not going home this weekend," Deedee admitted. "Mom must be so upset."

"You'll call her from out there," Todd said, breathing a sigh of relief because at last traffic was moving. "Or call her now on the cell phone."

"I'll call from the house." The house loaned to Todd by a managing director at Wheeler, Rhodes, and Smith—where they were lowly but highly paid analysts—was right on the beach, Deedee remembered. At intervals off-season it was loaned to various—favored—employees. Todd felt triumphant to be so honored. This hinted at a huge end-of-the-year bonus. "I can't get over Dad's doing this!"

"By the time I was fourteen, I was living with my third stepfather." Todd shrugged. "It's the times we live in." And that, Deedee knew, was his mantra.

"Mom and Dad would be celebrating their silver anniversary in a matter of days." She sighed in frustration. "What's she going to do with her life now? What kind of a job will she be able to find—and fill?"

"And it's tough for the wife to be granted alimony these days. But hey, women's lib is responsible for that."

"Mom had a job," Deedee said stubbornly. "Running a big house, raising Zach and me, being Dad's hostess at endless dinner parties. But turning her loose in the corporate world is like—like dropping off a deer in the middle of Manhattan."

50

"Look, millions of women face divorce. Even at her age. She'll survive."

"It's a well-known fact—the man goes along his merry way, but the divorced wife's scale of living plummets." Deedee shuddered. "She's talking about moving back into the city. She has no idea of the crazy rents today."

"You could give her your apartment, move in with me." Todd moved one hand from the wheel to fondle Deedee's knee.

"I'm not sure I'm ready for that." Deedee reiterated her set response. She'd known Todd almost a year, had been involved with him for the past five months. She'd thought her life would be wrapped around Cliff— but with her crazy hours and his equally crazy hospital resident schedule they had no time for each other.

"Think about it," Todd coaxed. "We'd have a chance at some decent time together—instead of maybe a weekend every two or three months. And your mother would have a place to live."

"But how long will she be able to pay that kind of rent?" What kind of a job could Mom land? A saleswoman in a boutique—in a department store?

"She's got to come out with some cash at the closing," Todd argued. He knew the situation. "She'll have to play it by ear."

"Todd, you're hitting seventy-five," she

protested, glancing at the speedometer.

"And other cars are passing like we're standing still," he shrugged.

"This is the weekend. There'll be cops out," she warned.

"Oh shit!" He groaned at the sound of a police siren, then blew in relief. "He's got another sucker." But he slowed down, like everybody else on the road.

At twelve twenty Amelia Blair pulled into the driveway. Helen geared herself for a casual approach. She came outside with a pair of shears—ostensibly she was about to cut some 'mums to bring into the house. She knew to keep her distance after Amelia introduced her to the clients. Let Amelia do her thing.

In barely half an hour Amelia ushered her clients out of the house. Their faces were noncommittal. *This is supposed to be such a great market? Why are we getting this response?* And then Helen chided herself for impatience. Amelia had had the listing only about seventy-two hours.

Helen waved as Amelia pulled out of the driveway, then returned to her spurious efforts at trimming back the 'mums. As soon as they disappeared from sight, she went into the house. As usual when she was uptight, she went to the kitchen to put up coffee. Amelia would be in touch later. It was the weekend—prime selling time. Maybe Amelia would bring out other possible buyers today or tomorrow.

Restless, too tense to settle down to read, she was about to call Gerry when the phone rang.

"We've had a nibble," Amelia began cautiously. "Better than the Denver man's offer, but low." She named a figure. Helen flinched. It was far below Amelia's original estimate. And every extra dollar counted. It would devastate Zach to have to transfer in the middle of the school year.

"Let's turn it down," Helen said. She wouldn't even mention it to Paul. He was so hungry for cash—and that would get him off the hook—but it would leave them so little. "It's still early in the game," she said with shaky bravado.

"I'd rather not call the Denver man," Amelia said. "Let him call us."

"Right. After all, he seems rather desperate to settle on a house."

But would it be their house—or someone else's? It would be wrong, her mind warned, to jump too fast. She had to think ahead. She needed enough to see her through until she had a place to live, had a job—and, most important, to see Zach through this year at Columbia. Later she'd worry about the last two years. She was his mother. That was her obligation.

Five

The borrowed house in East Hampton was a small gem, Deedee thought as she lay on a chaise on the wrap-around deck and gazed at the sunkissed ocean. How wonderful to escape—even for a couple of days—the insane frenzy of the long working hours, the nerve-wracking noises of the city. Wrapped in serenity, she turned to gaze at Todd, asleep on a chaise beside her—seeming younger than his twenty-seven years and oddly vulnerable. Awake he was so vibrant, she thought—so enraptured with the life he saw ahead of him. Impatient, she conceded—he wanted tomorrow to happen today.

Her eyes focused on the cordless phone he'd brought out of the house in the event anyone—meaning, anyone from Wheeler, Rhodes, & Smith—needed to contact him. God, she was tired from this insane grind of theirs! Yet she knew—as Todd kept reminding her—that at the end of their two-year apprenticeship, a handful of their group would be selected to move up. The rest would be dumped. He was convinced they were the two out of ten that would make it upward.

Call Mom, she told herself guiltily, and reached for the phone. Mom would be home—she was expecting prospective buyers to show up. She dialed, feeling a surge of tenderness. How could Dad do this to Mom? How would Mom survive?

"Hello—" Her mother's voice. Calm, cordial, as though her world was not falling apart.

"Hi, Mom. I'm out at East Hampton with some friends for the weekend. It was kind of a last-minute decision." So Mom would think she was out here with women friends.

"I'm glad to see you're having some time off from the office. You work much too hard," Helen scolded.

"That's the deal these days," Deedee said. "Technology was supposed to give us more free time. Hah!" She paused for an instant. "Any buyers yet?"

"Amelia Blair has a couple of possible sales," Helen reported, but Deedee sensed her tension. "These people haven't heard that this is a sellers' market."

"Would you like to come into the city for a few days? You could have my bedroom. I can sleep on the sofa," Deedee offered.

"Thanks, darling—but I should be here at the house."

"You could give Amelia Blair the key—people do that." Deedee felt sick, envisioning her mother floating around that big house alone. Dad wouldn't hang around in these circumstances, would he? "I gather Dad has moved out."

"He's moved out."

"I hate to think of you alone out there." *Where is Dad living? Hotels are madly expensive, and he's short of cash. Is he shacked up with some woman?*

"It's civilization, darling." Helen's chuckle sounded almost real. "I'll be fine." *But she doesn't sound fine.*

"We'll be driving back tomorrow afternoon. I'll call you when I get into the city," Deedee promised. Mom liked Cliff, she remembered—she'd been disappointed when they broke up. She hadn't met Todd. There never seemed to be time.

Off the phone Deedee's thoughts lingered on her mother. She felt as though her own life had been turned upside down. Sure, half the marriages today ended in divorce. She'd grown up with kids who lived with one parent or the other—or commuted like a yo-yo between mother and father. But you didn't expect it to happen to you.

She searched her mind for signs that her parents' marriage had been in trouble. Dad worked long hours—but so did a lot of other fathers. Mom was always there for Zach and

56

her. In battles with Dad, Mom usually took their side. Dad could blow up under almost no provocation sometimes—but Mom stepped in to protect them.

Face it, Dad had never been much of a father. He'd been a rotten father—an absentee father. But most of the kids they grew up with were in the same situation. The fathers dashed to the Metro North Station at 7 a.m., arriving home fourteen hours later.

All at once, clouds seemed to dart across the sky, blocked the deliciously warm sun. Like their lives, she thought painfully. She couldn't bring herself to come out and ask, "Mom, is Dad really having a thing with another woman?" She felt oddly uncomfortable envisioning her father in such a situation.

Todd stirred on his chaise, uttered incoherent words in slumber. Todd made it clear he wasn't ready for marriage. Neither was she. Maybe at thirty she'd be ready. But Dad's behavior made her all at once distrustful of men in general. If she married Todd, would he want a divorce in ten or twenty years?

Involuntarily she thought about Cliff. Sometimes she'd teased him about being a creature of habit. Yet instinct told her Cliff would wear well through the years. But it had been right to break off with him, she told herself defiantly. With his mad schedule and hers, what chance did they have to see each other?

"Hey, where did the sun go?" Todd's voice brought her back to the moment. "Didn't I tell you to order a full weekend of sun?" He flashed the charismatic smile that had attracted her at their first meeting.

"I've lost the power," she flipped. "Sorry."

"You're still upset about your mother," he said, a glint of comprehension in his eyes. Born, she realized, from having survived his mother's three marriages.

"I don't know how she's going to handle this. No alimony. She'll lose her health insurance. Dad will probably shift his life insurance—if he hasn't already cashed it in. Todd, how is she going to support herself?"

"Forget it for the weekend," he ordered. "This is refueling time." He sat up, reached for her hand. "It's getting cold out here. Let's go inside and warm up." His eyes said, "I want to make love."

"Let's," she whispered in instant response.

Helen glanced at the kitchen clock. It was almost 6 p.m. Nobody would be coming to look at the house this late, would they? She crossed to the coffeemaker, poured herself another cup. She'd have to think about dinner. Something light and quick. Maybe a cheese omelet and stir-fry vegetables.

The phone rang, startling her. She reached for the kitchen extension. "Hello."

"It's Amelia Blair." A hint of excitement in her voice. "I had a second offer from that last couple—still a bargain-basement deal. I told them I wouldn't even take the offer to you. But the Denver man called. I gather he's being pressured by his wife. He gave me a new figure." She quoted it casually.

"It's low for today's market," Helen pointed out, her heart pounding. She knew, though, that Paul would say, "Take it!"

"Exactly. I can try to push him up another ten thousand—"

"Twenty thousand," Helen instructed. She'd been doing some frenzied figuring. The money for Zach's college must come out before Paul and she divided what was left after the loan sharks were paid off. "Another twenty thousand and he has a deal."

"I'll try to reach him. I may not get through until tomorrow," Amelia warned, but Helen sensed she was already counting her commission.

"I'll be here," Helen said.

He'd want an early closing. Amelia said she could probably get it through in a month. Helen fought against panic. So soon she must gear herself to move out of this life into a frightening new world.

She prepared her omelet and vegetables,

popped an onion roll into the oven to warm up, then carried her dinner on a tray into the living room. She'd watch the news on TV while she ate. Unless the news was another horrendous famine or flood. You heard so little that was good or heart-warming on the news.

Around 8 p.m. Gerry called. They hadn't spoken this often in months, Helen thought while she listened to Gerry's efforts to cheer her up. Gerry had done well for herself, she realized. But there had been desperate times before she settled in to a life on her own.

Was the divorce her fault? Helen asked herself for the hundredth time. Had she let herself go? It was clear that Paul no longer found her attractive—but then he hadn't stayed twenty-one, either. All at once she heard a click on the line. "Gerry, I have another call—"

A moment later she was talking with Amelia Blair.

"The Denver man put up a fight, but he's coming through," Amelia reported in triumph. "He's driving up tomorrow to give me a binder. He'll go to contract as soon as we can prepare the papers. He wants to be in the house by Thanksgiving."

"Can everything be managed by then?" Helen's heart was pounding.

"Have your lawyer give me a call in the morning." The office was, of course, always

60

open on weekends. "We'll get cracking."

She ought to call Paul right away, Helen told herself. Yet she dreaded calling him at that woman's apartment. She'd have another cup of coffee—then she would call.

Paul sprawled on Iris's queen-sized bed and watched the baseball game. They'd gone out for an early dinner, returned to the apartment because Paul insisted he had to see the night's baseball game. So Iris was pissed. She'd get over it.

He heard the shower turned off in the bathroom. When Iris was in an amorous mood, she showered. He grinned, visualizing her efforts to woo him away from baseball. And he knew how to make her hot as a pistol.

"Hi—" She emerged from the bathroom a few minutes later, wearing only gold-hooped earrings. Though she had been born after Marilyn Monroe had died, she made a point of playing up her resemblance to the sex-goddess.

"Hi," he drawled, inspecting her with obvious approval. "Going somewhere?"

"Sure—" Her smile was an eloquent invitation. "On a short trip to paradise." She strolled to the bed with a provocative thrust of her hips.

"Why short?" He reached to pull her down beside him. Hell, with Iris he felt about twenty. "I'm still good for the long haul."

"Show me," she commanded, throwing one leg across his hips. "I'm available."

He manipulated her slim, perfumed body to his satisfaction, knowing just how she liked to play this game. Already he was aroused. This one was always ready for action, he thought, rejoicing in her reciprocation.

"Oh, Paul, you're great," she murmured after a few moments. "So cool!"

"No," he said, his breathing uneven. "Hot. Hot as hell."

The phone was a jarring intrusion. "Don't answer," Iris said.

"I have to—it might be important." He leaned towards the night table to pick up the receiver. "Hello—"There was silence for an answer. "Hello?" Annoyance in his voice now.

"I called to tell you we have a deal on the house," Helen said and hesitated. "Is this a bad time?"

"No, of course not." He was all alertness now. "What are they offering?"

Helen sat motionless beside the phone. Her face hot. She'd interrupted Paul and his slut in the middle of sex. She knew that breathy, faintly hoarse, tell-tale quality in his voice.

How do you erase from your memory

62

almost twenty-five years of living with a man? But it was ridiculous for her to feel betrayed. Their marriage was over. In a way she was lucky—it hadn't happened when Deedee and Zach were small—or when they were vulnerable teenagers. Dee was twenty-three, Zach was nineteen. They were adults. This was her problem to deal with—the kids were in the clear.

She'd make sure the money for Zach's sophomore year at Columbia came off the top of what they had left from the sale of the house. She'd have a few thousand from the sale of the SUV. Somewhere in the city of New York she'd find an apartment for herself. Somewhere she would find a job. But the prospect was unnerving.

Six

Helen awoke Sunday morning with an instant realization that her days in the house were numbered. The sale would go through, wouldn't it? It was incredible to have made a sale this fast! But the Denver man was pressed to buy.

Amelia said he would be up this morning to give her a binder. He'd go to contract as fast as the papers could be put through. Amelia talked last night about a projected closing on the Monday before Thanksgiving. Helen suppressed a shudder. By then she must have found a place to live in Manhattan.

All at once—remembering the phone call to Paul last night—she felt faintly sick. She tried to block from her mind the sound of Paul's voice—that told her he was in the midst of making love to his young slut.

Focus on what was important. Check with Jeff Madison about a lawyer to handle the closing. She glanced at the bedside clock— and remembered the summer they'd spent in a rented house near Geneva when the kids were small. They'd bought the clock there.

She would take nothing from this house except her clothes and her books, she told herself in silent rage. She wanted nothing that reminded her of Paul. Nor would there be room in a one-bedroom apartment for any of the large-scale furniture that filled the house.

Try to arrange to sell the furniture to a dealer as a package deal. Hold a weekend tag sale to dispose of the linens, the cookware, appliances—the collection of almost 25 years. The kids would have to come up and salvage what they might want. Maybe they'd be able to help her with the tag sale.

It was too early on a Sunday to call Jeff. Have breakfast, drive into the village to pick up the *Sunday Times*, read the Apartments for Rent columns. Get an idea of what she would be facing. Deedee had talked about the insane rents in the city.

Two hours later—after forcing herself to eat breakfast—she sat down with the Apartments for Rent columns in the *Times*, was horrified by the prices of rentals. She would run out of funds fast at these rates. Maybe she should look for something in Queens or Brooklyn.

In a burst of frustration she thrust aside the classified section of the *Times*, decided it was late enough to call Jeff about the name of a real estate attorney. And if the Denver man came through with the binder as planned, she'd take the train into the city tomorrow and start the search for an apartment.

Deedee stirred into wakefulness, turned to glance at the bedside clock. Oh God, it was almost noon! She'd vowed to be up no later than 8 a.m., to take a long walk on the beach. Todd was making inchoate noises, coming reluctantly awake.

"We shouldn't sleep the day away—" But she stifled a yawn as Todd reached out to pull her close.

He dismissed this. "We needed the sleep.

Did I ever tell you that you talk in your sleep?" A teasing glint in his eyes.

"Do I say anything exciting?" She tried for a lightness she didn't feel. She was plagued by recurrent bouts of anger and frustration. How could Dad wreck a marriage after twenty-five years?

"Last night you worried about your mother." His voice was compassionate. As a small boy he'd suffered through his mother's two divorces. "She's not like my mother—she has her feet on the ground. It won't be easy," he conceded, "but she'll survive the divorce."

"I hate my father for doing this to her." He hadn't even bothered to call Zach and her, she thought with fresh outrage. Did he plan on leaving for California without even seeing them?

"What did your mother do before her marriage?" Todd pulled Deedee into his arms but without amorous intent.

"She married right out of college. While Dad went to law school, she was an editorial assistant in a publishing office. After I was born, she did some freelance work. Proofreading, editing, typing—whatever came along. Todd, she's forty six—what chance does she have in today's job market?"

"Shhh, she's going to be all right," he soothed. "For starters, move in with me and give her your apartment. That'll solve a major problem. And consider the perks. Like this morning. You turn around and there I am—and vice-versa. Consider how much time we'll save in travelling—I'm much closer to the office." Todd's apartment was in the East 60s. The office a dozen blocks south. "Time we can use for better things," he reminded, an eloquent glint in his eyes.

Mom would be shocked if she moved in with Todd, but she wouldn't say that she was. She'd try to be sophisticated and casual. But Todd was right—it would solve a major problem. "Todd, I don't know—"

"I know," Todd insisted. "Call her tonight and tell her to stop worrying about an apartment."

Early in the afternoon Amelia Blair called Helen to say that the Denver man was in her office and had given her a binder. He wanted to come over and get the dimensions of the rooms to send to his wife.

"So she'll know what furniture to have shipped from out there. Their house was sold—as you know—but they were able to rent it for three months while the new owners are in Europe. He had to buy," Amelia confided. "Their rental is up the end of November."

"Bring him over." Helen sighed in relief. She'd been haunted these past few days by the specter of the loan sharks barging in to take over the house—leaving them with nothing. At least, this way they could salvage something.

The prospective buyer exuded enthusiasm as he moved about the house. At occasional moments she sensed a curiosity in him. Why were they selling this perfect house? When he was about to leave, she told him.

"I've loved this house since the day we moved in. But my husband and I are divorcing." There, that startled Amelia. "It's a house that begs for a large family," she said with a wistful smile. "I'm sure you'll enjoy living here." And by tomorrow it would be all over town. *Have you heard? Helen and Paul Avery are getting a divorce. After so many years!*

Alone she debated about calling Paul to tell him they had a binder, would go to contract right away. No, she rejected—wait until tomorrow morning and call him at the office. *I'll never call him at that slut's apartment again.*

Focus now on what must be done in the days—weeks—ahead, she ordered herself. Make notes. Myriad details had to be handled. No chance that the deal could go awry, Amelia said. By the Monday before Thanksgiving they would go to closing. She would celebrate Thanksgiving somewhere in Manhattan. Hardly a celebration—but she and the kids would greet Thanksgiving together. They were still a family.

With a need to be busy, she went through the huge upstairs linen closet, earmarked what she would offer Deedee for her apartment, check if Zach could use more linens and towels for his dorm use. So absorbed in the tasks ahead, she was startled to realize it was past 8 p.m.

She was making a pretense of having dinner when the phone rang.

"Hello—"

"I'm back from East Hampton," Deedee reported ebulliently. "We drove in early to avoid heavy traffic. Any news on the house?"

"It's amazing—we have a sale. A decent price. The buyer wants to close the Monday before Thanksgiving."

"Wow! That was fast."

"Did you enjoy the weekend?" Helen felt a surge of tenderness. The marriage might be ending in a disaster, but it had given her two great kids. "How was the weather out there?"

"We had a marvelous time, and the weather was wonderful. Todd borrowed this gorgeous house from a friend—" All at once Deedee sounded tense.

"Todd?" Why had she assumed Deedee had gone out to East Hampton with girlfriends?

"You know Todd. The guy from the office

that I've been seeing for a while."

"Yes, I've heard you mention him." Helen's mind leapt into alertness. Deedee had spent the weekend with a man. "I've never met him."

"Well, you know our insane work schedule—" Unease in Deedee's voice now.

"Yes." Cliff, too, had an insane work schedule—but Deedee had managed to bring him out for occasional weekends. She'd liked Cliff, Helen remembered.

"Anyhow, this was kind of a test run." Deedee cleared her throat in that nervous gesture so like her father's. "I'm going to move in with him—for a while. So—" She paused with a dramatic flourish. "I can loan you my apartment for two or three months at least. I don't think I'm ready for marriage just yet," she admitted. "Neither is Todd. So we'll just give this a whirl."

"When is this going to happen?" Helen tried to conceal her shock. This was the twenty-first century—such arrangements were acceptable these days.

"Right away. So any time you're ready, you can start moving in. If I'm not caught up in the rat-race next weekend, I'll come out to help."

"That would be great." But her mind was in turmoil. Deedee living with some man named Todd? *I don't even know his last name!* "Everything will be moving fast now."

"I'll have extra keys made up." Deedee sounded relieved. She'd been afraid, Helen surmised, that her news would cause a row. Deedee was twenty-three—she made her own decisions. A mother could only pray that it was the right decision. "Oh, the sofa is a convertible. On school holidays Zach can sleep there."

"Fine." She wouldn't fall apart over this, Helen ordered herself. She was surviving the divorce. She could survive Deedee's living arrangements.

"Mom—" Deedee hesitated. "If you're going to be short on money, I can help some."

"I'll be all right until I find a job." Helen contrived to sound confident. "But thanks, darling."

In a corner of her mind Helen realized that the frenzied demands on her in the coming days were, in truth, a blessing. They left little time for her to agonize over her situation. There were meetings with the divorce lawyer and with the real estate lawyer, endless calls, "to-do" lists to be made and followed. Gerry phoned every night. Deedee and Zach phoned. It was almost as though she was an invalid—in fragile health, Helen thought in a moment of wry humor.

On a Friday morning—after much urging from Deedee—she took the commuter train into New York to check out Deedee's apartment. *"Most of my gear is out Mom. I left some stuff behind because there's no room in Todd's apartment, but I think you'll have plenty of room for your clothes and books."*

She'd made a point of telling the kids she was taking nothing else from the house. This was to be a fresh start—no ugly reminders to taunt her. Deedee ordered her to start moving in by bits and pieces instead of waiting for the closing. "Before you sell the SUV, Mom."

She boarded her Metro North train at slightly past 10 a.m.—avoiding the commuter rush. And avoiding conversation with anybody she knew from the community—all of whom must know by now about the divorce. She was relieved that few passengers were on board at this hour. She made an effort to read the morning's *New York Times* as the train sped towards its destination.

At Grand Central Station she took a cab to Deedee's Upper West Side apartment. Deedee had left word with the doorman that "my mother will be staying with me for a while." She went up to Deedee's apartment with no trouble.

Her hands were trembling when she unlocked the door. She'd been here several times—but she hadn't really seen it, she thought as her eyes swept around the living room. She'd forgot how small rooms could be in so-called luxury apartments. Deedee always said the only luxurious things were the prices.

Deedee was paying $1,300 in rent, considered herself lucky. The same apartment was going for $2,700 in other buildings. New York apartment rents were going through the roof. But Deedee drew a fabulous salary. How many 23-year-olds earned $70,000 a year?

Helen shuddered, visualizing the kind of salary she'd need to support this rent—along with all the other expenses. She would no longer have health insurance once Paul left his job at the end of the month. No more dental insurance. She'd need a new wardrobe to join the work force. And Zach had two more years of college after this year. She doubted that Paul would help with this.

She glanced at her watch. She'd told Gerry she'd call as soon as she arrived in the city. They were to have lunch together. Feeling herself in foreign territory, she glanced about the living room, located the telephone. Gerry was the assistant to a prominent publicist, loved her job, Helen recalled.

"I love working for Ted," Gerry had said. "I was so bitter after the nasty divorce—but then, thank God, I realized that was a deadend street."

The secretary Gerry shared with her boss reported that Gerry was in a meeting but would call back shortly. Now Helen inspected the rest of the small apartment. As Deedee had said, she'd emptied the closets except for several cartons stashed in the corners, the drawers of the double dresser.

It seemed so tiny, yet she and Paul had started their married life in a similar apartment only four blocks south. *What happened to us in the intervening years? Where did I fail Paul?*

The ringing of the phone startled her. She hurried to reply.

"Let's have an early lunch," Gerry said. "Before the mobs descend. There's a place not far from the office that has good food, great service and tables that aren't three inches apart."

Helen left immediately, found a cab to take her to their meeting place. Gerry was already there, but at this early hour few patrons had arrived.

"I can't believe how long it's been since we saw each other. Not since that weekend in the Hamptons." Gerry searched her face. "You look fine." Her voice was gentle. "I know you're not. It takes time to bounce back. But you will," she said with confidence.

"I'll sure as hell try." Helen's smile was defiant. She was not going to spend the rest of her life moaning over her divorce. She'd seen too many women do that.

A waitress arrived, took their orders. When she'd left their table, Gerry leaned forward, her voice low. "This is one of the few places around here where we can have some privacy at lunch. Have you talked to your lawyer about the alimony deal?" She'd urged Helen to fight for alimony.

Helen shook her head. "I'd spend all my time running across the country and going into court. Gerry, I'm on my own now." She tried to brush aside the desperation that crept in at unwary intervals. "I'll have to find a job." She flinched. "One that'll pay the rent on Deedee's apartment. Of course, I'm only there temporarily." Gerry knew the circumstances.

"My apartment-mate—Sheila—runs an employment agency," Gerry told her. "We'll huddle with her once you're settled in." She paused. "Helen, I need to tell you something that—that may upset you." Her eyes were troubled. "You know how I felt after the divorce. I was so full of hate—"

"Who could blame you?" *Do I hate Paul? I'm hurt, humiliated, stunned. I'm furious—*

"I knew I'd never trust another man again as long as I live." Gerry paused, seeming in some inner debate. "I never said a word to anybody until now—not even to you, as close as we were. But Al abused me—physically."

Helen gaped in shock. "You never let on—not once." She felt sick, envisioning Gerry being abused by Al—7 inches taller and 60 pounds heavier. *Shouldn't I have been aware of it?*

"I gave Academy Award performances. I established myself as a klutzy mother." But rage since buried surfaced again for the moment.

"Gerry, why did you take it?" Fiercely independent Gerry an abused wife?

"What was the alternative?" Gerry countered. "I had two kids to raise. I promised myself once they were both in college, I'd walk out. But I was scared. How would I fare on my own in the outside world? Then Al decided he wanted a divorce—so he could marry his young whore. But I did all right," she said with a surge of satisfaction. "I had a couple of bad years—that's behind me. Yet I was terribly lonely out on my own," she acknowledged. "Some women enjoy living alone—having to cater to no one except themselves. I hated it. I missed the closeness with somebody else. I yearned for warmth and companionship." She paused, her face softening. "And love. I've had a relationship with Sheila for almost two years now. Then two months ago she moved in with me." Her eyes sought to convey her message. "Helen, do you understand what I'm trying to say?"

For an instant Helen stared blankly. Then comprehension took over. Gerry was in a lesbian relationship.

"If it works for you, then I'm happy about it," Helen said slowly. For a moment she had been unnerved, yes—but if Gerry found something that made her wake up in the morning without the hate she'd felt after the divorce, then it was good.

"It won't make any difference in our friendship?"

"Gerry, no," Helen scolded. Of course, she was taken aback—but Gerry had been her closest friend for years. "Nothing can change that."

"You'll like Sheila when you get to know her," Gerry promised with an air of relief. "She's warm and bright—and she runs a successful employment agency," she added with an attempt at humor. "She'll help you, Helen."

I'll need help. What job skills have I to offer in this crazy new world? Gerry survived after her divorce. Can I?

Seven

Gerry was warming up the vegetable lasagna she'd picked up at Citarella's—the salad on a shelf in the refrigerator—when Sheila arrived home from the office.

"Dinner's ready whenever you are," she told Sheila with a welcoming smile.

"It was a long day." Sheila was at her health club by 7 a.m. every Monday, Wednesday, and Friday. "I need a glass of white wine to resuscitate me." She collapsed in a corner of the sofa, kicked off her shoes.

"Two white wines coming up." Gerry felt a sense of contentment. The work week was over—the weekend theirs. "Rough day?"

"We all know the healthy state of the job market." Sheila exuded a heavy sigh. "But why do workers who might make it flipping hamburgers at McDonald's expect to be sent out as administrative assistants in glamour jobs?"

"TV, darling." Gerry clucked sympathetically. "All these young things expect magic in their lives." She blew out softly. "Which brings up a problem—"

"You had lunch with your friend Helen," Sheila recalled, and Gerry nodded. "She knows about us?"

"She knows—she understands."

Sheila's eyes radiated relief. "You said she'd be in the job market soon."

"She's bright, conscientious—and I'm sure she'll be efficient once she brings her skills up to date. You know, becomes computer literate. Right now she's scared to death of getting out there."

"I was thinking about her today. I had a quick lunch with Liz Stratton. Liz is setting up a committee to plan our class reunion in the spring. She hasn't told Adam yet—but she's going to ask him for a year's leave. So she can take care of her mother at home instead of putting her in a nursing home. Her mother's Alzheimer's is advancing."

"Adam's going to be upset," Gerry guessed. "How long has Liz been with him?"

"Almost eighteen years. She came in right after he opened the agency. She watched him grow from a small-time publicist to one of the tops in the field." Sheila's face softened. "I think she's been in love with him since the beginning. After his divorce, he'd call her at home at night and ask her what to do with the pork chops he'd bought for dinner—or how did he cope with a tuna steak. He said he ate out at lunch five days a week—he couldn't face another restaurant in the evening."

"You're thinking of trying to place Helen

in her job?" Gerry was dubious. "Helen's never worked in publicity." She frowned. "Except for the few early years in publishing she hasn't worked at all—except for the usual volunteer deals."

"If she can take a crash course on the computer—using the software Adam's office has installed—I'd take a crack at trying to ease her into the job."

"I don't see it, Sheila—" Gerry squinted in thought. "I mean, Adam Fremont runs a high-pressured organization." Her own boss's main competition. "It would be like throwing her to the lions."

"Don't underestimate a woman like her," Sheila scolded. "As a volunteer—and you say she's handled major fund-raising—she's learned how to deal with people, work the phones. She's bright—she'll be able to handle the correspondence from Adam's notes. You'll teach her basic situations—like how to write press releases. You said she was an English major."

"He'll be expecting some bright young thing with two or three years' experience," Gerry warned.

"That's where you're wrong." Sheila smiled in satisfaction. "After working all these years with Liz, he'd hate a bright-eyed recent graduate of Vassar or Wellsley. Liz said as much."

"If it doesn't work out, Helen will be

crushed." Gerry was ambivalent. Adam Fremont worked harder than any man she'd ever encountered. He was a powerhouse in the field. Appearing taller than he was, streaks of gray in his slightly unruly hair, still slim and trim at forty-eight, he exuded a potent charm, but was known to be brusque—devastating—when faced with inefficiency. "She's in a vulnerable state right now."

"Despite the shortage of people it won't be easy to place her." Sheila was blunt. "Sure, companies are screaming for help— but the 'over-forty' workers are at the bottom of the list. This could be the perfect spot for her—if we coach her right."

"Okay—" Still, Gerry was conscious of a certain reluctance. "She's closing on the house the Monday after Thanksgiving. Once she's in town we'll work with her. How much notice does Liz plan to give Adam?"

"She'll stay till the end of the year. If Helen passes the two interviews—one with Liz, another with Adam—she'll be on the job the day after New Year's, 2000."

Liz Stratton sat in her private office in the luxurious suite that housed the firm of Adam Fremont, Public Relations. The rest of the staff—except for Adam, always the last to leave—were gone for the day. No point in delaying this, she ordered herself. Adam had to gear himself for her taking leave.

She reached into a desk drawer for her make-up kit, applied a fresh layer of lipstick—more from nervousness than need. She gazed for a moment at her reflection in the small make-up mirror she kept in her desk. Never a pretty woman, she conceded—but through the years she had learned to dress smartly.

All right. No more stalling. If her mother was to remain at home—and the doctors warned her condition was becoming severe enough to require nursing home care in a matter of a few months—she must be there full-time. *I owe this to Mama.*

Adam glanced up with a smile as she appeared at the open door of his spacious office. They were more than boss and employee, she thought with pride. They were friends. Close friends. She'd helped him through the divorce—and the painful two years that preceded it.

Only she knew his anguish when Zoe told him that Eric—whom he adored—was not his son. It never entered the divorce proceedings. In addition to hefty alimony— which Adam did not contest—Zoe had asked for full custody. It was she, Liz reminded herself, that had urged him to demand visitation rights. Eric came to him alternate holidays. At boarding school this year he would go to Zoe for Thanksgiving. He would be with Adam over the Christmas holidays.

"Why are you always the last to leave?" he scolded gently.

"Adam, we need to talk." Her voice revealed her tension.

"What's the problem?" He leaned forward, elbows on his massive desk.

"It's about my mother—"

"She's not getting better," he said compassionately.

"She won't get better. Adam, I hate having to ask this. But I need to take a year's leave of absence—to be with her." Her eyes pleaded for understanding.

"I guess I knew this was coming." His smile was troubled. "It's going to be hell without you to run things."

"I'll be here until the end of the year." She fought for poise. "I'll start interviewing right after Thanksgiving, weed out the impossible ones. By mid-December I hope to have a possible replacement."

"Liz, nobody can replace you. But don't bring in some pretty young kid fresh out of college," he warned. "Somebody mature and responsible. And I'll try to make do." His smile now was rueful. "I don't have to tell you—no one will ever be able to take your place."

"I'll be here to break her in," Liz reminded. "And if she encounters problems, she can always call me at home. Adam, I don't want to do this—but it's my responsibility to Mama."

"I know, Liz. But when the right time comes, you'll be back. There'll always be a place for you here."

Eight

To Helen's relief the Denver man—true to his word—went to contract immediately. Amelia Blair assured Helen there would be no slip-ups. In a phone call to Paul's office—she would never call his "home" phone again, she'd vowed—Helen conveyed the message to Paul.

"Great." Paul exuded relief.

"The closing is set for the Monday before Thanksgiving." *How can I talk so calmly to Paul?* "You'll have to be there, of course." The house had been bought in both their names.

"I'll be there," he promised, and cleared his throat in the familiar way that said he was uptight. "The creeps will be there to receive their checks, of course. I'll notify them—and the bank." The first mortgage, too, must be paid off.

"I've explained to Jeff that the balance is to be made out in two checks—half to you, half to me."

"Oh—" Paul sounded startled. "Yeah—"

"Is there any of the furniture that you'd like to take with you? I've talked to a dealer about a package sale. He's coming over on Friday to do an inventory and give me a price."

"No point in taking furniture across-country," he dismissed this self-consciously. "Just clue me in to how much we'll be splitting."

"I will," she agreed. Was he scared she'd walk off with the full amount?

"I have to go into a meeting now. Thanks for calling, Helen."

Now every hour of every day seemed crowded. She hadn't expected to be so busy. But that was good—less time to brood. She made lists, took care of each item and crossed it off. It amazed her that so many small matters needed to be handled. The utilities, the garbage collection, her cleaning woman. The list seemed endless.

She awoke on the morning of what would have been her silver-wedding anniversary with an instant—anguished—realization of the date. She'd been dreading this day. The morning was unseasonably cold. She ought to get up and turn up the thermostat, her mind exhorted. Instead, she huddled beneath the light blanket, drawing her body into a fetal position as though to find warmth in that fashion.

For the hundredth time she asked herself, *When did our marriage begin to fall apart?* How many women in Paul's life that she never knew about? Paul's ego had destroyed their marriage. He couldn't stand growing older. He wanted to be thirty for ever. He wanted to be rich and powerful. He sold himself to law partners—then unsold himself.

What do women alone in suburbia—divorcees, widows—do with their lives? Volunteer work, gardening? What about their social lives? Dinner party invitations are extended to couples—it's like Noah's Ark. No hostess wants to bother digging up extra men—and what extra men are there in suburbia?

Amelia mentioned that today young women were buying houses alone—though nothing as large as this one. They probably imported their company. They commuted to their jobs, entertained friends from the city on weekends. They weren't part of the community.

Even if she could afford it, she wouldn't want to live here alone. She'd be an outsider. How would she fill the empty hours?

There never used to be enough hours in the day—now there were too many.

She knew this day would drag on for ever. It was a wake for their marriage. But there was no room in her life for self-pity, she scolded herself. She had to move out into the world and care for herself.

It was scary to consider job hunting—even though Gerry told her that Sheila would be of enormous help. Society put such value on the young. On the rare occasions when she and Paul had gone to a movie these last few years, the faces were strangers to her. The national weekly magazines were constantly touting a "debut novelist."

Paul had been obsessed by stories about the new millionaires in their twenties, who arrived there via the dot.com craziness. She knew about middle-management executives in their community who were put out to pasture because of the "over-forty syndrome." Paul was lucky to have a job lined up in Silicon Valley. *But I won't be put out to pasture. I won't.*

In mid-afternoon a colorful bouquet of flowers was delivered. For a startled instant she thought they might be from Paul. They were from Zach. He remembered this was her wedding anniversary. The card read: "Mom, I love you."

Early in the evening Deedee called. "I'm on my dinner break," she explained. "Both

Todd and I will be here till dawn, the way things are going." She hesitated. Recognizing the date, Helen thought. The kids were so sweet, so anxious about her. "Mom, consider you're beginning a new life. You're going to be fine."

On the next to the last Saturday before the closing, Helen scheduled the tag sale. Friday evening Gerry and Sheila came up to help, would stay for the weekend. On Saturday morning—well before the arranged time—the three women carried out the items to be sold, arranged them on tables, on a pair of racks rented for the occasion.

Helen strived for calm. How strange to see possessions they'd acquired through the years being offered for sale. Linens she'd bought on vacation in Ireland, the blankets bought in Canada, sweaters from Bermuda that she knew she'd never wear again because that trip was supposed to have been their second honeymoon.

The anger that Deedee and Zach expressed at intervals upset her. The kids shouldn't harbor such rage at their father— yet could she expect anything else? It wasn't just her life that had been turned upside down. They were affected, too. Their family had been disrupted.

The Saturday morning before the closing Deedee and Zach came out to the house to help with the final packing. As prearranged,

Helen met them at the train station. The three of them would drive back together in the SUV—to be sold immediately. Saturday night Helen would sleep in her new residence.

"Did you have breakfast?" Helen was solicitous. "All the pots and pans, the dishes went at the tag sale last week—except for the coffeemaker and one place setting."

"We had breakfast," Deedee soothed. "Hey, won't you enjoy being able to go downstairs for breakfast without having to drive three miles? You can walk around the corner to pick up a container of milk instead of driving to the mall. And Citarella is just two blocks down on Broadway—and a few blocks up there's Zabars and Barnes & Noble—and great little shops everywhere."

"The city has its advantages," Helen conceded, determined to offer a casual façade.

The day fled past, with occasional moments of nostalgia that almost unnerved Helen. With a laugh at herself, Deedee decided it was time to drop off her Barbie dolls at the library thrift shop. Zach conceded that he didn't need the souvenirs he'd brought back from his hiking trip at fourteen on the Appalachian Trail or those from the summer camp in Spain the previous year. They'd join Deedee's Barbie dolls along with roller skates and baseball equipment that had never been discarded.

"What about Dad's computer?" Deedee asked while they lingered in the den. "Isn't he taking it?"

"He said it was a dinosaur," Helen recalled. "He'll get a new one—"

"Mom, if you're going out into the business world, you'll need to know computers," Zach said pensively. "Take it with you. And don't consider it the enemy," he warned. "This is almost the twenty-first century."

"I suppose I'll have to take a course." All at once Helen was fighting panic. There was a world out there that she didn't know.

"Take the fax, too," Zach ordered. "Get familiar with it. It's part of the everyday business world." But his eyes were troubled as he regarded his mother.

"I'll take the computer and the fax," she agreed—almost defiantly. But she was terrified at the prospect of having to deal with them.

Zach drove into town to leave off their contributions at the library thrift shop, returned with take-out dinner for the three of them. By dusk they had eaten and were transferring to the SUV everything that Helen was taking with her to the Manhattan apartment.

"Dad called last night," Zach reported grimly. "He wanted to say good-bye before he left for California. He said he'd probably be too busy with the closing to have time to see Deedee and me. You know that's a crock of shit! But when did he ever have time for us?"

"He left a message on my answering machine," Deedee said with contempt. "I'll bet he was glad I wasn't there."

Nine

Alone in the apartment, Helen forced herself to hang away clothes, to empty valises into dresser drawers. She was sure she'd lie awake for hours, but moments after she hit the bed she was asleep—exhausted from the day's activities.

Sunday morning—feeling as though she was performing in a stage production, she went downstairs for breakfast. Afterwards, she went into a supermarket to shop—and was startled at how much she bought.

"A delivery, please," she told the clerk at the checkout counter. One of the perks of living in the city, she thought with a wry smile.

With the *New York Times* in tow she returned to the apartment. Involuntarily she allowed her mind to dart back through the years to the first apartment she'd shared in New York with Paul while he studied at NYU Law—only a few blocks from this apartment.

She'd thought Paul was so wonderful, so ambitious. She'd been so in love with him, proud of their passion for each other. She'd known that the passion seemed to go out of their marriage—but she'd told herself that happened after a number of years. She'd always felt that in any marriage one partner led and the other followed. Paul led—she followed. Or so she had thought.

She'd worked to see Paul through law school, then afterwards because they needed the money to keep up the front Paul considered necessary to launch a successful career. She had worried that he moved from one firm to another—bitter at not receiving the recognition he felt he deserved. All through the years he had focused on moving up in the legal profession. She had managed their personal lives.

They'd bought and sold five houses in the course of their marriage—and it had been her responsibility to track down suitable houses, handle all the details of the financing, hire the lawyers who handled the closings. She'd checked out schools for the kids, from nursery school on. Paul insisted on frequent entertaining—"for business"— and this had been her responsibility. She'd hired the parade of contractors who made improvements on each of the five houses. Paul couldn't be bothered with deals outside of his profession. No, she told herself, she hadn't been a follower. She'd been a partner. But how could she use that life experience in the business world?

Sunday seemed endless. After she'd finished reading the *Times*, Helen busied herself with what Gerry used to refer to as "donkey work." She ironed every item of clothing she'd brought from the house. She sewed on buttons, sewed hems where the thread had broken—mindful that tailors were expensive in her present financial situation.

Earlier than usual, she went to bed. Again, feeling as though she was playing a role in a stage production. In her mind she was trying to gear herself to encounter Paul at the closing tomorrow morning. The SUV was in the garage downstairs, would stay there till Tuesday, when she had an appointment with a used car dealer. With a flicker of amusement she remembered that used cars were now referred to as "preowned."

Doubting that it would be necessary, she set her alarm. She was taking an early train in the morning. The lawyer handling the closing would pick her up at the station and drive her to his office—where the closing was to be held. And after the closing she'd never see Paul again.

She stared into the darkness of the bedroom until the first gray streaks of dawn infiltrated the drapes. At last she fell asleep—into chaotic dreams, awoke with a sense of falling through space. This was the day that wrote the end of her marriage, she thought in a haze of pain. Not the day the divorce became final. The day their house belonged to others.

Well before her commuter train was to pull into Grand Central, she was pushing her way through the rush hour crowds. All at once she wished she had accepted Deedee and Zach's offer to accompany her to the closing. But she knew she would be pulling Deedee away from work and Zach from school—and that would be wrong. And she knew, too, that they were relieved not to have to encounter their father.

She was grateful that the train was lightly populated. The *Times* that she had picked up at Grand Central to occupy her on the trip lay unread. She gazed out the window at the passing scenery—bathed in glorious sunlight—without seeing. This was the last time ever that she would be riding a Westchester-bound train.

At her destination she found the real estate lawyer waiting beside his car in the parking area, as arranged.

"Perfect weather." He greeted her with a

brilliant smile. "And we're right on schedule."

They exchanged pleasantries on the short drive to his office. He probably had a thriving practice, what with all the turnovers in suburbia, Helen surmised. All the company executives transferred at regular intervals.

He briefed her on the procedures that would comprise the closing. She didn't need to be told this, she thought fretfully—this was the fifth house she and Paul had sold in the course of their marriage. From a technical standpoint, they were still married, weren't they? Until the final papers came through.

She felt herself growing tense as they left the car to enter the office. Paul wasn't here yet. No sign of his car. But when was Paul ever on time?

Amelia Blair was in lively conversation with the others already about the conference table. Instinctively Helen knew that the pair of men in expensive Italian suits— saying nothing and wearing wary expressions—were the holders of the second mortgage. The buyer was in high spirits— his family was at this moment airborne, en route to New York.

"I hope this won't go on for ever," he said, glancing toward the door in faint apprehension. "I have to pick up my brood at the airport in four hours."

"I'm sure Mr Avery will be here any moment," Amelia soothed and shot a swift, nervous glance at Helen. She had a huge commission on the griddle.

Helen felt a surge of relief when she heard a car pull up outside. Paul, she surmised. A moment later he charged into the room—in jeans, black turtleneck, and denim jacket. Clothes she'd never seen him wear. His "young guy" look, she thought derisively.

"I'm sorry to be late," he apologized ingratiatingly. "The old jalopy wouldn't co-operate this morning." Old jalopy? He drove a 1998 BMW.

His eyes grazed Helen for a moment—an obligatory recognition, she told herself. But of course, Amelia knew about the divorce—and no doubt the others around the table knew.

With a fixed smile Helen participated in the routine closing. Everything was going smoothly. Paul signed the necessary papers, passed them to her for her signature. He gave no indication of the strained feelings between them. Then the two checks allotted to Paul and her were presented. Didn't the others wonder at this arrangement?

In moments the group was disbanding. Paul was the first to leave.

"I'm running late for a business appointment down in the city," he explained. *In jeans and denim jacket?* He turned to the

Denver buyer. "I'm sure you'll enjoy the house. We did." He managed a brief smile in Helen's direction as he hurried to leave.

Amelia Blair was struggling to hide her annoyance at Paul's behavior. After some visual exchange with the real estate lawyer she offered to drive Helen to the station.

"Thanks, that would be nice." Helen assumed this arrangement had been set up before the closing.

"You'll have a wait. Why don't we stop in somewhere for coffee?"

"I'd like that." Helen gathered together the papers that had been assigned to her as former owner. Paul had never bothered with such trifles.

It was over. Would she ever see Paul again? Let him at least keep in touch with the kids. Though at this point both Deedee and Zach felt only contempt for him. Children shouldn't feel that way toward their father, she thought in anguish. But Paul was no longer a part of this family.

On the train back to Manhattan—to her new life—Helen tried to assess her feelings about Paul. Love had long ago eroded—but she'd refused to face that fact. No, she thought in sudden defiance. Love hadn't eroded— Paul had smothered it through the years. The real Paul had emerged, and he was not the man she'd loved and married.

Paul had become a stranger—but he was

woven into the pattern of her life. He was her husband, the father of her children. They were a family. She'd thought that was the way it would be for ever.

She knew the divorce statistics in this country. She knew many families divided by divorce. But why, she asked herself with sudden rage, were you so sure this would never happen to you?

Ten

On the way back to Manhattan Helen was filled with a sense of leaving one life behind and embarking on another. Remembering the rents of apartments in Manhattan, she shuddered. For now, at least, she had Deedee's apartment. But she worried that Deedee was living with a man she'd never met. The world was on the cusp of the twenty-first century—it was old-fashioned, antediluvian to be concerned about such arrangements, she rebuked herself. But where was Deedee headed with this man named Todd?

First thing tomorrow morning she would open a bank account in Manhattan, deposit the certified check from the closing. No need to do anything about the charge plates in her name except advise of change of address. And keep them inactive for now, she cautioned herself. No running up bills.

Then she'd have to settle down to job-hunting. The prospect was a thunderous, ever-present cloud that hung over her head. But other women coped, she told herself defiantly.

She arrived at the apartment to find a message on the answering machine. She pushed the "message button."

"Hi, I guess you're not back yet from the closing. But come over to our place for dinner. We should be home around six. Sheila's a gourmet cook. See you then." Gerry and Sheila's apartment was just four blocks away.

Gerry knew how desolate she'd feel after the closing, Helen thought tenderly. She winced at the prospect of preparing dinner for herself alone. But women did that. Millions of women came home from work, sat down to a solitary dinner—usually on a tray before the TV set, Gerry had said once. *"And thank God for the 'mute' button on the remote. How did we live without it?"*

Needing activity, Helen decided to run down to the supermarket, shop for a few basic items she'd forgot to pick up yesterday morning. Back in the apartment forty minutes later, she settled down to read until it was time to leave for her dinner date. But the words before her were blurs, her mind too chaotic to focus.

Her marriage wasn't a total loss. She had Deedee and Zach. To be able to love was a precious gift. And she loved the kids so much. They were her wealth.

A few minutes before six she left the apartment. A touch of winter in the air this evening. She was glad she'd worn a warm coat.

Thursday would be Thanksgiving. It would be so strange to have Thanksgiving dinner in a tiny apartment. But it would be a regular Thanksgiving, she promised herself—turkey, pumpkin pie, the works. If Gerry and Sheila had no other plans, she'd invite them. The first Thanksgiving without Paul, her mind traitorously pinpointed.

This was a fireplace night, she thought in a corner of her mind. In the early years Paul, too, had enjoyed a roaring fire in the grate. Later he'd decided it required too much effort. At intervals Deedee or Zach had assumed the task of building a fire on nights when Paul was staying in the city. On business, she'd thought.

She was conscious of an odd solace in the bustle in the streets as she headed for her destination. Once she had loved living in Manhattan. Paul had never liked city living. *"Hell, it's dehumanizing,"* he'd scoffed. Why

100

did she allow Paul to keep creeping into her mind? He was out of her life for ever.

Gerry and Sheila were both home. Already, appetizing aromas were emerging from the small kitchen.

"Sheila's cooking up a storm," Gerry reported in high spirits. Yet Helen sensed a certain insecurity in her. Couldn't Gerry understand she wasn't turned off by her relationship with Sheila?

"Hi," Sheila called from the kitchen. "I hope you like salmon steaks—"

"Love them," Helen called back. Sheila was bright, warm—and appealingly vulnerable. She'd endured a lot of hurt in her life, Helen guessed. But who went through life without hurt?

"We've mastered the fifteen-minute dinner preparations," Gerry said, setting the table in the dining area. "Between the microwave, the George Forman grill, and stir-fried vegetables, it's a cinch."

"Do you two have plans for Thanksgiving?" Helen asked on impulse.

"No. Sheila's family lives in a small town in Iowa. My kids are both living out in Texas," Gerry reminded. "My brother and his wife haven't spoken to me since the divorce. To them I'm a fallen woman." Helen knew about Gerry's brother and his wife, who belonged to some weird cult.

"My mother barred me from the house,"

Sheila said with a tense smile. "She's staunch Catholic, sure I'll end up in purgatory."

"Then come over and have dinner with us," Helen invited.

"Great!" Gerry exchanged an approving glance with Sheila.

Dinner seemed almost a festive occasion, Helen thought. The conversation was light—mostly revolving around amusing anecdotes about Gerry's office and its clients. The other two eager to lift her spirits.

Not until the table was cleared and the dishes stashed in the dishwasher did the conversation take a serious turn.

"You said you were bringing in a computer, didn't you?" Gerry asked.

"Yes." Helen's smile was wry. "Paul's discarded it. It's almost three years old—a dinosaur, he said, in the computer world. I don't know the first thing about it. Zach will set it up when he comes over on Thanksgiving. I suppose if I'm to work in an office, I'll have to learn to use it. I still use an IBM Selectric." On occasion she typed for Paul. He'd considered a computer beyond her talents. "I admit it scares me to death—" She managed a shaky laugh.

"You'll have to learn." Sheila made it seem an amusing effort. But her eyes were serious.

Haltingly Helen briefed Sheila now on her experience. "I'm good at organization," she said and explained her efforts as a volunteer. "I have a substantial knowledge of proofreading. I was an English major."

"Helen has always been the most disciplined person I've ever known," Gerry said. Helen was startled. Gerry had said that before. She'd never considered herself especially disciplined—she just did what had to be done.

"We have a possible job in mind," Sheila said. "There's no guarantee, of course—but we want to coach you to take over for Liz Stratton in—"

"Who's Liz Stratton?" Helen was conscious of the pounding of her heart.

Sheila explained the situation, outlined the job requirements. "Adam Fremont won't be an easy boss to please," she warned, "but he's fair and he pays well. The major problem is to make you computer literate in a hurry."

"I don't know much about publicity—" Helen glanced anxiously from Sheila to Gerry. "I did some minor publicity as a volunteer."

"You don't have to know a lot," Gerry soothed. "You have to be diplomatic on the phone, able to write letters from Adam's notes. And he'll want somebody mature. Someone who won't be awed by meeting entertainment and publishing celebrities."

"How long do I have to learn the computer?" Could she take a crash course somewhere? Deedee never had free time, but maybe Zach could help her— "I suppose there are schools?"

"You'll need one-on-one instruction considering the time element," Sheila said. "I can find someone for you. It'll be expensive," she warned, "but necessary for any office job."

"Liz is giving Adam a month's notice. She'll handle the initial interviews. Weed out the applicants she knows he won't like. By the time you reach the interview with Adam, you'll have basic knowledge of the computer, the program Liz uses. And if it doesn't work out with Adam, then Sheila will send you out on other possible jobs. But you still have to be computer literate." Gerry chuckled at her air of consternation. "Darling, it's not like learning to be a concert pianist."

The following morning Helen received a call from a computer instructor. She scheduled daily appointments—except for Thanksgiving day—at hours when he had open time. He sounded younger than Deedee, she thought self-consciously—but Sheila said he was a great teacher. All right, this was her training period. If she bombed out with Adam Fremont, Sheila would send her out on other interviews.

In the course of the afternoon Zach and Deedee called—both anxious about how she was handling the situation.

"I'm fine," she told each—though that was a blatant lie, she conceded to herself. She was a nervous wreck. "Stop worrying about me."

She was taken aback when Deedee suggested she go to a hair stylist.

"I know this guy who's sensational. He charges a lot, but wow! Make an appointment with him, Mom."

The computer instructor—an early-twenties college drop-out enthralled with the world of technology—arrived Tuesday morning, set up the computer, and began her instruction. She was grateful for his patience, that he assured her she wasn't a complete idiot. She felt mildly reassured.

On Thanksgiving day Zach was the first to arrive. She'd expected him to sleep over during the school holiday, but he explained that he'd stay in the dorm.

"It'll be quiet with almost everybody gone—I can do some real cramming." He glanced about the apartment. "Anything you need me to do?"

"I haven't got around to putting up a hook on the bathroom door. Deedee never bothered. I bought one—it's in a kitchen drawer."

"Okay, so I'll work for my dinner," he said, grinning. He sniffed appreciatively. "Hey, you've put the turkey up already."

The alarm was a raucous intrusion. Without opening her eyes, Deedee leaned over to turn it off. God, she felt as though she'd just fallen into bed an hour ago. She swung to the other side, was startled to discover that Todd wasn't there. Now she became aware of the sound of the shower running.

She reached for the other pillow, thrust it behind her head. Why couldn't Todd come with her for Thanksgiving dinner? His mother and stepfather were skiing in Canada.

She hadn't told Mom she'd invited him. She knew Mom wouldn't mind. But what was this nuttiness about going in to the office today? It was Thanksgiving. Nobody would be there.

Moments later—while she debated about getting up—Todd emerged from the bathroom.

"Ah, sleeping beauty's awake. Happy Thanksgiving." He grinned, dropped his towel, posed provocatively.

"I would be happier if you were coming to dinner with me." Her eyes were reproachful.

"Honey, I'll have a chance to do some spade work at the office. Like you said, nobody'll be there. I can snoop."

"You'll be caught and fired," she warned. But like Todd, she was ambitious to be among the small clique that would move upward at the end of this apprenticeship.

"I've got great plans for us, baby—you know that." Todd said they had the kind of ambition that couldn't be stopped. "But we need to learn things." He strode to the bed—amused that she was ignoring his obvious passion. "Let's have our own Thanksgiving party now."

"I'll be worried about you all day—" But she didn't stop him when he pulled the straps of her nightie away, drew the soft material down about her waist. "Sometimes you scare me—the chances you take."

"Oh, shut up," he scolded amorously. "I want to make love."

Aware of the time, Deedee searched for a taxi to take her across town. Few drivers were out today, she realized impatiently. Then she sighed with relief. An empty cab had just swung around the corner. She lifted an arm in signal.

With so little traffic, the taxi made the trip in record time. She tipped heavily in honor of the holiday and hurried into the building. It was almost 1:30—she'd meant to arrive much earlier. Mom must be so upset today, though she'd hide it. Thanksgiving had always been special for them. But Todd had a way of making her forget everything else.

Zach opened the door when she rang.

"You've got a key—why didn't you use it?" he scolded. Zach, too, was upset. Their first Thanksgiving ever without Dad. Damn him!

"So I'm lazy," she drawled and swept inside.

Her mother peered from the kitchen. "I hope you're hungry. We have a huge turkey."

"Can I do something to help?"

"Everything's under control. Gerry and Sheila will be here any minute." Helen paused. "Flowers came for you. I put them in a vase on the dining table."

"Who from?" Todd?

"The card's on the table—"

"Oh, they're lovely!" A bunch of delicately blue forget-me-nots spilled over from a small vase. She reached for the envelope that said "Deedee," withdrew the card.

"Happy Thanksgiving. I miss you. Cliff."

Eleven

Helen told herself not to ask who had sent Deedee the exquisite bunch of forget-me-nots. Modern mothers were not supposed to ask questions. But instinct told her they were from Cliff. He wouldn't know that Deedee had moved in with Todd, that she was living in Deedee's apartment—for now.

Deedee was trying to appear amused, Helen interpreted—but she was unnerved. She still felt something for Cliff. That was good, Helen told herself. He was sweet, warm, intense. He and Deedee had seemed so right together.

What is Todd like? Am I feeling hostile toward him because I resent never having met him? Isn't it natural for me to want to meet him? It didn't have to be today—I can understand his wanting to go to his family for Thanksgiving. But what about some other time? Can I just casually say to Deedee, "Why don't you and Todd come over for dinner some evening?" It wouldn't mean a long hike out to Westchester. She was living in Manhattan now.

A few minutes later Gerry and Sheila

arrived. Sheila was introduced to Deedee and Zach.

"Put this in the fridge," Gerry told Zach—handing him a package from a neighborhood liquor store. "Are you old enough to drink?" Her raised eyebrow said "no."

"If I can vote at eighteen, fight in a war, how can the government tell me not to drink?" Zach drawled. "Besides, freshman year at college is the introduction to serious drinking." He whistled. "The campuses reek from puke from first-year students who haven't learned to handle the hard stuff."

"To the fridge," Helen ordered and turned to the others. "There may be a short wait for the pumpkin pie. I don't have two ovens here like at the house." She saw Deedee's face tighten at mention of the house. *Why did I mention it?* "I'll take out the turkey, throw in the pie."

"I hope your throwing arm's in shape," Zach flipped.

In a burst of conviviality Gerry and Sheila insisted on setting the table while Deedee helped in the kitchen. Zach hovered at the kitchen door.

"Mom, I'll take out the turkey when you say it's ready. I saw it through the window—it's awesome. Thirty pounds?"

"Eighteen," Helen told him, trying to share in the convivial atmosphere. He was remembering that it had always been Paul's duty at other Thanksgiving dinners. "Everybody will go home with 'care packages.'"

While Helen tested the turkey to see if it was done, Deedee brought the cranberry sauce—this year the canned variety—and the bowl of salad from the refrigerator, took the yams out of the toaster-oven. Zach had wandered off.

"Ma?" Zach called from the bedroom. "You're using Dad's old computer?" he said with approval.

"I'm learning," she called back. "I have a tutor."

"I would have taught you—" He appeared in the dining area with an air of hurt reproach.

"Zach, when would you have time? But once the tutor's gone and I run into trouble, I'll be calling you," she warned. She understood his dismay. For the first time he realized that she would, in truth, have to become a wage earner. "But right now, come take this bird out of the oven."

They gathered about the table—extended with one leaf to accommodate the five of them. The atmosphere properly festive, Helen told herself—yet she couldn't erase from her mind the knowledge that for the first time in twenty-five years Paul wasn't sitting at the Thanksgiving dinner table. But the ghost of him was here.

Zach made a production of opening the

bottle of wine Gerry and Sheila had brought, and poured it with an air of sophistication that was somehow touching. He was so conscious of being the man of the house, Helen thought. So young to assume that role.

"Tell us about this fabulous job of yours," Sheila ordered Deedee.

While Deedee carried on lively conversation with the others, Helen found her thoughts focused on Paul—no doubt having dinner today with his "girlfriend." She'd always been too blind to realize that she was forever deferring to his wishes. She was always the one—all her life—who compromised.

Not just with Paul, she realized with new clarity. Whenever there was an impasse with her mother, it was she who gave in. She winced in recall, hearing in her mind what her mother had said when told that she was to become a grandmother for the second time: "You'll close up shop after this, I hope." Mom had resented the children; they were competition. Mom always had to be center-stage.

Paul alternately spoiled and ignored the kids. More often he had no time for them. It was a miracle that they turned out so well, she thought gratefully. How sad that Dad didn't live to see Deedee and Zach. He was so warm, so loving—and, like herself, he always gave in to Mom—trying always to appease her.

She remembered Thanksgivings when both her mother and Paul's mother—two widows who loathed each other—had come to them for the holiday dinner. She'd always felt as though she was sitting on a keg of dynamite until both left the house.

Both Paul's mother and hers sat out the last segment of their lives—just waiting to die. As though life was a burden to be endured. Didn't a lot of people do that?

Life's a precious gift. It shouldn't be wasted. I won't waste it.

"The stuffing's great," Zach said enthusiastically, reaching for a second helping.

"You like it better than the turkey." Helen brushed aside introspection. Don't reflect on the past—enjoy this time. Both kids with her, Gerry and Sheila here. "But you'll still get a 'care package.'"

Zach grinned. "Remember when Doug and I went on the Appalachian trip the summer we were fifteen? You mailed all those packages of food to post offices we were supposed to hit—and half of them we missed. What do you suppose happened to all those packages?"

"They went to auction," Gerry surmised. "And some poor suckers got stuck with them."

"How did you do with the SUV?" Zach

113

asked.

"Not as well as I'd hoped," Helen admitted. "And much of it went to pay off the loan. Still, it's a help."

She knew Zach had harbored a fantasy about inheriting the SUV—but she needed the money. Besides, parked on the streets around Columbia—because he could hardly afford the fancy garage prices—it would be stripped or stolen in no time.

Last summer he drove to California with two buddies—in Paul's retired car. The year before he went with a school group to Paris —ostensibly studying French but mainly carousing, he'd admitted. No fancy school vacations this coming summer.

"Mom, you're getting thinner," Deedee said in sudden astonishment. "I knew there was something different."

"That's good," Helen said with an air of defiance. "I hated my pudgy look. I really should have some of my clothes taken in. No," she said with sudden determination. "I'll buy new ones."

"Great," Gerry applauded. "Get yourself a whole new look."

"A few new clothes," Helen stipulated— because she sensed a certain alarm in both Deedee and Zach at the prospect of a shopping spree on her part. They worried about her finances, she thought tenderly. And Zach worried about college money.

In high school and college she'd had a passion for smart clothes. But to please Paul—once he came into her life—she wore little black dresses. Sportswear had to be beige or gray because that was Paul's preference. She'd always loved earth tones.

"Soccer mom outfits aren't quite what you'll need on the job." Sheila intruded on her musing. "Allot wardrobe as a business expense."

"How long before the pumpkin pie comes out?" Zach demanded. "And I trust," he drawled, "that you have chocolate Cherry Garcia to go with it?"

After dinner Deedee and Zach insisted on handling the clean-up. The other three settled themselves in the living room with second cups of coffee.

"Another Thanksgiving almost behind us." A hint of bitterness lurked in Sheila's voice. "My mother's eighty-one, but she will have cooked dinner for my horde of sisters, my brother, the in-laws and the assorted grandchildren." Her face tightened. "And they'll act as though I've died and gone to purgatory."

"At the rim of the twenty-first century they still feel that way?" She felt amazement earlier, Helen reproached herself, though it was short-lived. But what could she say to alleviate Sheila's pain?

"I was born and raised in a small Midwest

town," Sheila reminded. "No room in their lives for anyone outside the pale."

"One day they'll wake up and realize the world has changed," Gerry said. But her eyes were somber. "My boys don't know about Sheila and me. All they know is there was an ugly divorce."

"It may come as a shock to them at first," Helen admitted. "But they're bright kids—and they love you. They'll understand you have a right to live your life as you see fit."

"I tried to be a good mother to them. I was a good mother," Gerry said defiantly.

"Of course you were," Helen said. "You're still a good mother." Gerry had always been there for her sons. Even with both living out in Texas, deeply involved in their careers, there was a closeness between Gerry and her sons. Nor would they allow her living with Sheila to destroy that bond, Helen told herself.

"I married because my mother nagged me into it." Gerry was in a reflective mood. "Al was a catch—a professional man. We'd have a good life together, she kept telling me. But from the very beginning he cheated on me. I pretended not to see. It was so humiliating. I thought, *We'll have children and he'll change*. He didn't. I should have been happy when he asked for a divorce. He was setting me free. I didn't understand that until I met Sheila." Her eyes softened. "In my late forties I found myself." All at once she chuckled. "All the years I damned 'Al and his whore'—when in truth they gave me back my life."

Long after the others had left, Helen roamed restlessly about the small apartment. She tried to settle down to read for a while, but this was futile. Close to midnight—aware that her computer instructor would be here at 9 a.m. tomorrow—she prepared for bed.

Lying sleepless, she considered her situation. Millions of women were divorced—that didn't mean an end to their lives. Mom had been a widow for years. That was akin to being a divorcée, wasn't it? But that was another era—and Mom and she were so different.

Mom had lived on capital and later on that and Social Security. When capital was exhausted, she had made weekly contributions. That had been her responsibility.

There had never been a question of Mom's going to work—not even in her younger years. Mom had spent her time sitting in the park, going to movies, reading magazines in the library, whiling away time in cafeterias. She'd recoiled from the thought of becoming involved in volunteer work, was insulted at the suggestion she spend time at a senior citizens' center. Didn't she die of boredom?

117

On the street below a boom-box shrieked into the night. Helen felt a flicker of amusement. Nobody was ever truly alone in the city, she told herself—though the philosophical talked about the loneliness of city life. She'd have no time to be lonely, she admonished herself—too much had to be done.

The prospect of invading the working world was intimidating. Out there everybody was so young! It was a young, young world. Television screamed this at you every hour of the day—all the sit-coms that dealt with teenagers or twenty-somethings. All the models in magazine ads. It was as though nobody over thirty existed. When would TV sponsors realize that the over-thirty generations bought detergents and cereals and pet food and cars?

Gerry was four years older than she, she told herself defiantly. Sheila, too, was pushing fifty. *If they can make it out in this young, young world, so can I. Am I going to waste all the years ahead? That would be stupid! Use them well.*

Number one—stop being fearful of the computer. George is a great teacher—even if he's so young.

"Hey, stop being scared." His voice echoed in her mind now. *"The computer's your friend. You should see the class that I teach at a senior citizens' center. They're twice your age—and*

they're learning." Not twice, she thought—but she appreciated his pep talk.

Go to sleep, she ordered herself, and tried meditation. But her mind was a traitor. Where had Paul spent Thanksgiving? With his young slut? When was he leaving New York?

What does it matter to me? Our marriage is dead. Accept that.

In truth, she mocked herself, it had not been a great marriage—not after the first three or four years. She'd been important to Paul—seeing him through law school. She'd been so grateful to feel she was important to someone. That had been the basis of their marriage. To feel good within herself because she was needed.

The only good thing that came from their marriage was becoming a parent. Thank God for Deedee and Zach. They made life worthwhile.

Twelve

Adam Fremont swung over on his side to inspect the clock on the night table beside his bed. It was almost 3 a.m., and he was as wide awake as if it was 9 p.m. God, he loathed spending holidays alone. He couldn't bring himself to go alone to a restaurant on Thanksgiving day—he'd ordered dinner to be sent in.

Thanksgiving was a family holiday—and, except for Eric, he was alone in the world. Sure, all he had to do was hint that he would be alone today and he would be swamped with invitations. But it would be wrong to invade a family, he'd scolded himself each year since the break-up with Zoe.

Face it—he'd been relieved when Zoe demanded a divorce nine years ago. He'd known at the end of the first year the marriage had been a mistake. His mind swung back through the years to those hectic weeks when Zoe had been in blatant pursuit. He was thirty-three, just hitting his stride in the business. She was in a heavy scene with a rock star he represented—and all shaken up when she discovered he was bisexual and enthralled by his drummer, Adam recalled...

Adam finished signing the letters Liz had just brought in, returned them to her.

"You'd better get out of here," he said at the sound of summer thunder. "We're going to have one hell of a storm any minute."

"You have a visitor." Liz's eyes radiating distaste. "Zoe Matthews."

"What does she want?" Adam was surprised. Zoe was on the fringe of television. She did occasional commercials, soap-opera bit roles. He didn't handle people in that category.

"I think she's had a blow-up with Rolfe and wants to cry on your shoulder." Liz grimaced. "Get rid of her fast."

"Okay. Send her in. And leave the door open." It was a sultry Friday afternoon, the heat breaking late-July records. Most people he knew were en route to the Hamptons—or already there. He was staying in town to do some work over the weekend. Liz complained he was becoming a workaholic.

"Hi—" Zoe paused in the doorway. "I need you to be my messenger boy," she drawled in the sultry voice she hoped would move her up from bit parts to leads in the soap-opera field.

"To whom?" Rolfe, of course.

121

"I want you to tell Rolfe I never want to see him again." Her huge green eyes—that managed to seem inviting and vulnerable at the same time—were all at once tearful.

"Why can't you tell him?" Adam hedged. He was tired from a long, hectic work week—but not too tired to be aware of Zoe's slim yet voluptuous body, the never-ending legs on display in the briefest of miniskirts.

"We were supposed to leave for East Hampton two hours ago. When he didn't pick me up on schedule, I went over to his apartment. You know, I thought he might have fallen asleep—what with his crazy hours. I have a key—I let myself in. He was in bed with his drummer. The bastard's AC/DC!"

"I thought everybody knew that." Adam squirmed uncomfortably.

"I didn't. Oh Adam, I couldn't believe he could do this to me. He—he talked about our getting married—"

"Look, Zoe, you're young and you're gorgeous," Adam soothed, rising to his feet to cross to her. "You'll find somebody else who'll make you forget all about Rolfe."

"Could we go somewhere and have coffee?" She lifted limpid eyes to his. "I—I'm scared to be alone."

"All right." He brushed aside reluctance. He didn't want her to start trouble for Rolfe. "Let's run around the corner to—"

"Could we have it at my place?" she broke in, flinching. "I look so awful right now." She dabbed at her eyes with a tissue. "My studio's just a few blocks away. Adam, I'm scared to be alone right now. I don't know what I might do when I feel so—so destroyed."

"Sure—" This was screwy, he thought in a corner of his mind. Why did he have to play nursemaid to Rolfe's cast-offs? And this wasn't the first time in the two years that he'd been handling Rolfe's publicity. But it was part of the job, he taunted himself— protecting a client from an embarrassing situation. Not that he truly believed Zoe might try suicide. But there was always that faint possibility that she was upset enough to try it—sort of a cry for help. Wasn't that what the shrinks called a lot of suicide attempts?

By the time they arrived at Zoe's studio apartment, the sky had unleashed torrents of rain. Thunder roared. Lightning flashed. They were both soaked. Zoe hurried to flip on the air-conditioner.

"Take off your jacket and kick off your shoes—they must be sopping wet. I'll change into something dry, then put up coffee." Zoe's smile was wistful, apologetic—as though she was responsible for the storm, Adam thought compassionately.

She couldn't be more than twenty-two or

123

twenty-three, he thought. These kids came to the city with such dreams—that few of them realized. She'd been enthralled at being pursued by a young rock star.

She'd never believe that Rolfe was a dozen years older than she. That was part of the scene he'd built for Rolfe—the 23-year-old singer who burst on the scene from nowhere. In truth, Rolfe had played the Hollywood scene for almost ten years—getting nowhere.

Together they'd built up a whole new façade for him—and it had worked. Rolfe was his first major client. Whatever he had to do to keep Rolfe clean, he'd have to do.

He draped his jacket over a chair, took off his shoes and socks, went into the tiny kitchen. He found coffee beans, a grinder. Okay, make coffee. He remembered an affair when he was right out of college. He'd shared an apartment with a girl who woke him every morning by grinding coffee beans. And before she brought him coffee in bed, she'd slide beneath the covers to make love.

Her name was Alison, he recalled. He was devastated when she decided she hated living in Manhattan, would not remain another week. He couldn't see himself becoming a publicist in an upstate town of 11,000. After that, he'd confined himself to occasional brief encounters. No room in his life for marriage. He had a career to build.

"Oh, let me do that—" Zoe stood at the entrance to the tiny kitchen in very short denim shorts and a white blouse. It was clear she wasn't wearing a bra. In bare feet—without the high-heeled sandals she'd worn earlier—she looked small and appealing.

"I'm talented at grinding beans." He was astonished to find himself aroused.

"Women's work," she clucked. No feminist, this one, he thought with surprise. "Go stretch out on the sofa and relax. Put on some music—it'll drown out the thunder."

"You don't like thunder?" he teased, walking to the stereo.

"It fascinates me—and frightens me," she said, frowning in thought. "It's something I can't control."

"There're a lot of things we can't control in life—" He brought out a handful of CDs, lifted an eyebrow at the eclectic selection. "You like Gershwin," he noted, holding *Rhapsody in Blue* between his hands.

"Play the *Rhapsody*," she ordered. "It's that kind of day."

She dumped the ground beans into the coffeemaker, flipped it into action, came to stand beside him while the tempestuous Gershwin music poured into the room.

"I never realized until just this minute that you're terribly sexy," she whispered, and all at once unbuttoned her blouse to display the lush rise of her breasts.

"We shouldn't be doing this—" His eyes clung to her while she stripped away the denim shorts to bare, golden-tanned skin.

"Why not?" She reached to unhook his belt. "We're both over twenty-one. We're single—and hot as hell—" Her voice dropped to a whisper. "Adam, make love to me. This minute. Or I'll go out of my mind!"

That was how it started with Zoe. In truth, she was twenty-eight and desperate for permanence—at the moment. And he didn't kid himself—she'd hoped he'd promote her into TV stardom. She had a very limited talent. By the end of their first year he knew he was being used. Oh, in the beginning the sex had been great. She was an artist in bed. Until she realized he couldn't publicize her into her own TV sitcom.

Still, he'd been joyous when she came to him and said she was pregnant. He was the only child of parents who themselves had been only children. He had always been envious of friends who had large families. And then—drunk as a skunk one night, when Eric was five—she told him Eric was not his child. And she wanted a divorce— with a large settlement.

Still, he loved Eric. He'd fought for part-time custody. Bless Liz for pushing him to do that. Adoptive parents usually loved the adopted children as if they were their own. He considered himself a loving adoptive parent.

But damn, he dreaded Liz's leaving him. She was part of his life. She said the doctor predicted her mother would have to go into a nursing home within a year—and she'd be free to return. But it was going to be hellish not to have her as his right hand in the year ahead. But he'd warned her—no sweet young thing fresh out of college as her replacement. He expected a thoroughly experienced mature woman who knew the business.

Damn, this would be a rotten year without Liz to depend upon. He loathed the prospect of working with a strange woman—who'd probably be set in her ways and generally a pain in the ass.

Thirteen

Helen focused on her self-imposed work schedule. For one hour a day—whenever her computer instructor could fit her in—she worked with him on becoming computer literate. More hours were devoted to practice. Only on Sundays—when he was unavailable—was she free from this chore. Gerry brought her endless folders from her office to study, to help her gain some understanding of the publicity field.

"You know more than you realize," Gerry told her on the Thursday evening a week after Thanksgiving, when she was to have dinner at Gerry's apartment along with Liz Stratton. "I mean, all those deals you worked up to raise funds for your Friends of the Library group, the local senior citizens' center, the youth center. Don't just be afraid because now you'll be doing it on a professional basis."

"Sheila said if—if this doesn't work out—" Helen paused. Admit it—this was a long shot. "If it doesn't work out, she'd be able to line up some 'temp' jobs. She said those sometimes wound up into permanent positions." *This is a great job market—remember that.*

Helen started at the sound of the intercom.

"That's Liz." Gerry rose to respond to the doorman's summons.

A few minutes later Liz was at the door. Gerry greeted her warmly.

"Sheila has to work late," Gerry told Liz with a sigh of regret. "You know how it is. Something comes up and you can be stuck for hours. But she hopes she'll be here to have coffee with us later."

"Oh, the 35-hour work week these days is just for drone jobs." Liz grunted in distaste, yet Helen sensed that she didn't truly resent this.

"Liz, this is Helen Avery," Gerry introduced them. "Liz Stratton."

While they exchanged pleasantries, Helen felt that Liz was making an evaluation that was pleasing. The first bridge had been crossed.

"I'll have dinner on the table in a few minutes," Gerry said casually. "You two sit down and get acquainted."

The two women discussed the merits of life in Manhattan versus life in suburbia. Helen made a point of sounding upbeat about her move. Sheila said that Liz's approval would go a long way in Adam

129

Fremont's decision about her replacement. Temporary replacement, Helen reminded herself. But Sheila said Liz would be gone at least a year.

"To the table for one of my fifteen-minute dinners," Gerry effervesced. "Thank God for microwave ovens and George Forman grills."

Over dinner Liz launched into blunt discussion of grooming Helen to take over.

"Adam's not the easiest boss in the world," she warned. "But he's a great guy. I'd rather work for him than anybody else." And Helen remembered that Gerry—or Sheila—had said that Liz had been in love with him for almost eighteen years. If she said he wasn't an easy boss, what would other women think of him? *I'll probably hate him—but it'll be a good job. If I can land it.*

"I know it's a totally different world—but dealing with groups of volunteers, I've learned to overlook a lot." She was searching for words. "I had to be diplomatic to keep them together. After all," she said with a wry laugh, "they weren't getting paid."

"It's a high-pressure job," Liz warned. "Sometimes I don't get out of the office until ten or eleven. But I meet exciting people. I'm never bored."

"It sounds great." *Am I being too self-assured? I know I don't have the job yet. I don't even have Liz's approval. Sheila warned*

130

there'll be some testing.

Helen felt herself grow increasingly tense. She was being evaluated—for a job that could be very rewarding financially. Sheila had assured her of this. No matter what she thought of Adam Fremont—and Liz's warnings ricocheted in her mind—she wanted this job.

Sheila arrived as they dawdled over dessert—Black Forest cake brought in from Citarella's.

"I'll have to spend an extra half-hour at the gym tomorrow," Sheila sighed, digging into the luscious slab Gerry put before her. "But it's worth it."

Now the talk became purely social. Sheila announced she'd had a phone call from Kathy Beckmann, the real estate broker in Montauk who was searching for a small house for them.

"Kathy says the house is three minutes from the beach. And she thinks the seller will drop another ten thousand."

"Let's drive out Saturday and have a look," Gerry said. "It would be great if we could have a house by Memorial Day weekend."

"Why don't you two drive out with us?" Sheila invited Helen and Liz.

"I can't leave Mom," Liz reminded. "But thanks for asking."

"I'd love it," Helen said after a startled

moment. This was her decision to make—she didn't have to confer with Paul.

"It's beautiful." Gerry was enthusiastic. "You walk on the beach—and it's all yours."

"Ours and the seagulls and an occasional town dog," Sheila amended whimsically.

The phone was ringing as Helen let herself into the apartment. She rushed to pick up ahead of the answering machine.

"Hello—"

"Liz was impressed," Gerry said with satisfaction. *Because I'm not a beautiful young thing? Just the way Liz looked when she talked about him said she was in love with him. I won't be any competition.*

"I was scared to death," Helen admitted.

"I could tell right off that she liked you. She'll start interviewing on Monday. She'll wait until the end to interview you officially. That means you'll be one of the last that Adam sees, gives you a little more time to cram."

"I hope the job isn't more than I should tackle." Helen forced herself to be honest. "From what Liz says, I gather Adam Fremont is a demanding boss."

"He works very hard—and he expects the same of his people. He's a fascinating man—but wary of women after a nasty divorce. I understand his ex-wife was a bitch."

132

"Can't blame him for that," Helen conceded. "I'll never trust another man as long as I live." Her face softened. Only Zach. The only man in her life from this point on.

"Look, if this doesn't work out, there'll be other jobs," Gerry soothed.

But not jobs that paid what Adam Fremont was willing to pay, Helen warned herself. Not jobs that would handle the rent on Deedee's apartment. She was terrified to keep digging into her limited capital. Zach's next quarter at Columbia was coming due—an astronomical amount in her situation. "Liz seems awfully nice."

"Are you going to that hair stylist Deedee talked about?"

Helen was startled. That was to remind her to smarten up her image. "I'm calling him tomorrow."

Deedee had warned her the stylist— Gregorio—was very busy, that she might have to wait weeks for an appointment. She was astonished to be told that she could come in at 3 p.m. the following afternoon.

"You're so fortunate, madam," the receptionist cooed over the phone. "Just minutes ago I had a cancellation. An actress was summoned out to the Coast immediately for a screen test."

Helen was in Gregorio's salon five minutes before her appointment. She fought off self-consciousness as she viewed the scene around her. Attractive, self-assured young women emerged from the private booths. Even the pair of older women seemed confident of their looks. The hairstyles were smart, she observed approvingly. Right.

Then she was ushered in to what the receptionist referred to as "Gregorio's studio." Pretentious, she conceded—but it was part of the picture.

"Oh, we have serious work here." But Gregorio's attitude was indulgent. "But before we style, have you considered coloring?"

"Well, no," she stammered.

"I'd suggest a hint of auburn," he said, studying her with startling intensity. "For your skin, your eyes. And the gray," he clucked. "You're much too young to allow this—"

An hour and a half later—after a dizzying consultation, coloring and cut—Gregorio handed her a mirror with an air of triumph. "Madam, this is you."

Helen gazed in the mirror in shock. A stranger stared back at her. Here was a hint of the girl she had been twenty years ago.

"Madam is pleased?" A touch of indulgent laughter in Gregorio's voice.

"I'm delighted." Her smile was brilliant.

On the bus back to the apartment she knew that she would have to dig into capital and refresh her wardrobe. A new person was being created. A woman Paul wouldn't recognize. She felt more capable of filling the job for which she was being groomed.

Some of Helen's earlier euphoria wore off in the course of the evening. First, she received a call from Jeff Madison.

"Paul asked me to notify you that he'll be leaving for Silicon Valley in the morning." Why couldn't he just say "California"? Silicon Valley sounded so pretentious. "If for any reason you need to contact him, you can do that through my office."

"Thank you, Jeff. I'll make a note of that."

They talked briefly, then Jeff was off the phone. Why was she trembling this way? Paul was out of her life. He couldn't marry his young slut for at least a year. It would be that long before the divorce was final. *But Paul is out of my life now.*

Ten minutes later the phone rang again.

"Hello." *It's absurd of me to be upset because Jeff called. Be logical.* "Yes?" she said because there was silence at the other end.

"May I speak to Deedee, please?" Uncertainty in the young male voice at the other end. Cliff, she realized.

"Deedee is out of town for a few days," she lied. "On business. May I take a message?" He didn't recognize her voice.

"No," he said hastily. "Thank you, no."

Cliff didn't know about Todd—didn't

135

know Deedee had moved in with him. Cliff was such a good kid! Why had Deedee broken up with him? She'd been so vague—something about their not having any time for each other. But she was finding time for Todd.

It disturbed her that she'd never met the man Deedee was living with—but a mother was supposed to be sophisticated about these things. *I worry about Deedee. Will she marry Todd? Will he be a decent husband?*

I don't want her to end up in a divorce court—like me.

Fourteen

Deedee smothered a yawn, glanced at her watch. It was 9 p.m. She had been here in the office since 7 a.m. One of her shorter days, she thought with grim humor. She ought to call Mom, she told herself guiltily —she hadn't spoken with her in several days. But she was exhausted and hungry.

Call, she ordered herself, and reached for the phone.

"Hello—"

"How're you doing, Mom?"

"Keeping on my schedule. I went to Gregorio—like you suggested. He's terrific. Oh, there was a call from Cliff. I told him you were out of town on business."

Deedee tensed. "He wouldn't know I'm not at the apartment now."

"I hate to call you at the office—unless it's a real emergency," her mother apologized. "I figured I'd be hearing from you soon." *Mom wouldn't call me at Todd's place—she wouldn't feel comfortable calling me there.*

"It isn't important," Deedee said—overly casual. She'd kept his forget-me-nots on her desk until they were totally dead. *Okay, so I'm a sentimental freak sometimes.* "I'd better run. I'm famished—I haven't eaten since noon. I'll call you soon, Mom—when I have more time."

"Sure, darling. Take care of yourself. You work much too hard." Her usual complaint.

"Keep plugging, Mom." She tried for lightness. "You'll soon be a working woman." *Would she? It's weird—to think of Mom working in an office.*

"Hi—" Todd hovered at the entrance to her cubicle. "Ready to knock off?"

"I'm starving," she said, reaching in a desk drawer for her purse. Todd was already holding her coat for her. "Where shall we eat?"

"Let's order in," he said. "I called the car service—a car should be waiting downstairs for us by now." One of the perks provided by the firm.

"Why do we put up with these insane hours?" Deedee demanded in a moment of rare rebellion. "It's inhuman."

"But so rewarding," Todd drawled. "Just wait till the bonuses come in after the first of the year."

"Sometimes I ask myself if it's worth it." Deedee walked with him through the near-deserted floor towards the elevators.

"It's worth it." He slid an arm about her shoulders. "Despite all the shit we deal with. Don't ever forget that."

The car was waiting for them. While they drove through the city streets, Todd talked about his day's activities.

"Damn, I wish somebody would dump Daisy Merton," he bitched. "Or transfer her to another department. Hell, she must be pushing fifty—too old for this game!"

Deedee frowned. In less than four years Mom would be fifty. But there were other fields besides investment banking. Mom would find a job. Wouldn't she? "I hear Daisy's sharp."

"Not for the twenty-first century," he jeered. "Women like Daisy can't handle the new technology that keeps pouring out. That's our scene."

"What would you like for dinner?" She didn't want to hear any more of Todd's philosophy about the workplace. "There's a new spot just opened up near us. It sounds real gourmet."

"Okay, we'll give it a whirl."

Todd seemed restless tonight, Deedee thought. Bonus time was a lot of weeks away, but he was edgy about how much they'd see. He was talking about buying a condo. Prices were going through the ceiling—but he insisted they wouldn't drop, they'd just keep escalating.

In some ways, she thought involuntarily, Todd was like Dad. Always impatient to live higher than his means allowed. But Todd would make it big, she acknowledged. Dad had something missing in his make-up. He'd sell himself big, then undo it with some dumb remark or move. It was Mom who'd always been the stable influence in their lives.

At the apartment Todd called the new take-out place and ordered while Deedee headed for the bedroom to change into a nightie. Like most Manhattan apartments, theirs was overheated. She emerged—barefoot—in a spaghetti-strapped black chiffon nightie that in a gleeful mood Todd had bought for her at Victoria's Secret.

"You look like a twelve-year-old out to seduce an older man." He chuckled, reached to pull her close. "I like the barefoot touch."

"If I was twelve, you'd seem like a horny old lecher." *Why did I suddenly think of Dad? Does he have the hots for some sexpot half his age? Is he having a mid-life crisis? Is that all it is? But the divorce is real.*

"Horny, yes—" Todd was wriggling against her, his hand caressing her curvaceous rear.

"Todd, the take-out delivery guy will be here any minute—"

"It'll be at least fifteen minutes, probably longer." He released her, with swift movements pulled off his shoes, shed his slacks.

"So all you want is a 'quickie,' " she chided, knowing he relished hearing her talk this way. *I'm not in love with Todd—it's just the sex thing.* The realization was unnerving.

"Hey, let's play while I still have the strength." He reached for her again, pushed the spaghetti straps from her shoulders, slid the sheer black chiffon down the length of her.

"Honey, you'll have the strength on your deathbed." It was weird the way he could arouse her on a moment's notice. Foreplay, he joshed, was for people who didn't work eighty hours a week.

"Oh, shut up," he scolded, swept her in his arms and carried her to the king-sized bed that occupied a major portion of the bedroom.

She closed her eyes, forgot she was exhausted, and moved with him to passionate

140

satisfaction.

While they clung together in the ultimate moment of their lovemaking, they heard the doorbell. "The damn delivery man." At this specific hour the doorman was at dinner—delivery people knew to ring.

"You'd better buzz back." Her voice was breathy. "Or we won't eat."

While he went to the door, she pulled on a robe, slid her feet into the high-heeled backless slippers that Todd liked her to wear. Oh, set the alarm for tomorrow morning. Both of them had to be in early again. Outside she heard Todd kidding with the delivery man. He thought he had to charm everybody, she thought with sudden impatience —like Dad.

She heard the door close. They were alone. She went out into the living room. Todd was arranging food on plates. She glanced at the delivery slip. Wow, it was expensive!

"Taste this—" Todd extended a forkful of beef. "Great."

"At that price it should be."

"In this world you get what you pay for."

Mom didn't deserve what she got in this world, Deedee thought involuntarily. Dad treated her like shit. After almost twenty-five years of marriage. That wasn't fair.

She inspected Todd with new questions in her mind. If she married Todd, would he dump her in ten or fifteen or twenty-five years? *Knowing what Dad did to Mom, can I ever trust any man again?*

Helen glanced at the clock. Gerry had said, "Be here around 6:30." She had this obsession about being on time—probably because Paul was always late, she thought. She'd changed clothes three times—the new outfits she'd bought yesterday. Outfits that pleased her though the price tags were unnerving. The pundits said inflation was low—but it didn't seem that way when you shopped. Instinct told her the dinner this evening—when she was to meet Liz Stratton for the second time—was important to her future. Sheila wanted Liz to see her "new look."

"Liz is a doll," Gerry had reassured her. "You two hit it off at your first meeting." Both Gerry and Sheila were so optimistic that Liz would prod her into the job as her replacement. They didn't have to tell her— she knew the job market wasn't shrieking for 46-year-old women with little business background.

With the salary she'd earn in Adam Fremont's office she'd have a chance at survival. She couldn't afford to think at this moment about Zach's last two years in college. She'd never be able to afford Columbia. Maybe a state college, with college loans to help if she lived very frugally. Paul had talked vaguely about contributing—but she couldn't count on that.

It was important for Zach—and Deedee, even if she seemed so independent—to know they were a family. They could be a family without Paul. She'd always envied those with large families. It must be such a warm, wonderful feeling to have brothers and sisters, aunts and uncles, cousins.

The ringing of the phone was a jarring intrusion. Incoming calls were few since she'd moved into Manhattan. At the house, it had seemed the phone never stopped ringing—she was always on some committee, always busy with some campaign.

She reached for the receiver. "Hello—"

"How're you doing?" Deedee's always cheery greeting.

"I'm hanging in there. Running over to Gerry and Sheila's for dinner tonight. I'm meeting that woman again who'll be interviewing me for a possible job. If I pass her, then I move up to the boss." *Will I pass?*

"You're okay?" Deedee prodded. "Really okay?"

"I'm fine," Helen insisted. She was cramming with the intensity of a college freshman promised a car if she came up with all "A"s by the end of a term. She swore at the computer at intervals—but was learning.

"Oh, I had a call from Jeff Madison. He said everything's going on schedule about the divorce—he doesn't foresee any problems."

"Bully for him," Deedee derided.

"I suppose you're much too busy with the job to come over for dinner one night this week?" Helen tried not to sound wistful.

"Maybe we can meet for lunch on Saturday." Helen heard guilt in Deedee's voice. *I don't want Deedee to feel that way.* "If I don't have to go in to work."

"Darling, I know you're terribly tied up with the job. I just hope you find a little time for relaxation. Life shouldn't be all work."

"Everybody I know works crazy hours." Deedee sighed. "You have to put in the time if you want to move up in the world. Mom, I'm at the office—I have to run."

Off the phone Helen reached into a closet for a coat. She paused for a moment to inspect her reflection in the mirror. The new hairstyle and the color job had done wonders, she thought for the dozenth time. And the olive green pantsuit—two sizes smaller than her old wardrobe, she remembered with awe—was flattering to her new slimness.

Did Paul go chasing after that young slut because I let myself go? Is it my fault that he wanted a divorce?

Brushing aside recriminations, she left the apartment, hurried in the crisp December evening to Gerry and Sheila's apartment. Thank God for Gerry and Sheila—she would have been lost without them.

"My God!" Pulling the door wide, Gerry stared at her in astonishment. "You look marvelous!"

"Like you told me, I went to Deedee's hairstylist." All at once Helen felt self-conscious. "And he suggested the coloring."

"Sheila, come see Helen's 'new look.' It's just amazing." Gerry drew Helen inside. "And that's a new suit. Every time I saw you through the years you were wearing black or beige. Even your swimsuits," she said, giggling.

"That was Paul," Helen conceded. "I always dressed to please him." *That had always been my way—to try to please.*

"Welcome to the New World," Sheila joshed. "You do look great. Wow, you've slimmed down."

"You may have lost weight the hard way," Gerry said gently, "but less of you is so much better."

"Fourteen pounds," Helen confessed. "When I'm upset, I don't eat."

"Some people eat like pigs when they're upset," Sheila said, her eyes rueful. "Including me."

"Keep the weight off," Gerry urged. "But with exercise—not by starving yourself."

"I'll walk everywhere," Helen vowed,

145

remembering Sheila's dedication to her health club. "I may even invest in a stationary bike or a treadmill."

"Standard items in today's living rooms," Gerry flipped. "I see it coming in ours."

Ten minutes later Liz arrived. Helen was conscious of her startled scrutiny. In the brief time since their last meeting she'd become someone else physically. The new hairstyle, the tint job, the weight loss.

"Nobody would ever think you have two grown children," Liz said after a few moments of casual conversation. At their last dinner, Helen recalled, she'd talked about Deedee and Zach.

"Cosmetics are wonderful," Helen said lightly, and then realized that tonight Liz's face was devoid of make-up. She remembered Gerry saying that Liz had long been in love with Adam Fremont—though he was never aware of this. Would Liz prefer an older, frumpy woman to replace her?

Have my chances of landing this job just plummeted?

Fifteen

Zach dug ravenously into his hamburger at his favorite off-campus fast-food hang-out. Where the hell was Doug? His interview at the copy center must be over by now. They'd decided just yesterday to try for a weekend job advertised in the neighborhood freebie weekly newspaper. He'd been hired this morning—and the guy who did the hiring said there was an opening for one more. Some regulars had dropped out to cram for exams.

Zach's face lit up at the sight of Doug charging into the café. He was smiling, Zach noted—he'd been hired.

"The money is shitty," Doug said, sliding into a chair opposite Zach.

"It's lots better than minimum," Zach countered.

"Yeah," Doug acknowledged. "We can put in maybe twenty hours a week—Saturday, Sunday. Probably more over the winter break. In five weeks," he pointed out smugly, "we'll have our stake."

"You're sure we can operate with a couple

of grand?" Zach was uneasy. "All the stuff we've been reading—" They'd done mounds of research on day-trading. "They talk about a minimum of $10,000. What makes you sure we'll be accepted for online for less?"

"I showed you—right on the internet." Doug glared at him in exasperation. "You're in business with as little as $500. Of course, you won't get anywhere with that. We'll have to be sharp, play it smart—but we can do with $2,000. All you need to play on the market," he emphasized yet again, "is a PC and a modem."

"We can only day-trade on Fridays." Zach yearned to be convinced.

"Right now—but once we're on the winter break, we'll do it five days a week. Work at the copy center on the evening shift. The secret—my old man says—is to make sure to sell out before the market closes for the day."

"Some of the articles we read talked about training courses—"

"We haven't got the time or the money. Consider our research training," Doug said breezily. "Plus we've got a sharp mentor—" He grinned. "Of course, he doesn't know he's playing that bit."

"You're sure your old man will lead us in the right direction?" Zach was apprehensive. He didn't want to break his ass working at a copy machine, then lose his stash the first day out. Still, day-trading was grabbing a lot of followers.

"My old man's been working the day-trade scene for five months. He's cleaning up." Doug grinned. "Each night after dinner, my mother says, he sits down, does his homework, makes out his schedule for the next day." Doug's parents lived in a co-op on West End. Doug popped in for a sub-stantial—free—dinner at regular intervals. Neither he nor Zach was on the meal plan at the school. "Every Thursday night I'll be home for dinner. Dad loves to talk about day-trading. I'm a great listener."

"Yeah, but have you learned enough for us to play the game?" Zach alternated between unbounded enthusiasm and skepticism.

"Look, we just have to be sharp, watch where the numbers are going. Yesterday my father earned $27,000! Okay, we don't have his bankroll, but together we'll have a couple of grand as seed money from the job. We've got computers. We've got a phone. We set up business in the dorm." Doug pushed back his chair. "Let me get some food. I'll soon be a working stiff."

Zach returned to his hamburger. The anxiety that had plagued him at regular intervals since he learned about the divorce reared its ugly head again.

It scared him to think of Mom out there

trying to make a living—trying to deal with college tuition. Dad was a class-A bastard to dump her. To screw up so they even lost the house! How the hell did Dad expect Mom to cope in the business world when she'd never had to deal with anything except running the house and giving all the dinner parties Dad thought were important to his career?

Was Doug right? Could they make a humongous haul with day-trading—starting out with no more than two grand? How long before Mom ran out of money? Would she end up on welfare? He felt perspiration forming on his forehead. *I have to make a lot of money.*

Mom said she'd made sure his tuition and dorm fees for this year came off the top of the house sale—it was in a special account. But what about next year—and the year after?

"The cheeseburger special went up a quarter," Doug said indignantly, puncturing his introspection. "And we keep hearing about low inflation."

"The cholesterol special," Zach drawled. "Be a moderate—have straight burgers."

"I wish to hell we didn't have to wait a month to build up our seed money." Doug frowned, staring into space. "I wonder. I just wonder—"

"Wonder what?"

"If I could hit my mother up for an advance—you know, against the job?" Doug's face brightened. "I'll bet she'd go along with that. What about putting the same deal up to your mother?"

"Not a chance." Zach flinched in reproach. Doug knew the situation with Mom and Dad. "But—" He hesitated. *Do I dare? I'd be able to pay it off when the bill came in.*

"But what?" Doug demanded.

"I've still got the Mastercard Mom gave me when we drove out to the West Coast. I can get a cash advance," Zach pointed out in triumph. "I'll have money from the job to pay off when the bill comes in."

"My mom will come through," Doug predicted. "I'll talk to her tonight. How soon can you get your advance?"

"It's easy. I'll have a grand tomorrow morning!"

"Hey, we're in business," Doug crowed.

Mom didn't have to know about it until the Mastercard bill came in, Zach told himself. And by then he'd have the cash to pay it off. No sweat. *What can go wrong?*

Helen glanced at her watch as she approached the entrance to the building where Adam Fremont's offices were. She was ten minutes early. It was gauche to appear early, she reproached herself. Walk around the block—that would take up the time. A good day for walking—cold but crisp.

Everywhere were signs of the approach of Christmas—just twelve days away. Shop windows displayed colorful holiday decorations. Earlier she'd stopped to admire the awesome Christmas tree at Rockefeller Center, lingered to watch the figure skaters on the ice below. She inspected—along with an admiring crowd—the Christmas windows of Saks.

She tried to convince herself the interview today with Liz Stratton was just a formality. After their second dinner—when she'd been scared she'd turned off Liz—Sheila had talked with Liz at length.

"Don't worry," Sheila had insisted. "Liz was pleased by the copies of press releases, the campaign plans for fundraisers you handled in the past dozen years. You're at the top of the list."

Helen walked with compulsive swiftness, strived for calm. This job was the plum, but if it didn't work out, there would be others. She checked her watch again. All right, it was time to present herself at Adam Fremont's office.

Liz kept her waiting only a few moments. With an inquisitive smile the receptionist ushered her into Liz's windowed office. The window an indication of her ranking in the firm.

"This won't take long," Liz assured her with a warm smile. "Adam wants to be sure you're proficient in Word—which is what you'll be using here in the office." *That sounds as though I practically have the job—or am I jumping to conclusions?* "No need for graphics or spreadsheets—we farm that out."

"I've used Word for quite a while." *How easy it is to lie when it's necessary.* "I'm very comfortable with it. I've done considerable proofreading in the past—and some editing."

Liz talked about Adam's clients. "Some can be difficult on occasion," she conceded. "Diplomacy is important."

Helen smiled reminiscently. "Diplomacy I can handle."

All at once the door flew open. A man stood there. Charismatic, yet slightly imperious. Adam Fremont, Helen guessed. He might have knocked.

"Oh, excuse me," he apologized perfunctorily. "Liz, I need you to handle something—as soon as you're free." He spun around and left the room.

"That was Adam," Liz said. "I'll set up an appointment for you with him at the end of the week." She flipped open her appointment pad. "How's your schedule next Thursday morning?"

★ ★ ★

153

Adam glanced up as Liz came into his office.

"Close the door," he said tersely.

"Okay—" She closed the door, turned back to him. She could read him like a book, Adam thought. She knew he was in a personal rather than business crisis. "Problems, Adam?"

"Cancel all my appointments for tomorrow. I have to fly up to Boston in the morning. I'll be back in the evening." He sighed. "There's some trouble at Eric's school," he explained because Liz was waiting in her quiet way for an explanation. "The woman who called said they couldn't reach Zoe."

"Eric's not happy at boarding school. You said that would happen."

"Damn! I told Zoe it was a mistake to send him there—but you know Zoe. All she cares about is herself. I should have gone back to court, fought for full-time custody." *But how can I raise Eric on my own—with my mad schedule? How do I know she won't pull out the old routine about Eric's not being my child?*

"He'll be with you for Christmas," Liz soothed.

"Where did Zoe get the crazy idea that boarding school would be good for him?" Adam flared.

"She's having a thing with some young stud," Liz guessed. "A fourteen-year-old son is bad for her image. The affair dies out—she'll bring Eric home again."

"Why did she have to move to San Francisco?" For the past nine years—ever since the divorce— Zoe had been pulling up stakes at regular intervals. "When she lived in Southampton, at least I could run up and see Eric for weekends." But with Eric in school in Boston, he should manage a couple of weekends a month.

"If you cut back on the alimony, you could reel Zoe in," Liz scolded. "You're too damn good to her."

"I don't pay up for Zoe." He exuded contempt. "It's for Eric—so he'll have a semblance of a home life."

"I'll re-schedule your appointments. A death in the family," she improvised. "You had to rush out of town."

"How're you doing with the interviews?" He dreaded Liz's absence from the office. She was more than his assistant. She was a close, cherished friend.

"Not bad. You'll start your interviewing on Monday. Just four," she said quickly because he'd winced. "One a day—"

His mind shot back to the woman who'd been with Liz when he went to her office. "The woman with you just now—was she an applicant for the job?"

"Yes. The one I suspect you'll be hiring."

"You figure she's the best of the lot?"

There'd been something strangely appealing about her—in the moment his eyes had met hers.

"I would say so."

"Then forget about more interviews. Hire her," Adam ordered. "The more time you have with her the better."

Helen heard the phone ringing as she unlocked the apartment door. Of course, the answering machine would pick up, she reminded herself—but she rushed inside.

"Hello—"

"Helen?" The voice was faintly familiar.

"Yes—"

"This is Liz Stratton—in Adam Fremont's office. I've just talked with him. He's authorized me to make the decision about hiring. If you want the job, it's yours."

"Oh, Liz, that's wonderful!" Helen felt a glorious surge of relief. "When shall I begin?"

"Be here Monday morning at nine thirty. I'll start showing you the ropes. And Helen, good luck—"

"Thanks. I'll need it—"

"You'll be fine," Liz said with confidence. "But don't be upset if Adam seems impatient at times. He doesn't mean it. It's momentary. He works under so much pressure."

"I'll remember that," Helen promised.

"And thank you for everything, Liz."

Off the phone, she felt some of her excitement ebbing away. Could she handle this job? Were her skills up to Adam Fremont's demands? She was replacing a woman who'd been on the job for eighteen years, knew every aspect of the field.

Am I way out of my depth? Will I be fired by the end of the first week?

Adam sat in Dean Andrews' office and listened attentively to her complaints about Eric.

"I realize boarding school is a new experience for him," Dean Andrews acknowledged. "It's difficult for some students to adjust. He's bright. He's charming. And he's rebellious," she emphasized. "Being a teenager brings on its own set of problems —but these kids must learn to live by the rules."

"I realize that." *Is she trying to tell me the school's expelling Eric?* "How do I handle this?" *Throw the ball in her court. Admit I'm at a loss.*

"We're putting Eric on warning. I'd like you to talk with him, try to make him understand we're here to help him—but he must abide by the rules."

"I'll do that." Adam felt a flicker of relief. "When can I see him?"

"He's been suspended from classes for the day and grounded in his room."

Adam glanced at his watch. "May I take him out for lunch? Talk with him away from the school?" He managed an ingratiating smile.

"That would be good," she approved. "I'll send for him."

Half an hour later Adam sat with Eric in a booth in a charming restaurant not far from the campus.

"Eric, I know it's tough getting used to a sleep-away school," Adam conceded. *Poor little kid—he'd seemed terrified when we came face to face in the dean's office. Doesn't he know I'll never do anything to make him unhappy?* "And sometimes rules seem a little nutty—but there's a reason for them that you haven't come to understand."

"Am I gonna be expelled?" Eric seemed almost hopeful.

"No. Not if you stay with the rules. And that's for your own good. You know how sometimes I'm stuck with business—but I promise you that after New Year's I'll try to be up most weekends. We'll do things together. And remember, you're coming to me for the school break between Christmas and New Year's."

"Yeah—" A wisp of a smile brightened his face.

"And now let's talk about Christmas presents. You have something special you want this year?"

But fancy presents, Adam taunted himself, wouldn't guarantee happiness.

Sixteen

Back in her apartment—torn between euphoria and apprehension— Helen called Deedee at her office. Miraculously, Deedee picked up on the second ring. Haltingly, Helen told Deedee that she had joined the ranks of the employed.

"I'm not earning your kind of money," she admitted humorously. She'd never earn the kind of money Deedee saw from her job. But Liz had assured her raises would be fast in coming if "you and Adam are on the same wavelength." *Will we be?* "But it's a job."

"Mom, that's really great!" Underneath Deedee's enthusiasm Helen sensed some anxiety. "When do you begin?"

Not until evening was she able to catch up with Zach. He expressed equal enthusiasm.

"Wow! My mom, the working lady! Remember, play it cool," he urged.

"I'll be cool," she promised.

Moments later she was on the phone with Gerry.

"You're right for the job," Gerry said with confidence. "Don't let Adam faze you. He's really a great guy."

"That's what everybody keeps telling me." But she was uneasy. Both Liz and Gerry admitted he could be difficult.

"Play it like Liz," Gerry urged. "If he blows his top, just smile sweetly and go on about your work. He's under a lot of pressure from demanding clients."

"Sure." Helen tried to reflect Gerry's attitude. *But if he's one of those men who use his office staff as whipping posts, I'll freak out.*

She continued to schedule hours with the computer instructor for the rest of the week. Liz would be with her until the end of the year—she wouldn't be on her own until after New Year's, she comforted herself. And in a way she did have suitable background. All the years of setting up publicity for volunteer groups, writing press releases. This would just be on a higher scale. *I can handle the job.*

On Monday morning she left the apartment with trepidation. Her initial shock was on boarding a loaded subway train. This wasn't Metro North. She'd forgotten the relentless shoving of humanity, the scent of expensive and cheap perfumes blending with the aromas of food and stale tobacco.

She didn't have to ride the subway—she could take the bus, she reminded herself.

160

No doubt crowded too—but not this madness. She shuttled from the West Side to the East, emerged at last into the sharp cold of mid-December. She realized she was at least half an hour early, detoured into a coffee shop.

Liz was at the office when she arrived. She was relieved not to come face to face with Adam Fremont until late in the morning.

"Welcome aboard, Miss Avery." He paused, his smile warm. "Actually, we're very informal around here. I'm Adam."

"Helen." She returned his smile. "I'm happy to be here."

She had no further contact with him for the rest of the day. But then this was her learning period. It was clear that the rest of the staff—so young, she thought—were confident in their jobs. She sensed an intense loyalty to Adam Fremont—despite his reputation for being demanding. And she was aware—even at a distance—of his potent charm, no doubt instrumental in his success.

Heading home—standing on a crowded bus—she admitted to being exhausted. From tension, she told herself—she wasn't exactly decrepit. She glanced about at the faces on the bus. Women considerably older than she were working.

I can handle this.

★ ★ ★

Helen dreaded the imminent approach of Christmas. Holidays were the bad days for those who were alone. But she wasn't alone, she rebuked herself. She had Deedee and Zach. They would both sleep over on Christmas Eve and spend Christmas day with her. She suspected they'd arranged this between them—knowing how she'd feel.

She'd thought that Zach would stay at the apartment for the long winter holiday at Columbia.

"I'll be at the dorm," he'd said. "I'll be working at this copy place on a full-time basis while there're no classes—it's right near campus. It'll be easier that way." Poor baby, he understood their straitened finances. On his own he'd decided he could handle his daily needs from the job he'd lined up. He wasn't on the food plan this year—his own decision.

"Oh, sure." If they'd had the house, would he have come up as he had last year? But there'd been no money problems then—they thought.

She'd casually suggested that Deedee invite Todd to Christmas dinner. *"Oh, he's going home for a four-day weekend."* Would Deedee have gone with him except for her?

At intervals she replayed the scene when she learned about Todd. Deedee had said that neither of them was ready for marriage. Her mind hurdled back through the years.

She'd been sleeping with Paul for a year before they were married—but they both knew they'd be married after graduation. Deedee was going nowhere. The knowledge was disturbing.

Determined to make this a normal Christmas despite Paul's absence—and not even a card from him thus far—Helen bought a small Christmas tree, shopped for decorations. She'd donated the horde of decorations they'd collected through the years to the Friends of the Library thrift shop. Gerry and Sheila would be with them for Christmas dinner. She bought inexpensive presents for the children and Gerry and Sheila.

The office was to close the Wednesday before Christmas. There was to be an afternoon party.

"A few clients pop in for a drink with Adam. The rest of us have a late catered lunch," Liz explained. "And the bonus checks are handed out." Her face was luminous. "Adam's so generous."

On Wednesday morning Helen arrived at the office at nine thirty sharp, as always. Liz was always there earlier. The other four on staff straggled in minutes before ten. Liz was with Adam in his office, Helen realized as she headed for Liz's office—where she reported each morning,

"Kelly, behave yourself," Adam was saying

to someone on the phone. That would be Kelly Olson, Helen pinpointed. The sexy singer in Adam's stable. "Your life is not over because that skunk walked out. Now you listen to me—" There was a pause. "Kelly, stop that, I'm coming right over." He slammed down the phone.

"Adam, Eric's plane is due in at 10:50!" Liz reminded.

"Pick him up at LaGuardia," Adam ordered. "Damn it, why did Kelly pick this morning to pull another 'I'm about to have a nervous breakdown' scene?"

"I'll leave in a few minutes," Liz promised, and hesitated. "Eric's going to be disappointed that you're not there—"

"I don't have much choice." A sharpness in Adam's voice now. "Oh God, Liz, how am I going to manage without you?"

Adam charged out of his office and down the hall. Moments later Liz strode into her office.

"Helen, I have to run out to LaGuardia to pick up Adam's son. He's coming in from boarding school to spend the holidays with Adam. I'll need you to check with the caterer about the lunch deal—and you'll have to phone the liquor store—" She pulled a sheet from a jacket pocket. "Here's the phone number and what we'll need."

"What about ice cubes?" Helen asked. She remembered Gerry had said that Adam had

164

a bitch of an ex-wife. She hadn't known about the son. "And what about glasses?"

"Damn, I forgot! Send Bill down to buy a couple of bags of ice cubes. You can store them in the fridge in Adam's office. We have loads of plastic cups."

"If clients are coming, should we have flowers?"

"We've never bothered," Liz admitted. "But that'll be a nice touch. There's a phone number for a florist on my computer—one where we have an account. Order whatever you think will be right. I'd better run—I don't want Eric arriving to find nobody is meeting him."

"How old is he?" Helen recoiled from the vision of a child arriving alone in the hectic pre-Christmas atmosphere at LaGuardia.

"Fourteen." Liz's face softened. "A sweet, sensitive, darling boy. I'd better run—it may be hard to get a cab this close to Christmas Eve."

Helen summoned Bill, their good-natured "go-for"—and sent him on his errand, phoned the liquor store, the caterer, the florist. Not much different, she comforted herself, from what she'd handled in her volunteer capacities.

Gerry said Adam's ex-wife had custody of their son. Why was he in boarding school? Why wasn't he with his mother?

★ ★ ★

Shortly before noon Liz returned to the office, accompanied by a slender teenager with dark, rumpled hair and blue-green eyes that seemed to reflect fear of the world.

"Eric, this is Helen," Liz said gently. "Stay here with her until your father returns. Helen has a son, too." Her eyes pleaded with Helen to take charge.

"Zach is five years older than you," Helen told Eric. "He's in college now."

"Adam called me on my cell phone," Liz said. "He's having all kinds of problems with Kelly. I've got to make a bunch of phone calls for him." She paused. "I'll make them in Adam's office." She hesitated. "Everything under control?"

"Ice cubes in the fridge. I checked with the caterer. Everything is on schedule. The liquor store and the florist should be delivering any minute."

"Great." Liz hurried from the office.

"Are you hungry?" Helen asked Eric—her smile ingratiating.

"Sort of—" He was uncomfortable with her, she realized. Poor baby.

"I'll order in for you. What would you like? A hamburger and French fries?" Zach would reject the French fries but succumb to the hamburger despite its fat content, she thought in a corner of her mind. He called himself a semi-health food nut.

"I don't eat meat," Eric said defensively.

"What about a veggie burger and orange juice?" she coaxed.

His face lighted. "Cool."

"I'll call right now." She reached for the phone, turned to Eric. "Do you like computers?"

"Yeah—" He was still wary with her.

"There's solitaire, hearts, minesweeper and some other stuff on the computer if you'd like to play."

He seemed hesitant. *What's he so upset about? Because his father wasn't at the airport to meet him?* "Okay—"

Eric settled himself at the computer. The modern-day babysitter, Helen mused. They'd probably be part of the nursery school scene soon.

She was oddly touched by the sight of Eric at the computer—alternately hitting keys and eating his veggie burger with enthusiasm. Thank God, Paul waited for the divorce until the kids were grown. Yet even at their ages, they were upset.

Liz was caught up in endless phone calls—something to do with arranging psychiatric care for pop star client Kelly Olson over the holidays, Helen gathered. "A publicist like Adam takes on the most personal of care," Liz had confided. "He's got clients who practically won't go to the bathroom without consulting with him."

Helen conferred with the caterer about the

buffet luncheon that was being set up for staff and visiting clients. She'd arranged the flowers delivered earlier by the florist, set up an improvised bar. The others were caught up in the festive spirit of the day. They traded good-humored insults, talked about plans for the long weekend.

"That looks great," Helen congratulated the caterer's staff when they were done. "Thanks so much."

As they rushed out to their next assignment, Adam charged into the reception area. He looked harried, Helen sympathized.

"Is Eric here?" he asked Helen.

"He's in Liz's office," Helen told him. "Playing computer games."

"Thanks—" His face aglow, Adam strode past her. "Eric?"

Helen hesitated about returning to Liz's— soon to be her— office. But Liz had deposited the plastic cups atop the file there. They should be out in the reception area. According to the others, clients should be dropping by soon.

"No, I'm not hungry," Eric was telling his father. "Helen ordered me this humongous veggie burger and a big orange juice. I was starving."

"Would you like some cookies?" Helen offered now. "There are plates of them set up out on the buffet table." He seemed

168

ambivalent. "It's a holiday—you can have cookies today," she coaxed, remembering the period—at the same age—when Zach had "gone off sugar."

"Well, just a couple." With an infectious grin Eric hurried from the room.

"You've taken great care of him," Adam said gratefully. "Thanks." She was disconcerted by the intensity of his gaze.

"I have a son—a little older than Eric," Helen told him. *Are those tears in his eyes?* "He's in his sophomore year at Columbia."

"Eric's had rather a bad time." He gazed into space now, as though visualizing painful moments. "His mother and I were divorced when he was five. It—it was an ugly divorce. I haven't seen as much of him as I'd like. Zoe is constantly moving from one city to another—each one more distant than the last."

"My divorce isn't final yet," she confided after a moment. "But my two—I have a daughter, also—are very hostile towards their father. It's obvious that Eric loves you very much."

"Adam, you old bastard!" A man in jeans and ski jacket rushed towards Adam. Helen was startled for a moment to recognize a top TV anchor man. "Why are you hiding away? Come out and have a drink with me!"

Helen went to turn off the computer.

Adam Fremont loved his son very much, she thought tenderly. The divorce wasn't his fault. Gerry said his wife was a bitch.

Seventeen

The ring of the alarm clock was a raucous intrusion. Without opening her eyes, Helen groped to shut it off. From habit she must have set it last night. She frowned in rejection at the sound of a garbage truck grinding away downstairs. Further down the block a segment of roadway was being attacked.

Yesterday—the first day of her long weekend off—she'd slept until almost 10 a.m. The day had sped past. She'd been caught up in shopping for this evening's dinner, for their more festive Christmas day dinner tomorrow. She'd shopped for more decorations for the Christmas tree that seemed huge in the apartment's small living room—tiny compared to the house, she mused.

In the evening she'd baked fanciful cookies—as though Deedee and Zach were small kids. But baking was a time-pusher. She'd talked on the phone with Gerry for almost an hour. How did people survive before the invention of the phone?

Gerry was feeling a kind of emptiness because both of her sons would not be with her for the holidays. She'd invited Gerry and Sheila for Christmas dinner, but they were going to friends in the Poconos for the weekend.

She loved Gerry and Sheila—they were real friends. But she recognized that they led a second life that excluded her. A life with a cluster of women who shared something she couldn't feel. She respected their need for this other life. In no way did it intrude on their close friendship.

The heat was coming up strong. She relished the comforting warmth. Her mind hurtled back through the years to other Christmases. Always a special time. Her enjoyment came from seeing Deedee and Zach's pleasure in the holiday—the gifts, the festive atmosphere, a sense that all was right with the world.

When the kids were small, so many Christmas presents required assembling, she remembered. She found pleasure even in this. On rare occasions Paul participated. In truth, he was a part-time father. He either spoiled them rotten—or ignored them. And of course he spent much of each day away from the house. She'd always told herself this was necessary to provide the kids with the good things of life.

Adam Fremont was a great father—he exuded love and concern for Eric. How sad that—as Liz had said—Eric's mother kept moving to distant parts of the country. *"Adam kills himself to arrange time to be with Eric."*

How did Deedee and Zach feel through the years when Paul saw so little of them? But then most of the kids they knew had almost-absentee fathers, who dashed out of their suburban houses to catch an early commuter train, returned to a late dinner. When they were little, Deedee and Zach were often asleep by the time Paul arrived home.

She'd tried to arrange vacations that would please both Paul and the kids. But Paul liked resort hotels where every moment was filled with activity. The kids— and she—preferred lazy vacations. It was Paul who decided on shipping the kids off to fancy summer camps or summer tours. She'd deluded herself into believing he wished for time alone with her.

She ought to get up, give the apartment a real cleaning. At her insistence, Deedee had called a halt to her once-a-week cleaning woman. That was one expense she could avoid.

Allowing herself extra time in the shower this morning, she began to relax as the hot spray massaged her back. What kind of Christmas would Adam Fremont and Eric have? The office would be open only three days next week—and Liz said Adam would be in only for an hour or two each day. He was eager to provide Eric with a happy Christmas, she thought with a surge of tenderness. What a nice man he was.

Deedee stretched blissfully under the comforter. It was great not to be rushing to the office. To be away from that insanity for four days. But Todd—in the shower now—was in a rotten mood. He had been all week. He'd wanted to beg off going home to his mother and her current husband.

"Why can't we run down to the Bahamas for a long weekend?" he'd groused at regular intervals all week.

She couldn't do that to Mom. Not at Christmas. Families belonged together on holidays. Todd couldn't understand that. She felt a surge of fresh rage that Dad wouldn't be with them this Christmas. Not on any Christmas in the future.

Wrapped in a terrycloth robe, Todd emerged from the bathroom. "God, I hate holidays!" he said contemptuously. "Three times a year my mother gets sentimental. Christmas, Thanksgiving, and Easter she's suddenly aware that she's a mother. I have to show up at the dinner table."

"Not this past Thanksgiving," Deedee reminded. "Your mother and stepfather were skiing in Canada." And Todd had done what he'd called serious snooping in the office. He'd bought some stock on Friday morning, she recalled—and said he'd made a bundle. That was dangerous. But Todd loved living dangerously.

"So I got off the hook one year." Todd shrugged. "But Christmas is a 'must.'"

"Mom suggested I invite you to have Christmas dinner with us. Maybe come over for Christmas Eve, too." She giggled. "The only way you could sleep over would be to bring a sleeping bag."

Involuntarily she thought about last Christmas. Cliff's father was recovering from a heart attack, and his mother insisted that the two of them go down to Florida for a month so he could recuperate away from the winter cold in Manhattan. Mom had been delighted when she asked to bring Cliff to the house over the holidays.

Cliff could be so endearing, she admitted reluctantly. But there'd been no time between his mad schedule and hers for them to see each other. And all he thought about was medicine. And then Todd came into her life.

"I think I'll leave right after breakfast," Todd intruded on her introspection. "Everybody will be traveling today—I'd like to miss the traffic." His mother and current step-father had just bought a ski lodge in southern Vermont. "It's going to be a bitch of a drive—over five hours."

"Remember, you're not to open your Christmas present until morning," she told him. She'd bought him an absurdly expensive watch.

"Yours is on the top shelf of my closet." He grinned. "You can model it for me my first night back." Another nightie from Victoria's Secret, she guessed. In a corner of her mind she remembered the forget-me-nots Cliff had sent her on Thanksgiving. "Aren't you going to get out of bed and make breakfast for me?"

"I'll consider it," she flipped. Truantly her mind darted back to the one night she'd spent in Cliff's apartment. In the morning he'd brought her breakfast in bed.

"Oh, there's a problem about New Year's Eve." He was overly casual—alerting Deedee to some unpleasant revelation. "Thompson's invited me to a houseparty at his country house. I can't refuse—not with the bonuses coming."

"No," Deedee agreed after a moment. Oliver Thompson—a vice-president—had a nubile daughter who was causing her father serious headaches. Was he seeing Todd as a possible husband?

"Before breakfast," Todd drawled, pulling

off his robe, "I've got another present for you."

"I thought you were in a rush to hit the road," she mocked.

"Not that rushed." He flashed what Deedee called his "invitation to sex" smile, tossed aside the comforter. "God, you make me horny."

By 2 p.m. Helen had finished cleaning the apartment, had already set the table—though dinner was five hours ahead. She was fighting a wave of depression. She worried about Deedee's living with Todd. Zach had alarmed her two days ago when he talked about maybe quitting school at the end of his sophomore year. He wouldn't be thinking that way if their lives hadn't been thrown upside down.

The phone rang. She rushed to pick up. Probably Deedee or Zach. Gerry and Sheila had left for the Poconos this morning.

"Hello—"

"I hope you don't mind my calling you at home this way," Adam apologized. "I found your phone number on the computer. And you did say you have a son who's nineteen."

"Yes, I have a nineteen-year-old son," she said gently, "and I don't mind your calling me at home." Some problem with Eric, she surmised with sympathy.

176

"I want to make this holiday from school a treat for Eric," Adam said. "But it's tough for me to figure out what kind of activities he'll like. Last Christmas we went skiing—and he said that was cool. But traveling at this time of year can be so wild—and I didn't make any reservations. I'm desperate for suggestions."

"Hold a minute while I get the *New York Times*," she said and hurried to locate this. She flipped through the sports page, pinpointed happenings. "Adam—"

"Yes," he said eagerly.

"Eric likes sports?"

"Some," Adam told her.

They focused now on sporting events, then Helen suggested taking Eric to the Museum of Natural History.

"Oh yes, he'd like that." Adam seemed less anxious.

They discussed other holiday activities that might appeal to Eric, and then Helen brought up the matter of restaurants.

"I gather Eric's into health food. Zach's partially committed," she said chuckling. "But from him I've learned about a few choice health food restaurants—"

"Let me write down the names."

Off the phone Helen felt an unexpected serenity. Adam Fremont might be a hellion in the office—as the younger crew had confided, though with an air of indulgence—

but he was a warm, charming man.

All at once she was in the grip of self-consciousness. *I'm not attracted to Adam Fremont as a man. That part of my life is over.* But women could have male friends without the man/woman involvement. She'd enjoyed Adam's turning to her for help. Hadn't Gerry said that Liz was more than Adam's assistant? They were close friends. Why couldn't she have the same relationship?

But Gerry's words darted disconcertingly across her brain now: *"Liz has been in love with Adam for almost eighteen years."*

Adam was startled to find himself thinking about Helen Avery at regular intervals in the course of the afternoon. There was something serene and unaffected about her that he found appealing. She was a beautiful woman who probably had no idea that she was, he thought with admiration.

But enough of this. No room in his life for an affair—even if she was willing. God knows, he had plenty of opportunities. Kelly —twenty-eight and drop-dead gorgeous— was ready to climb into his bed at the slightest invitation. But he knew enough not to mix business and pleasure. He knew enough to keep himself clear of personal attachments.

In a corner of his mind he sensed Helen was attracted to him—as he was to her. A

178

man usually recognized the signs. But hell, his life was complicated enough. No involvement with women for him. He'd allowed moments of kindness to Eric turn him on. Not for him, he reminded himself grimly. *No room in my life for a woman. Don't ever forget that.*

Eighteen

Focused on Christmas Eve dinner preparations in the kitchenette, Helen heard the lively conversation between Deedee and Zach in the living room without fully comprehending what was being said. At least, she thought gratefully, they weren't fighting like mortal enemies. Gerry used to say the fighting was normal—just sibling rivalry. Paul used to get furious with them—but he'd made no effort to intercede. He just walked out of the room.

She smiled in retrospect, recalling Gerry's assessment of sibling rivalry. "Oh, it goes on forever. My brothers and I didn't have a civil word for each other until they were both married and had kids. I fell in love with their kids—that did it." But now Gerry was a pariah to her brothers, who belonged to some crazy cult that believed divorce was a sin. And they'd never understand her relationship with Sheila.

She'd been upset at first when Zach said he'd be staying at the dorm over the winter break. If they still had the house, he'd be up there. But he said Doug was staying at the dorm, too. Kids these days liked a lot of freedom. At least, he wasn't going to a college a thousand miles away. He wasn't into drinking and drugs.

Helen tensed. The conversation was taking a bellicose turn.

"So you're making a ton of money on the job," Zach scoffed. "You have no life."

"This is an apprenticeship—another year of this and I'll be an associate. The hours will drop to maybe sixty a week—and the money goes up." Triumph in Deedee's voice.

"You hope," Zach jeered. "Doug won't be twenty for another three months. He's talking about going into day-trading while he's still in school." Why did that make her feel uneasy? Helen asked herself. "One day last week his old man made $28,000 in one day."

"Kids!" Helen called from the kitchen moments later. "Set the table. Dinner's almost ready." Zach and Doug were thick as thieves. Zach wasn't going to get crazy ideas about day-trading, was he? Lots of stuff in the papers about it these days. No, she reassured herself instantly. Where would he get the money to start?

With dinner on the table in the dining area—the lights on the tree in the living room blinking cheerily— Helen was able to brush aside some of the depression that had hovered over her much of the day. She wouldn't think about other Christmases. After dinner the three of them would finish decorating the tree. They'd bring out presents and put them underneath—to be opened in the morning.

"It was shitty the way Dad just sent a group Christmas card to this apartment," Zach blurted out at a momentary pause in table talk. "As though he didn't know where anybody was except Deedee." He grunted. "And didn't care." He glared at Deedee. "You were always his favorite."

"Now don't get on that track again," Helen ordered. But Paul had played games with the kids. One week Deedee was his pet, the next Zach. More times than not, she forced herself to admit now, he ignored both.

"Why didn't he put down a return address?" Deedee demanded. "Was he scared we'd go chasing after him?"

Helen fought for calm. "He's out of our lives. If he wants to keep it that way, so be it."

Liz hated Adam's ex-wife, she remembered. But he never missed sending the alimony checks, Liz said. Adam had principles. He didn't love his child only in spurts —when it was convenient.

"So how's the job, Mom?" Zach was making an effort to return to safer ground. "You think you'll stay?" A hint of indulgent laughter in his eyes.

"I won't be on my own until after New Year's. But yes, I think I'll stay." *I'm glad both kids resemble me. I can look at them and not see Paul. He was a habit—love went out the window long ago. I just didn't recognize that.*

"Mom—" Deedee paused, seemed ambivalent about what she was on the point of saying.

"Yes?" Helen waited for her to continue.

"I was wondering about Gerry—"

"What about Gerry?" All at once Helen felt defensive. Gerry was like a member of the family to the kids.

"I mean this thing with her and Sheila." Deedee was groping for words. "Has Gerry jumped over the fence?"

For a moment Helen stared at her in incomprehension. Then the inference crept through. "If you're asking me if Gerry is in a lesbian relationship, I don't think it's any of our business." Helen dared a negative response.

"Mom, I didn't mean it in any derogatory

fashion." Deedee was defensive. "I just wanted to make sure I don't say something wrong. You know, something that could be misinterpreted. If that's what makes Gerry happy, then okay. She's still like part of the family—nothing's changed."

"What's for dessert?" Zach asked. "I hope it's frozen yogurt. Low fat, natch."

They were all trying to pretend this was a normal Christmas Eve, Helen thought as they focused on Zach's favorite frozen yogurt—but it wasn't. Each of them knew that. It wasn't just that Paul was missing from the scene—though each of them was sharply conscious of that. The pattern of their lives had been disrupted.

Millions of people had to adjust their lives at one time or another. Millions in this world would look on them with envy. They weren't living in hovels. They had food on the table, clothes to wear. They were living in a country that provided freedom.

She was conscious that Deedee and Zach were sparring again.

"This is Christmas Eve," she scolded. "Take off the boxing gloves."

"But Deedee's dumb to say there's no future in day-trading." He sought for the last word. "We're living in a whole new world—where technology is shooting down the old ways. Wow, would I love to get into day-trading with Doug!"

"That's pie in the sky." Deedee insisted on having the final word.

After dinner—as though it was a normal Christmas—Deedee and Zach decorated the tree while she commented at intervals. She turned on the TV. The sound of Christmas carols filled the room. It almost felt like Christmas Eve, she thought. Almost.

How were Adam and Eric celebrating this evening? He'd sounded so anxious to make it a good holiday for Eric. Did they have a Christmas tree? Had they gone out for dinner? She flinched at the vision of Christmas Eve dinner in a restaurant. What a desolate image.

Where are Paul and his young slut having dinner? Why should I care? For the children I care. Oh, why am I thinking this way? Paul is out of our lives. We don't need him.

She was touched later—when they prepared for the night—by the disarming efforts of the children to make her understand they were here for her. They worried about her, she thought lovingly. They were scared that she couldn't cope alone.

Zach deserted his sleeping bag to settle himself on the sofa—insisting he was comfortable there. Deedee recalled how when she was very small and there were thunderstorms, she insisted on sleeping in what she'd called "the big bed." The queen-sized

184

bed in her parents' bedroom.

Later Deedee tried for lightness as she settled herself beneath the comforter. "It's been a long time since we shared a bed. It's almost like we're having a slumber party."

It was far into the night before Helen fell asleep. Still, she found poignant comfort at having both Deedee and Zach here in the apartment with her.

Christmas day was pleasant, Helen congratulated herself as evening approached. Zach had just left for a party at a friend's apartment. Deedee had left a little earlier. *"The apartment is a disaster area. Todd and I were both in such a rush to get out yesterday, and the cleaning woman didn't come in this week because one of her kids was down with chicken pox."*

Helen settled herself on a corner of the living-room sofa, switched on the radio to WQXR and leaned back to enjoy the classical music. She felt as though she'd passed a major hurdle—Christmas without Paul. She and the kids had survived this.

On Monday Helen went into the office with the uneasy knowledge that Liz would be on the job only three more days. On the following Monday she would be on her own. An unnerving realization.

"Hi—" Liz emerged from Adam's office to greet her. "This is going to be a slow day. We

185

can use these three days for a crash course for you," she said with a suspect air of optimism.

"Sure." How much more could be crammed into these three days?

"I've typed a list of our major clients," Liz continued, "and some of the problems that arise with them." She chuckled wryly. "Sometimes I think we're as much their nursemaid as their publicist. But let me clue you in."

Helen gathered that little would be happening in this period between Christmas and New Year's. Liz gave word to the others that she and Helen were not to be disturbed—"unless there's a real emergency." Helen was conscious of Liz's ambivalence about taking time off—even while this was a "must." Deep inside, Helen sensed, Liz felt she was deserting Adam—and it was painful.

Adam surfaced in mid-afternoon. With Eric at his elbow, he hovered in the doorway to Liz's office to give her some last-minute instructions, then turned to Helen.

"Thanks for the tips—they're working out just fine."

"Great." Helen smiled in sympathy.

She was astonished that the short work week was passing so fast. Liz made farewell calls to clients, introduced them to Helen.

"You'll do fine," Liz reassured her. "And

don't be afraid to act on your own if Adam is unavailable. Your instincts are right."

On Wednesday afternoon Adam came into the office for a warm farewell to Liz.

"We'll keep in touch," he comforted, embracing her. "Hey, we've got a lot of years behind us."

"We'll keep in touch," Liz agreed, close to tears. "What are you doing over the long weekend?" She was trying for a casual touch.

"I'm driving with Eric out to Montauk." He turned to Helen with an apologetic smile. "I know that sounds crazy—going out to the beach in winter—"

"Oh, no," Helen protested, her face luminous in recall. "I took my two kids out there some years ago—when my 'ex' was out of town on business—and we had a marvelous time. This time of year. They loved walking on the deserted beach, watching the sunrise and the sunset."

"Nobody there but the seagulls and a town dog or two out for a stroll," he picked up. "I'm looking forward to it."

"Enjoy." All at once Helen was disconcerted by the intensity of his gaze. By her sense of encountering a kindred spirit. And she was conscious, too, of Liz's stricken face—

Nineteen

Thursday Helen woke up with the instant realization that she wouldn't be going into the office today, was startled that she missed this routine. She thought about Adam and Eric, probably en route right now to Montauk. East Hampton had been more Paul's style.

He'd never been one to enjoy solitude. She remembered his defiant retort when she'd suggested a Montauk retreat for last summer. "Hell, no! I work hard and I play hard. Who wants to sit around staring at the ocean? We'll rent in East Hampton."

Both Gerry and Sheila would be working a half day, Helen recalled. The three of them would have lunch together. Gerry and Sheila were leaving tomorrow morning for a houseparty in Putnam County. She'd be alone—she couldn't expect the kids to spend New Year's Eve with her. At their ages partying was the big thing on New Year's Eve—and the next day they'd sleep into the afternoon.

Her mind darted back to last New Year's

Eve. Zach and Deedee both stayed in the city, called on New Year's day. At Paul's insistence—as usual—they'd had a party for eight couples. Why was it always couples? And looking back she was conscious of all the nights Paul stayed in the city this past year—"on business."

The morning dragged until it was time to leave to meet Gerry and Sheila for lunch. This whole long weekend would drag. She'd drop by the library, pick up a couple of suspense novels to see her through. But at least she didn't have the headache of arranging for a New Year's Eve party.

They were having lunch at Michael's—on Sheila's expense account. *"I love all that modern art—and the tables are far enough apart so we can hear ourselves talk."* As usual—always recoiling from being late—she arrived first. There was a festive air in the restaurant that she enjoyed. The last New Year's Eve of the century was coming, she mused. Would the next be better?

Gerry and Sheila arrived together within a few minutes.

"I think half the town is closing down this afternoon," Gerry effervesced as they joined her at their table.

"And everybody's braced for a wild break-down in the computer world," Sheila drawled. "Oh, we've done our share of preparing for possible problems," she admitted. "A dozen jugs of bottled water, loads of batteries, more cans of tuna than we'd usually eat in a year—"

"We did the same thing at the house." Helen winced in recall. "And in the apartment. I notice Deedee put in the usual jugs of water and cans of tuna—but whatever happens we'll survive."

"Sometimes technology scares me. I mean, so much has happened so fast. The young take it in their stride—" Gerry shrugged this away. "Still, it's kind of exciting to know we're on the threshold of a new century."

Their waiter arrived. They focused on ordering. She was glad Gerry and Sheila had suggested lunch, Helen thought. It gave her a sense of belonging to this urban life.

After lunch she detoured to the library to pick up a couple of suspense novels to read over the long weekend. It would be a cozy, restful New Year's Eve, she told herself. She'd be extravagant, order in dinner tonight and tomorrow night.

It would be the first time in her life, she thought self-consciously, that she would be alone on New Year's Eve. No, there was one other time, she remembered. Her last year in college. But even now she didn't like to think about that.

Thursday evening she ate her ordered-in

dinner before the TV set—on a tray. She slept late on Friday morning— luxuriating in her idleness. She lay in bed—conscious that the year, the century, had only hours to go—and plotted those hours. It was weird, she mocked herself, that she needed some structure in each day.

Were Adam and Eric enjoying their stay in Montauk? After the pressure he endured on the job, he needed the quiet out there. And it would be good for Eric, too, to have this time alone with his father. Paul would have filled every moment with frenzied activity. Instinct told her that after the days of diverse entertainment in New York, both Adam and Eric would welcome the oasis Montauk would provide.

Her mind darted off to memories of the years ago trip to Montauk in winter. They'd stayed at Gurney's, lain on chaises on the deck or walked along the empty beach—its smoothness broken only by occasional human footprints and swatch of seagull imprints. They'd lingered over gourmet meals. Oh yes, the serenity of those few days had been beautiful.

All at once she was unnerved that her thoughts had focused yet again on Adam. She remembered the way he'd called her at home, thanked her for her suggestions. It astonished her that it was so comfortable to be with him. She'd been uneasy at first. The others in the office made cracks about his mercurial temper—yet they did so with indulgence, she remembered. He was warm and kind and unpretentious.

Enough of this. Get up, have breakfast, vacuum, dust. Greet the new year—the new century—in an immaculate apartment.

Early in the afternoon Deedee called.

"Interested in company for dinner?" she asked, overly casual.

"I'd love it," Helen said. *Todd won't be spending New Year's with her?* "I'll be ordering in—so think about what you'd like." One of the pleasures of Manhattan living.

"The office is closed today—I slept till a few minutes ago." Deedee giggled. "Wow, was that a break. Shall I bring anything?"

"Just yourself." *What kind of man is Todd to leave Deedee alone on New Year's Eve?*

"Todd got dragged into a weekend house-party with one of the big guys. He couldn't refuse." Deedee made an effort to dismiss this as inconsequential—yet Helen sensed she was upset.

"One of those things." Helen played along with her. In a corner of her mind she recalled again the New Year's Eve long ago, when Paul had behaved in a similar fashion. "It happened to me my last year in college—right after I moved in with your father. There was some judge that—"

"You and Dad lived together before you

192

were married?" Deedee was astonished.

"Just our last year in college. Couples did that even twenty five years ago—"

"You never said a word about it!"

"It isn't quite the thing you discuss with your kids." Helen was disconcerted. "We knew we were going to get married, but that wasn't the time—" But Deedee and Todd shared no such commitment. "Anyhow, this judge invited him—it was considered an honor for a prospective law student. So he went." She'd tried to rationalize it, but even now—all these years later—she remembered her sense of being abandoned.

"What time should I come over?"

"Darling, any time you want," Helen told her. "I'll be here."

Helen paced about the apartment. Todd was wrong for Deedee—she was sure of that. But you weren't supposed to interfere. That was a cardinal rule in today's world.

Without having met him, she suspected Todd was a carbon copy of Paul. Ambitious as hell—career ruled his life. But where were he and Deedee going?

When Deedee was seeing Cliff, she'd felt no such worries. Cliff, too, worked endless hours—Deedee complained they had no time for each other. But there was a warmth and compassion about Cliff that was endearing. Todd was there—available, she thought impatiently. Was the sex so great that Deedee couldn't resist him?

She started at the sound of the doorbell. The doorman never called up to announce Deedee, of course. She hurried to respond.

"Happy almost-New Year." Deedee held up a package from the neighborhood liquor store. "I figured for New Year's we should celebrate with a bottle of bubbly."

"Good thinking," Helen approved. How long since she'd spent New Year's Eve with Deedee? Not since Deedee was in junior high, she thought tenderly. In high school there were already New Year's Eve parties—with strict rules about curfews. "Are you hungry? Would you like a snack before dinner?"

"Yeah—" Deedee threw off her coat and headed for the kitchen. Helen chuckled at the familiar gesture—Deedee opening the refrigerator, inspecting the contents, then checking the freezer. "I'll have a sandwich," Deedee decided, bringing out the makings. Rye bread, the remainder of yesterday's sliced turkey, mustard.

"I'll put up coffee for us. And let's live dangerously. I have Ben & Jerry's Chocolate Cherry Garcia in the fridge."

"I know." Deedee grinned. "We'll leave a little bit in case Zach surfaces tomorrow."

For the first time since the approach of the holiday Helen was conscious of a flicker of festivity. It felt good having Deedee here. She wouldn't be welcoming the new year alone. The new century. Why did that seem so awesome?

Over their afternoon snack Deedee talked animatedly about her job. It was almost as though she was trying to convince herself that she loved her work, Helen thought. The money was astounding for one so young, fresh out of college—but what kind of a life did Deedee have?

"With a little luck I'll become an associate in less than a year," Deedee seemed to read her mind. "The hours will drop down. Well, maybe to sixty hours a week," she acknowledged. "But anybody on the upward trail expects to put in long hours. And the money will go up."

"I'd like to think that you have time to enjoy living," Helen said gently. "I know—in this world money is important—but there has to be time for something besides work."

"That's what Cliff used to say." Deedee stared into space. "But his life revolved around the hospital. He had no time for anything else."

"That's until he finishes his residency." So Cliff was still in Deedee's thoughts.

"We'd go to a movie, and he'd fall asleep on my shoulder. We'd try for a day at the beach, and the same thing would happen."

"It'll be different when he's in practice.

Everybody knows how hard residents work—the crazy back-to-back shifts—" *I shouldn't be trying to push her back to Cliff, should I? But deep in her heart Deedee still cares for him.* "It'll be different when he's in practice," she reiterated.

"No." Deedee was brusque. "Cliff is one of those rare, dedicated doctors. With him medicine—his patients—will always come first. It just didn't work for us." *And it does for Todd and her, when she's so upset that he's left her alone on New Year's Eve?*

Earlier than normal—because they suspected there would be a rush at the send-out places, they ordered dinner. One of the magic gifts of city living, Helen thought again. She wildly over-tipped the delivery man. How sad, to be working on New Year's Eve.

With WQXR sending Strauss waltzes into the dining area, they ate their New Year's Eve dinner. But it was far more pleasant, Helen told herself, than the endless dinner parties she'd endured through the years—guests were always couples Paul thought would be useful in some way or other.

After dinner they turned on television, watched the usual holiday programming. It was a good New Year's, Helen told herself, because Deedee was here. She didn't feel like a woman whose husband had walked out on her after almost twenty-five years.

She was beginning to believe that there was life ahead.

"I'll stay till just past midnight," Deedee said. "Then I'll hit the trail."

"It'll be late to be out alone," Helen worried. *Should I suggest that Deedee sleep over?*

"On New Year's Eve?" Deedee laughed. "This is Manhattan—the streets will be jammed. I'll get a cab and be home in minutes. I'll probably sleep till afternoon again."

"Call me when you get home," Helen urged when the new year had been rung in with the usual hoopla, and horns and whistles echoed throughout the city. "Just to put my mind at rest." People worried about electrical power going out because of computer glitches with the arrival of January 1, 2000. No traffic lights, the city—the country—in darkness.

"Happy New Year, Mom," Deedee said once again, and exchanged a warm embrace with her mother. "Let's make it a great one."

Tired and sleepy, Helen nevertheless lay awake far into the night. Monday would be the beginning of her new year—when she went into the office to try to fill Liz's shoes. How had Adam and Eric spent New Year's? Had it been a happy holiday for them?

Why am I thinking about Adam? I'm not Liz—I'm not in love with my boss. I barely know him. All right, I like him—a lot. But there's no room in my life for anything more. Nor in his. It's the holiday. Holidays have a weird way of making me feel sentimental. No room for sentiment in this world. Remember that.

Twenty

Preparing to leave for the office this first Monday in the new year, Helen was conscious of a sense of relief. The world seemed past the dire predictions that chaos would descend because computers wouldn't be able to cope with the year 2000. But this feeling was momentary. In another ten minutes she must leave the apartment and head for her first day on her own at Adam Fremont, Public Relations.

It wasn't going to be bad, she exhorted herself. Liz was a phone call away if she ran into trouble. The others on staff—all four so very young—would be supportive. But they must recognize that she was taking Liz's place. It was her responsibility to make sure everything ran smoothly.

As Liz had done, she arrived at the office ahead of schedule. She'd just removed her coat when the phone rang.

"Adam Fremont Public Relations," she responded in the prescribed cordial tones.

"You're not Liz!" an indignant, faintly hoarse voice greeted her.

"No." She was sweetly apologetic. "I'm filling in for Liz while she's on leave." The approach Liz told her to use. All of Adam's clients knew this.

"Where's Adam?" the caller demanded. "This is Rod Langley." The leading man in a hit Broadway musical—with a movie contract in negotiation, Helen pinpointed. "I have an emergency!"

"He isn't in the office yet. May—"

"And he's not home," Rod pounced. "I called him there first. Where the hell is he when I need him?"

"I expect to hear from him soon," Helen soothed. She hesitated. "What's the emergency? Perhaps I can help—" Despite the calmness of her voice her heart was pounding. Liz would know how to handle this.

"I've got a ghastly sore throat—and I have to sing tonight! And I'm supposed to audition for a Hollywood big shot at three tomorrow afternoon! How can Adam let me down this way?" Adam said his clients expected him to be all things—sometimes coming to him when they'd be expected to lean on their agents.

"Are you running a temperature?" she

asked, as though talking with Zach.

"I don't think so—but my throat hurts like hell."

"Do you have any honey in the apartment?"

"No—" He seemed mollified by her sympathetic tone.

"Lemon?" she pursued.

"Yeah—"

"Start drinking hot tea and lemon," she ordered. "And gargle in-between with warm salt water. And in the meanwhile I'll call a pharmacist and have a cough medication sent over." His address would be on the computer—along with names and phone numbers of neighborhood pharmacists. Liz was accustomed to playing surrogate mother. "Start right now," she ordered. "And when Adam gets in, I'll have him call you immediately."

"Who're you?" he rasped.

"Helen," she told him.

"You're okay, Helen," he approved. "I'll get on the routine right now. God, I don't want my understudy to go on tonight. The Hollywood guy—the one I'm auditioning for tomorrow afternoon—" He groaned. "The one I'm supposed to audition for— he's coming to the performance tomorrow night. Isn't this a bitch?"

"If you're not running a temperature, you'll probably get better quickly. I'll get the medication over to you right away."

"Okay." He seemed a bit calmer now. "My agent wasn't in," he said grimly. "Nobody there offered to help."

"Hot tea and lemon, gargle with warm salt water," she repeated. "And take the medication according to directions on the package."

"Will do, Helen—and tell Adam to call."

"He's driving in from out-of-town," Helen improvised. "But he'll call as soon as he arrives."

Helen pulled up the necessary information on the computer, ordered medication from the pharmacist to be delivered immediately. She'd managed this "emergency" all right, hadn't she? It was a reassuring thought.

It was almost 11 a.m. when Adam walked into the office. He looked more relaxed than she'd ever seen him, she thought while they exchanged greetings. He'd enjoyed his holiday. Immediately she advised him of Rod Langley's call and her efforts to calm him.

"I'll call him. He's a nervous wreck about this movie deal. He always develops a sore throat before important auditions."

Helen was disconcerted by the sudden intensity of Adam's gaze. "Shall I get Rod for you?"

"Please." He paused. "Oh, Eric asked

about you. He thinks you're terrific."

"He's a wonderful boy," she said softly and reached for her phone.

Why did her heart begin to pound this way when Adam looked at her as he was doing now? She was over-reacting, she scolded herself. To Adam she was just Liz's replacement—temporary, at that. Yet she couldn't erase from her mind the suspicion that something more was developing between them.

She'd started the week off well, she congratulated herself at the end of the day. Still, she was discomforted the following morning when Adam—clearly in a bad mood—yelled at her for some minor gaff. She knew the others were watching for her reaction—but she realized, too, that they hoped she'd stay. They didn't know how desperately important this job was to her. She'd be here—unless Adam fired her.

His muscles aching from tension, Zach leaned back in his chair in one of two rooms in the minuscule dorm suite he shared with Doug. God, he was tired! They'd been at this since 8 a.m. this morning. Scanning the Internet for the latest stock figures before the market opened. At intervals watching CNBC on the TV set placed next to the computer monitor.

Now his eyes focused on the TV screen. It

was moments before 4:30 p.m.—the stock market was closing for the day.

"Hey, how did we do?" he asked Doug with apprehension. Doug was at the calculator figuring out their first day's results as day-traders.

"We lost 182 bucks," Doug admitted. "Plus the cost of our trades. That's less than ten bucks each on the Internet." Zach flinched. They'd made nine trades in the course of the day. "But this is our first day," Doug pointed out defensively. "We've got a lot to learn."

"Shit." They couldn't afford the time or money for training courses, Zach reminded himself. But they'd studied stock fundamentals. They'd pored over e-mail newsletters. They'd got involved in chat rooms. And Doug's father—unknown to him—was their advisor.

"Look, school's out for the winter break." Doug refused to relinquish enthusiasm. "We'll be playing every day—I'll go home for dinner more often, pump Dad. He thinks it's great I'm so interested."

"He doesn't know we're playing." *Mom would freak out if she knew I was day-trading —on money I borrowed on her Mastercard.* "He'll be pissed if he finds out."

Doug grinned. "I'm not about to tell him. But he gave me his day-trading software when he bought new. Just so I could see

203

what it was like."

They couldn't afford a steady losing streak —not with their small stash. With online brokers you had to put up cash for half your trades. It used to be a $10,000 minimum— then they'd discovered brokerages that settled for as low as $500—which put them in business. He felt guilty, Zach acknowledged to himself, that he'd taken that advance on Mom's Mastercard. But he'd put away his salary check each week to cover what he'd drawn out. Mom wouldn't be losing anything—and with a little luck he might end up with a bunch of money. It happened to people every day. He'd give her a commission.

"All right, we jumped a little too fast today," Doug said. "We need to remember Dad's rules. We shouldn't have bought that first stock this morning—not the way it had been hyped. Dad said, *'Never buy any stock when the market first opens if it's been hyped. It'll go up, then drop like a deflated balloon. And just because a stock is dropping, don't rush to buy it without checking how the company's doing. It may never go up again—'"*

"Let's knock off for now." All at once Zach was ambivalent about the whole deal. But that was because he was beat, he alibied. He'd feel differently in the morning.

Close to dawn, Zach was vaguely conscious

of fire trucks racing through the streets. He pulled the comforter over his head. It was Saturday—his morning to sleep late. Doug would get up early and jog—he was on a fitness kick. In moments Zach was in deep slumber again.

"Zach, wake up! Come on, return to this world!"

"What? What?" Zach struggled to open his eyes. He managed a glance at his night table clock. "Are you nuts?" he demanded of Doug in outrage. "It's just seven thirty!" Sure, they worked at the copy center today —but they were both on the 4 p.m. to midnight shift.

"You heard the fire trucks last night?"

"The dorm's still here," Zach shot back.

"Yeah." Doug was grim. "But the copy center burned. An electrical fire. I went over there. It'll be at least two or three weeks before they can reopen, John—the guy who hired us—told me."

Zach was instantly awake, felt panic closing in on him.

"We'll have to look for new jobs fast!" *I have to have the money before Mom's Mastercard bill comes in.*

"John's paying us—*would* be paying us— ten bucks an hour," Doug reminded. "Anything else we line up will be minimum— maybe seven bucks at the most. If we're lucky enough to find something right away."

He uttered an agonized groan. "I'm already in the doghouse with my old man. I can't screw up with my mom, too."

"So we'll be a little late in paying back." Zach struggled for calm. But he could visualize Mom's shock when she saw her Mastercard bill—and he wouldn't have enough to cover it. She could borrow from his college account—from next term's tuition, he tried to rationalize. It wouldn't be a total catastrophe. But in a corner of his mind he wondered about where he'd go to school next year. *Would he go to school anywhere?*

"We still have cash in the brokerage account," Doug conceded. "We can withdraw that, split it between us." His face brightened. "Add that to what we can earn, and we'll pay back on schedule. Hey, we'll be off the hook."

Zach felt a momentary rush of relief. "But what about the day-trading? The money we can make if we handle ourselves right?" *How long will Mom hang on to that job? Deedee worries about that, too.*

Doug hesitated a moment. His face tightened in determination. "Yeah. Let's go for it. All we need is one great day, and we'll see more than the two of us could make in a month. It's our big chance—before the winter break's over. Okay?" His eyes dared Zach to turn him down.

"Yeah, let's go for it." They had Doug's father as a mentor—though he didn't know that. His father was cleaning up, Doug said. So he had a few bad days—he came back and really scored.

"Let's go over to Butler and do more research." They'd already researched like crazy at the college library, but more couldn't hurt. "Figure out why we goofed up yesterday. Come on, Zach, move your butt!"

Helen was conscious of hunger as she sat at the computer. She shot a fast glance at her watch. Wow, almost 2 p.m. She'd finish this press release and order in. No time today to go out for lunch. Not with the pile of work Adam had thrown at her this morning.

Liz said there'd be rush days like this. But she could handle it. Almost a whole week on her own, she realized with satisfaction—and she hadn't called Liz once for help. So far no major catastrophes. Liz had called twice just to offer words of encouragement.

She heard exuberant voices in the reception area. Linda, their vivacious young receptionist, was clearly delighted with the new arrival. Linda had confessed that one of the perks of the job was meeting celebrities.

"I have to see Helen," a vaguely familiar voice was booming. Rod Langley, she pinpointed. "That little doll saved my life."

"I'll tell her you're here." A giggle escaped Linda.

"No need," Rod dismissed this in high spirits.

Moments later Rod strode into her office —a bouquet of red roses in hand.

"For the beautiful lady who saved my life," he said with a dramatic flourish.

"Thank you. They're gorgeous." Startled, she accepted the roses. "My favorite of all flowers—"

"I dropped by to tell Adam—I'm flying to Hollywood in the morning for tests. I wouldn't be doing that if you hadn't played Florence Nightingale." He leaned forward, his eyes amorous. "When I come back, let's have dinner."

"Rod, get into my office and let's do some work," Adam said briskly, hovering in the doorway. But his eyes said he was annoyed with Rod. *Because he asked me out to dinner?*

Helen sat motionless, her mind trying to accept the realization that a man almost twenty years her junior had just called her beautiful, had suggested she have dinner with him. Oh, he wasn't serious, she rebuked herself. He was just being charming.

Adam had been annoyed, she thought again. He rejected socializing between clients and staff, she alibied. But instinct told her his annoyance went deeper than that—

Twenty-One

It was almost 8 p.m. by the time Helen left the office. There'd been a last-minute rush of work that had to go out. Adam was still at his desk. She suspected he'd be there for at least another hour or two. In an odd way she understood his passion for work. It was a way of avoiding worrisome incidents.

She waited impatiently for a bus. Why did they always arrive in bunches—with a long wait in-between? At least, at this hour the buses were uncrowded, she thought with relief when the 104 finally arrived. Why hadn't Adam sent out for dinner for himself? Would Liz have done that if she'd been on the job?

It had been so sweet of Rod Langley to bring her roses. Linda had been absolutely awed—she'd taken one rose home to show her roommate. *"Beth saw Rod's play last month—she's mad about him."* But then actors were known to make dramatic gestures.

She suspected Linda had overheard Rod's invitation to take her to dinner when he returned from the Coast. In Linda's eyes, she taunted herself, she was *old*. Why would a handsome young Broadway star want to take her out to dinner?

Still, it was good for the ego—even though she was sure he'd forget he'd ever mentioned dinner once he returned to New York. And why, she asked herself again, had Adam reacted that way? Because he didn't like staff socializing with clients. Her initial interpretation.

In the lobby of her apartment house she stopped to collect her mail. The box stuffed with the usual assortment of bills, ads, and catalogues. God, the wasted paper—the trees that were cut down for this garbage. Zach kept saying that e-mail was the best thing that ever happened for the environment.

Then—sifting through envelopes—she froze. She recognized the handwriting on a letter addressed to Deedee. *Paul doesn't know that Deedee is living with Todd. That I'm living in Deedee's apartment. Why is my heart suddenly pounding this way?*

She'd call Deedee, tell her about the letter. Whatever Paul had to say, he'd say to Deedee—Zach had made it clear that he was furious with his father. Deedee had been more diplomatic—but she, too, was furious with Paul. It was natural that Paul would want to keep in touch with the kids, she rationalized. The marriage might be dead, but he was still their father. When he cared to remember.

What is Paul writing to Deedee about? I don't want to know about his new life—about his young girlfriend. Are they annoyed that they have to wait so long for the divorce to go through? Does Paul plan on marrying her? It's strange—I don't truly care.

Again, she thought, love died a long time ago. Paul was a habit. When did it die? Not all at once—it eroded through the years. She'd thought that was how it happened in long-time marriages. Of course she'd realized early on that Paul was totally self-centered.

At the apartment she called Deedee's office. Voicemail told her Deedee was gone for the day. A rare early departure. She put down the phone. She'd been avoiding calling Deedee at home. *Suppose Deedee doesn't answer? Suppose Todd picks up? I don't want to talk to him!*

She was conscious of hunger. Have a quick dinner, then call Deedee. Relieved at this small delay she dug into the refrigerator, brought out the replica of last evening's dinner. Gerry had clued her in to the practicality of cooking two dinners at a time.

She finished off the heated-up chicken cutlet and stir-fried vegetables, poured herself a cup of tea and carried it into the living room. She couldn't stall any longer. Call Deedee.

She reached for the phone, felt a tightness between her shoulder blades as she punched in the unfamiliar numbers. She'd never called Deedee at Todd's apartment. All right, it was Deedee's apartment, too. But Deedee was there on a temporary basis— that was what she'd said.

The phone was ringing. *Deedee, pick up!* For a moment she was on the brink of hanging up—but then it was too late.

"Hello—" A male voice. A con man voice, Helen thought in instant appraisal—too startled to reply. "Hello—"

"May I speak to Deedee, please—" She struggled to sound casual.

"Sure thing. Who's calling, please?"

"Her mother—" *Is this what people mean when they talk about "being civilized"?*

"She's in the shower," he replied after a startled silence. "May she call you back?"

"Of course." This was weird—talking to the man Deedee was living with as though he was a total stranger. But he was just that, wasn't he? "I'll be home the rest of the evening."

She put down the phone, felt herself encased in ice. Her hands were trembling. Modern mothers were supposed to be sophisticated about these situations. She couldn't always manage to call Deedee at the office—she felt guilty when she called her there.

She tried to settle down to read—but Todd's voice kept filtering into her mind. It had been Todd. Who else could it have been? But maybe the young were right. Better to live together, learn if they were right for each other than to end up in a divorce court five years later. Or twenty-five years later.

She leapt to her feet when the phone rang, crossed to respond. "Hello—" She frowned as some telecommunicator began her spiel. "Sorry, I'm not interested." God, she loathed these intrusions. It was like somebody walking into the apartment without knocking.

A few moments later the phone rang again. She rushed to reply. "Hello—"

"Hi, Mom."

"I didn't mean to disturb you, darling, but—"

"Mom, you're not disturbing me," Deedee scolded. "What's up?"

"There was a letter for you in the mail box." Helen took a deep breath. "From your father."

"So read it, Mom—" A touch of irritation in her voice.

"But it's addressed to you—"

"So what? I'm not really interested in what he has to say." Deedee's tone was scathing.

213

"If there's anything requiring a reply, call me back. Don't bother reading it to me."

Off the phone, Helen sat at the edge of the sofa, held the envelope in her hand as though it might explode at any moment. All right, open it. With a sudden decisive move she ripped open the envelope, pulled out the sheet of paper, scanned the familiar handwriting.

Fine, so he was getting settled in a great new job. For the moment it was great—the honeymoon usually lasted about six months.

"You wouldn't believe the cost of housing out here. It's unbelievable. Any house worth looking at costs at least a million. My salary's fine—if I was living back East. Here it's a matter of fighting to survive."

This was his way of letting her know—via Deedee—that she shouldn't expect any help with next year's college expenses. After all, he had an expensive young girlfriend to keep happy. *How the hell am I going to manage two more years of college for Zach—even at a state school?*

A conversation she'd heard on the bus this morning between two young women about Deedee's age invaded her thoughts.

"Oh, I just heard last evening about an apartment that'll be vacant in my building in three months. You said your cousin was desperately looking," one of the two said with an air of

excitement.

"*Let me call her right away.*" *The other pulled a cell phone out of her purse.* "*What's it like—and how much?*"

"*It's a good-size one bedroom—and it's only $2500 a month. And it's okay to share.*"

Helen shivered in recall, calculating how much pre-taxes earnings were needed just to pay that rent. And she felt a fresh alarm because she'd be apartment hunting if Dee-dee broke up with Todd. And rents hadn't gone berserk just in Manhattan—it was happening in all five boroughs.

Remember what Gerry always said. "These are weird times—the only way to survive is to live one day at a time." That was the way to go.

By the end of her third week on the job—with only one emergency call to Liz—Helen felt more secure. Adam seemed pleased with her work though at heady moments she felt his approval went beyond that. A disconcerting yet intoxicating assumption. Helen glanced up from her computer as Linda burst into her office.

"A call for you," Linda bubbled, wide-eyed. "I think it's Rod Langley!"

"Thanks, Linda." Helen reached for the phone. Why hadn't Linda put the call through the normal way? "Hello—"

"Hello, my serene beauty." It was Rod. He

215

was on leave from his play—in Hollywood to do a test for some major film, she remembered. "I'm calling you from my flight to New York. We'll be landing in about an hour. What about dinner tonight? I can meet you at Le Perigord at 7 p.m. You won't mind the old 'five o'clock shadow' will you? I suppose I could shave at the airport if it'll bother you," he wound up his breathy monologue.

"No need to shave." An undercurrent of laughter in her voice. She'd been sure he'd forget about the dinner invitation. For what he'd called her "Florence Nightingale routine." Why not? All that lay ahead this evening was a microwave dinner and an hour or two of TV. "See you at 7 p.m. At Le Perigord."

"I'll make a reservation. See you then, Beautiful."

Only now did she realize that Linda still hovered in her office doorway.

"You're having dinner with Rod Langley?" Linda's eyes widened in awe. "Wait'll I tell Beth!"

"It's a 'thank you for saving my life' dinner." Helen chuckled. "You know Rod—always dramatic. I sent over cough medicine when he was afraid he'd miss a performance of the play."

"When did he get back in town?"

"He'll be back in an hour," Helen explain-

216

ed. Linda stared blankly. "He called from the plane."

"Oh, wow!"

Alone in her office Helen pondered over her casual—swift—acceptance of the dinner invitation. It wasn't exactly a date, she reproved herself. He was almost twenty years younger than she. *Maybe I remind him of his mother.*

She hoped this would be a day when she could leave the office no later than six. A cab home for a quick change, a cab back to Le Perigord. Only now did she remember that Rod lived in the low East 50s—a short walk to Le Perigord. But instantly she scolded herself for the suspicious thought. No! That was ridiculous. Rod Langley wasn't making a play for her.

Adam would be annoyed, wouldn't he, if he knew she was having dinner with Rod? So Rod was a client—Adam didn't control his personal life. Rod was just making a sentimental gesture. Still, she was relieved that Adam was out of the office most of the day. He popped in for about an hour in the early afternoon, then popped out again.

She was handling the job fairly well, she comforted herself. Adam was a great boss— as the others kept telling her. At moments she reminded herself that he was her boss— not a personal friend. She'd refrained from asking him how he'd enjoyed Montauk with

Eric. She'd made his flight reservations for Boston next weekend—this was a weekend to be spent with Eric—but she hadn't pried, she congratulated herself.

She was conscious of his quizzical scrutiny at unwary moments. Why did he gaze at her that way? What was he thinking? It was absurd to react the way she did. As if she was twenty and on the verge of a towering infatuation.

Twenty-Two

At exactly 6 p.m. Helen closed the office for the day. Adam had phoned in to say he wouldn't be returning. It was absurd to be disappointed when Adam was away from the office for long stretches. But she liked to be able to hear his voice or to glance up from her desk to see him just a few feet away. She missed him when he wasn't around.

Ignoring her budget, she was in a cab a few minutes later. An accomplishment this time of day. At the apartment she changed from pantsuit to a beautifully cut grey wool dress bought in more affluent times. She dug into her jewelry box—which contained

218

the collection of years, chose three silver chains and matching earrings.

Inspecting her reflection in the full-length door mirror for a moment, she was assaulted by doubts. *Why did I agree to have dinner with Rod? This was ridiculous! Did he feel obligated in some weird way to take me out?*

She reached for her coat, headed for the door. Whatever, she had to see this through. Maybe she'd accepted out of rebellion. To prove that she wasn't crushed by being discarded by Paul. That there was life after divorce.

Again she was lucky. A cab pulled up to disgorge a passenger just as she reached the street. She charged forward. A rather distinguished man who appeared to be about fifty emerged.

"Perfect timing," he approved. "The gods were with you."

"A miracle this time of day." She stepped inside the cab while he held the door for her. "Thank you." She basked in recognition of his admiring inspection.

She arrived at Le Perigord before Rod, was seated. The brief encounter at the taxi had bolstered her ego. Still, she felt self-conscious at sitting alone at a choice table. Other diners would recognize Rod, she realized. Would they wonder why he was having dinner with an older woman? Perhaps they'd think she was his mother.

Oh well, she tried for a flippant mood—this would be an amusing story to tell Gerry and Sheila. Even Deedee would be surprised. But a small reproachful voice warned her that Adam would disapprove.

She spied Rod at the entrance—in conversation with the maître d'. She glanced about the room. Other diners were recognizing him. She managed a bright smile as he was led to their table.

"You look none the worse for wear," she drawled, "but then in California it's only just past 4 p.m."

"You're scolding me for being late. I apologize." He flashed the charismatic smile that intrigued theater goers.

"No," she denied. "You're only a few minutes late. I was lucky—I caught a cab immediately."

"You're looking beautiful—as always."

"You're flattering—as always." *What am I doing here? I'm too old to play these games.*

Now they paused to focus on ordering—though Rod managed to slip in amusing accounts of his days in Hollywood.

"I return to the play tomorrow night." His sigh managed to convey both approval and philosophical acceptance. "But we have no performances on Mondays." He leaned forward, his eyes amorous. "Save all your Monday nights for me?"

"Why?" Be cool, her mind ordered.

"Because I want to see a lot of you." His eyes were reproachful. "Are you otherwise committed?"

She remembered now that his gaze had focused on two occasions on her left hand. The wedding ring had been discarded the day Paul announced he wanted a divorce. "Technically I suppose I'm married—my divorce won't be final for another eight months."

"Why should we miss those eight months?" he challenged.

"Rod, you should be seeing some lovely young woman close to your own age." This was the time for candor, she told herself. Of course, she was flattered by Rod's attentions—but how long would that last?

"Honey, I'm with a lovely woman close to my own age." His eyes crinkled in laughter. "Don't believe the official bio—or the surface looks. My birth certificate will tell you I'm thirty-nine—even though Adam gives out my age as twenty-eight."

"I'm forty-six," she told him, and he shrugged.

"So what's a few years when I'm fascinated by the woman?" he countered.

"Why me?" she probed.

"Because you're beautiful—and so in control." *Oh God, he doesn't know how shaky I am ninety per cent of the time!* "You're the person I'd like to be with in a hurricane—or

221

in a plane about to dive into the ocean. And frankly, you turn me on."

"I'm still smarting from an ugly divorce," she said and he winced.

"I've been through that scene, too."

"Then you understand I'm not ready for any kind of commitment at this point." *I can't believe I'm in this kind of situation. Paul would never believe it.*

"Okay. I get the message—you're being slow and cautious. I can deal with that. But we can still have dinner on Monday nights, can't we?"

"Some Monday nights," she agreed after a moment. "Dinner," she emphasized.

Helen lay sleepless long after she was settled in bed, the lights turned off. It was heady, she admitted to herself, to be pursued by a man like Rod Langley. A suburban wife with grown kids—and dumped by her husband. But it wasn't Rod who invaded her thoughts at unwary moments.

Why am I allowing myself to become emotionally involved with Adam? Misreading signs because I want to believe he finds me special. Don't I know by now that people in the entertainment field—and that includes Adam—are apt to dramatize the smallest things? He's just grateful that I was managing to handle the job fairly well.

How can I be feeling this way about Adam? I

barely know him. It's part of the divorce syndrome—that's it, isn't it? I felt this way about Paul in those very early years. The Paul I know now is a stranger—he isn't the man I loved so passionately twenty-five years ago.

People do change. I was too busy trying to be the perfect wife to realize how he was changing. And when passion disappeared, I told myself this was how it was meant to be after long years of marriage. But I can feel passion again—for Adam. I feel the way towards him the way I felt all those years ago for Paul.

She reached for the pillow beside her, brought it into her arms. She remembered the way Adam's eyes lit up when he was with Eric. This was a man who knew how to love. A man who knew how to give.

Paul never thought beyond himself. Even this girl he ran off with to California was someone to build his ego. What was the phrase? A trophy wife. If he ever got around to marrying her. Still she was unhappy that Deedee and Zach felt such rage toward Paul. Children shouldn't feel that way about their father.

She should have made it clear to Rod that there was no future for them. But how long would his infatuation last? It was a game he was playing. Or was he just seeking refuge?

Her mind shot back to the moment Adam had walked into her office when Rod was there. He heard Rod ask her out to dinner—

he'd been annoyed. Because he disliked staff socializing with clients? Or did he feel more for her than he wished to admit? There were moments when she was sure of that. When he seemed about to say something to her that was personal rather than business.

Oh, this is absurd! Go to sleep. Forget this insanity.

Adam listened impatiently to Zoe's dramatic pleas for an advance on her alimony. He glanced at the clock. It was past 2 a.m.—only 11 p.m. in California, where Zoe lived now.

"Zoe, I'll send a check to you tomorrow," he said when she paused for breath. "But there'll be no check next month."

"Wire it," Zoe ordered. "First thing in the morning. It's terribly important."

"I'll wire it first thing in the morning," he agreed. "Goodbye, Zoe." He hung up with greater force than he'd intended. But Zoe was impossible. Why did she suddenly need the money? To keep her boy toy happy?

He'd lie awake for hours, he taunted himself. Every phone call from Zoe was traumatic. Liz said a dozen times through the years that he ought to hire a detective, get the goods on Zoe that would make it possible for him to gain full time custody of Eric. But how much of him would Eric see each day? He'd be raised by a housekeeper.

Up until now he'd convinced himself that Zoe was providing a semblance of home for Eric. But this boarding school decision hit out of left field.

"Adam, a fine boarding school like this one will be great for Eric. He's getting to be more than I can manage on my own. We're so lucky they were willing to accept him at the last moment."

He'd be with Eric this coming weekend. He'd try to get up to Boston most weekends. Eric deserved more than he was getting out of life. He deserved a real home.

Helen had been wonderful with Eric. Watching them together, he'd felt the tenderness in her. What kind of a man was her husband to let her get away? Liz said her husband left her for some young slut.

It would be so easy to fall in love with her. Sometimes he had to fight with himself not to reach out to touch her. To feel her closeness. But there was no room in his life for Helen. He had his son and his business —that was enough.

Zach sat hunched before the TV set in the dorm room that was serving as their office during the winter school "break"—which was close to ending. The usual dramatic closing of the stock market was being telecast. Doug—scowling—was focused on his calculator.

Four days ago—after three weeks on a roller coaster—he and Doug had rejoiced in their first big deal. Their bankroll had leapt to over $6,000. But the stock they expected to make their fortune on had taken a nosedive.

Zach switched off the TV. "How bad is it?"

"We're down to $638," Doug said dejectedly.

"And we'll be back at school next week." *When will Mom receive her Mastercard bill? Wow, will she be pissed!*

"We need to make one big splurge." Doug struggled for an air of confidence. "I'll go home for dinner tonight, schmooze with Dad. And in the morning, I'm going to hock my watch."

"Your Rolex?" Zach stared at Doug in disbelief. That was Doug's claim to fame in their small circle. "Your grandmother will kill you if she finds out."

His grandmother had given the watch to Doug as a high school graduation present. His parents were horrified that he walked around with something so expensive. "In that neighborhood!" his mother moaned at intervals. But Doug told her the young thugs in the neighborhood would think it was a knock-off.

"This is our last chance. Where the fuck did we screw up?"

★ ★ ★

"Thanks for a lovely dinner," Helen told Rod as he gestured to the cab driver to wait. "You're spoiling me rotten."

"You're so good for me," he murmured. "With you I relax."

He walked with her into the lobby, managed a chaste kiss under the admiring eyes of the doorman. "You'll be all right now?"

"Oh, hordes of men are waiting in the elevator to kidnap me," she joshed. "Goodnight, Rod."

She crossed to the mailbox area to collect her mail. She hadn't come home to change for dinner—she'd been working too late for that. Anticipating this possibility, she'd stored jewelry in her purse to dress up her blouse, had worn a skirt rather than slacks with her suit jacket.

"Hot date," Linda had guessed, arriving at the office. Avid curiosity in her eyes. But Linda had refrained from asking if she was going out again with Rod Langley.

"Every once in a while I'm bored with wearing slacks," she hedged.

The mail was the usual assortment: catalogues, bills, solicitations for charitable contributions. She left the mailroom and headed for the elevator. Rod understood she had to be at the office in the morning—he hadn't been annoyed that she set an early curfew.

She'd had dinner with him two Mondays in a row—she'd put him off next Monday, she told herself. These dinners mustn't become a habit. Still, it was pleasant to spend an evening with him. He always seemed so eager to amuse her.

In the apartment she dumped the catalogues and the solicitation letter in the garbage pail in the kitchenette, stared with wry humor at her Mastercard bill. She'd used it to buy pantyhose at the drugstore last week. Nothing that would send her into shock.

She slid out of her coat, kicked off her shoes and opened the envelope. For a moment she was suffused with anger. What did they mean? She'd taken a cash advance for $1,000! First thing in the morning she'd call the bank.

Preparing for bed, she was assaulted by questions. Had Zach used his Mastercard for a cash withdrawal? No, that was absurd, she discarded this. The bank made some ridiculous mistake. But just to make sure, call Zach. She glanced at the clock. It wasn't too late. Call him.

Zach picked up on the first ring. "Chicken-lickin', what's cookin'?"

"Zach, I just want to check on something," she began tentatively. "I received my Mastercard bill today—and there's a cash advance for $1,000. It's probably a stupid mistake by the bank—"

"Mom, I'll pay it back." Zach sounded stricken. "I expected to have it before you got your bill—but then the place where I was to start working two weeks ago had a fire. I'll start next week though, and I can pay you back about—" he was juggling figures in his mind, "about a hundred a week."

"What did you need $1,000 for?" she demanded. Was somebody blackmailing him? Her imagination took a giant leap forward. Was there a girl—and she needed an abortion? "Zach, why?" She tried to keep alarm out of her voice.

"Doug and I were day-trading." His voice was anguished. "You know, we'd been reading all those stories about people making a fortune in six months. I thought if I made a bundle, you could stop working."

She felt love wash over her. This precious child was worried that she was working to support herself.

"It was not a smart thing to do." She tried to sound judgmental. "And I'll expect you to pay it back. I'll have to dig into your college fund—"

"Mom, I feel like such a nerd—"

"You won't do something like that again." A firmness in her voice. "You've learned your lesson. We can handle it." Her tone softened. "And, in truth, I love my job."

Do I love my job—or do I love Adam? This is the rebound scene, isn't it? It probably happens to a lot of women. I'll get over it. I don't need a man in my life.

Twenty-Three

Adam grunted in reproach at the insistent ringing of the phone. He swung over on his side to inspect the clock. It was minutes before 7 a.m. Now who was acting up? Or could it be Eric—so unhappy at boarding school?

"Hello—" Anxiety had prodded him awake.

"Adam, I'm in such a mess," Kelly moaned. "Jake and I had got together—and it was so wonderful—"

"Kelly, it isn't even 7 a.m.," he protested.

"But Jake's wife is crazy! She's been calling me every hour on the hour—warning what she'll do if I don't stay away from him—"

"Kelly, Jake's a skunk. So stay away from him!"

"She wouldn't believe me when I said I wasn't going near him—" She paused, took a deep breath. "I told her I had a heavy thing going—with you."

"Kelly, I'm twenty years older than you." He was fighting for calm.

"That doesn't matter. If you play along for a couple of weeks, then she'll be off my back. Let's have lunch today. At the Four Seasons. And Adam, be very attentive."

"I have a lunch date," he recalled. With a prospective client.

"Adam, you have to do this for me!" Kelly's voice was shrill. "I'm terrified of that woman!"

"Okay," he said tiredly. "I'll make a lunch reservation—1 p.m. Be there."

"Oh, I will, Adam," Kelly cooed. "And make sure it hits the columns that we're in the throes of a passionate affair."

Helen felt a surge of satisfaction as she arrived at the office this morning, January 31st. It was kind of an anniversary, she mused. The end of her first month on the job without Liz. She was doing all right—Adam was not about to fire her.

She was astonished when he stalked into the office minutes after she herself arrived. Normally he never arrived before ten thirty. Liz said he made some calls at home before he came in.

"Good morning," she greeted him with a brilliant smile that said all was right with their world. But he seemed upset, she thought.

"Good morning." He was terse. "Call Bob Adler and tell him something has come up and I can't meet him for lunch. No," he broke off. "I'll call him."

"Would you like coffee?" Her voice was sympathetic.

"Yeah—that would be nice." He left her to go into his own office.

An hour later he instructed her to make a lunch reservation for him at the Four Seasons. "And don't expect me back until well in the afternoon."

After Adam left the office, Linda sauntered in to Helen with a sassy grin on her face.

"Well, what do you know? The boss is having lunch with Kelly. She's been trying to get him into bed since she signed up with us. I guess you'd call that progress."

"It's probably a business meeting." Helen shrugged. "With Kelly everything has to be a production."

"With guys chasing her like tomcats after a cat in heat she can't figure why the boss doesn't join the pack." Linda giggled. "Wow, is she sexy."

"Are you going out to lunch now?" Helen asked and Linda nodded. "Will you please bring me back a turkey on rye?" She reached for her purse.

"Adam's really a cool guy." Linda squinted in thought. "I guess after his rotten marriage, he's kind of steered clear of women.

232

But maybe Kelly's finally getting under his skin."

"Go to lunch," Helen scolded. "I'm starving."

Is Adam becoming involved personally with Kelly? But why should that concern me? He's my boss—nothing more.

Yet she couldn't erase from her mind the way he gazed at her at odd moments. She couldn't erase the way she responded.

Adam was astonished to find Kelly waiting at their table when he arrived. She was always late for appointments. Jake's wife had really scared her.

"Hi, darling," she cooed and leaned forward to display the cleavage that mesmerized male fans.

In her mind, Adam thought, she was already reading a column item about the two of them. God, what he did for his clients. "Remember, you have a recording session next week. You should be rested for that."

"I'm going to be so good." Her smile was dazzling. Pointedly amorous—for the benefit of onlookers. "What are we doing this evening? And what about a ski weekend? That could be fun."

"I'm going to Boston for the weekend with my kid. And no," he read her mind. "You're not going with me."

233

"Spoil sport." She pouted, slid one foot across to rest against his. "A weekend in Boston would cause a lot of talk. And talk is great when I have a new CD coming out."

On the following Monday—after a drab, lonely weekend—Helen arrived at the office with a sense of coming alive. Over the weekend she'd fretted that Zach was so concerned for her, that he'd gambled away almost $1,000. She knew, too, he would repay the money from his part-time job, that it was a matter of honor to him. A nineteen-year-old shouldn't have to worry about such things.

She'd spoken to Zach and Deedee briefly over the weekend, had a phone call from Gerry last night. Gerry and Sheila had been out to Montauk to look at a house that was up for sale. They'd made an offer. "Kathy Beckmann's fairly certain they'll accept."

A few minutes before 10 a.m. Bill arrived. Helen sent him out to the post-office. Linda charged into the office as he took off.

"Wow, are things moving around here!" she bubbled to Helen.

"Like what?" Helen asked with an indulgent smile.

"Like Adam and Kelly—" Linda extended a folded-back copy of the *Daily News*. "They're an item in the columns!"

Helen took the newspaper, focused on the

segment Linda indicated. She struggled for an air of amusement as she scanned the words. Her heart pounding—her mind rejecting.

"Kelly's a client." She contrived to sound amused. *Adam and Kelly? I don't believe it!* "It's a public-relations ploy—Kelly has a new CD coming out."

That's all it was, she tried to rationalize. But beneath her casual façade she felt devastated.

Earlier than normal Adam strode into the office. Helen sensed that he was aware the others on staff had seen the column item about Kelly and himself—and wasn't happy about it.

"I've got a lot of calls to make," he told Helen after a terse "good morning." "I don't want to be disturbed."

"Right." She managed an impersonal smile.

"Eric said to say 'hi' for him." Adam's face seemed less tense now. "He said it was a good weekend."

"Does he feel better now about school?"

"Not really." Adam's eyes reflected his concern. "But we'll keep in close touch—that'll help." He glanced at his watch. "I'd better get cracking. This is going to be a rough day."

To Helen's surprise the day sped past. Adam had emerged from his office only

235

once—to ask her to order lunch sent up for him. But at intervals she heard his voice in animated phone conversation. He was in pursuit of new clients, she gathered.

At a few minutes after six—with the other staff members gone for the day—she knocked on his door. "I'm about to close up shop unless you need me," she said lightly.

"No, I'm fine. Go home." He smiled in friendly dismissal as the phone rang. "I'll get it."

She turned to leave, but Adam stopped her. "It's for you," he said, an odd glint in his eyes.

"Thanks." She hurried into her office, picked up the phone. "Helen Avery."

"Hello, Helen Avery," Rod drawled. "You haven't forgotten we're having dinner tonight? You're all clear?" He knew there were nights when she worked late.

"No, I didn't forget." She ignored her resolve not to see him every Monday. "I'm all clear." *Is Adam angry that Rod called me?* "The usual time?"

"Actually, could we move it up until 8 p.m. I'm stuck in traffic."

"That'll be fine." *Does Adam realize I'm seeing Rod? Why am I seeing him?* "Shall I call and change our reservation?"

"I'll call on the cell phone. See you later, Beautiful."

She put down the phone. Her heart

236

pounding. It was ridiculous to keep up this Monday evening dinner scene with Rod— on his one night off from the theater.

Yes, Rod was amusing. It was fun being with him, flattering to have him in pursuit. But she couldn't afford to have Adam angry at her. She needed this job. And it seemed clear that Adam disliked socializing between client and staff. That's why he was annoyed—wasn't it?

All at once the silence in the office was oppressive. She reached into a desk drawer for her purse, pulled on her coat. She'd have plenty of time to go home and change for dinner.

Adam left his chair, began to pace about his office. What the hell was the matter with Rod? Damn him for chasing after Helen. She was fresh from an ugly divorce—a divorce that wasn't yet final. She was so vulnerable.

But how can I warn her to steer clear of Rod? How can I betray a client? That would be unethical. And Rod's an important client—I don't want to lose him.

Helen heard the phone ringing as she unlocked the door. She hurried inside to pick up before the answering machine responded.

"Hello."

"Hi, it's me." Gerry sounded exhilarated. "I just got a call from Kathy Beckmann in Montauk. The owners of the house have accepted our offer!"

"Oh, great!" She knew how Gerry and Sheila had debated about where to buy—in the Poconos or at the ocean. The ocean had won.

"I don't think we'll have any trouble with the mortgage—I mean, two women. Maybe ten years ago—but not today. Anyhow, Sheila and I decided to run out for dinner to celebrate. Do you feel like joining us?"

"Normally I'd love it—but I have a date for dinner."

"Ah-hah! What are you hiding from us?"

"It's nothing serious," Helen said self-consciously and paused. "It's a client of Adam's—"

"Business?" Gerry sounded puzzled.

"No. I'm having dinner with Rod Langley—one of those casual dates. It's his one night off from the theater—and we've been having dinner together on Monday evenings. That's all," she pinpointed.

"Well, Rod Langley can take you to better places than we can afford." Gerry laughed, yet Helen felt an undercurrent of disapproval. "Enjoy."

Gerry and Sheila sat at a private corner table and ordered their dinner in their

238

favorite neighborhood restaurant.

"You're awfully somber when we're supposed to be celebrating," Sheila chided.

"I'm worried about Helen," Gerry admitted.

"It's not working out with Adam?" Sheila was instantly solicitous.

"It's not that." Gerry shook her head. "I think they're getting along great. But Helen met Rod Langley in the office—"

"So?" Sheila was puzzled.

"They're having dinner together tonight. I gather she's been seeing him for a while. Just Monday evening dinners, she said—his night off from the theater."

"He's using her," Sheila said angrily.

"You and I know that—but how do we tell her without crushing her ego?" Gerry countered. Only a handful of people in the business knew about Rod—and not one of them would utter a word.

"He's scared to death the Hollywood people will find out," Sheila surmised. "It would destroy his image as the new Great Young Lover if word got out that he's gay."

"What do I do?" Gerry sighed in anguish. "How do I tell her that Rod Langley would be happier with Zach than with her?"

"Maybe the whole thing will peter out," Sheila soothed. "Wait two or three weeks."

Twenty-Four

After a night of broken slumber, Adam awoke much earlier than usual. He heard the sound of sleet hitting the windows in his bedroom—an ominous symphony, he thought, reflecting his own feelings. What was he going to do about Rod and Helen? Rod was totally self-centered—wouldn't consider that Helen might be hurt. He was pretending to be infatuated—and she believed him.

He thrust aside the covers, headed for the bathroom to shower and shave. Heat was pouring into the apartment. Why were most New York apartments—from Park Avenue to projects—overheated? Without pushing aside the drapes to check, he knew this would be a rotten day weather-wise. This was one of those times when the weather people were correct in their predictions. They'd be hit with sleet and snow—and mush underfoot.

He wasn't over-reacting about Rod, he told himself. And it wasn't that he was upset that Helen was seeing another man. She had

240

no idea how he felt about her. How it required all his willpower not to reach out and pull her into his arms when they were alone in his office. He'd never felt quite this way about any woman—but hell, it was too late for him. That part of his life was over.

He knew when he emerged from his building that this was one of those mornings when he'd never get a cab. The sleet had turned into heavy snow. Dollar-sized flakes were descending with grim determination. Within a few hours the streets would be impossible. Buses would creep. Into the subway, he ordered himself—but with distaste...

He saw surprise at his early arrival in Helen's eyes as she greeted him. He wanted to be able to talk to her before the others arrived. He couldn't let this charade with Rod go on unchallenged.

"What a lousy day," he said, grimacing. "Except for cross-country skiers."

"It'll be ugly in the city tomorrow," she predicted. "When the snow turns dirty brown. But it's probably gorgeous out in the country."

"Oh, yes—" A nostalgic glint in his eyes. "I grew up in a small town that was a fairyland on days like this."

"Coffee?" she asked, already half-rising from her chair.

He hesitated. "I'd love it." He knew it was

politically incorrect to expect his assistant to serve coffee—but Liz hadn't minded and Helen made the suggestion herself on most occasions. "Join me?"

For a moment she appeared startled. He fought off an impulse to reach out to her. There was a sweet vulnerability about her that made him yearn to protect her.

"That would be pleasant."

Her smile said she was a woman who was insecure, unaware of her potent charm, he thought.

"It'll be ready in a few minutes—"

He settled in the chair at his desk and tried to frame in his mind what he must say to Helen. And if Rod figured out what had happened and fired him, so be it. He could survive with one less client. Rod mustn't be allowed to play games with Helen.

In a few minutes Helen came into his office with two mugs of coffee. Both of them, he thought whimsically, took it straight. They thought alike in a lot of ways.

"Sit down," he urged and saw alarm in her eyes. *Oh God, does she think I'm about to fire her?* "I want you to know that it's great to have you on board," he said. "I was a nervous wreck when Liz told me she had to leave—" He took a deep breath. "And in a way I feel guilty that Rod is presenting himself to you under false colors. I mean," he said, fumbling for words, "that he's obviously in pursuit."

"We've had dinner together a few times." She seemed uncomfortable, puzzled. "But what do you mean by false colors?"

"On Monday nights you've had dinner," he guessed and she nodded. "Because on every, other night—after the theater—he drives all the way out to his hideaway in the Poconos and stays out there until he returns for the next performance."

"I don't understand." She seemed to be searching her mind. "Are you saying he's married?" *She's upset. I'm handling this badly.* "There's nothing serious between us—I made that clear from the beginning." But she seemed uneasy. "Still, if he's married, I wouldn't want to—"

"You might call it that. Helen, Rod's gay. He drives out to the house in Poconos to be with his lover."

"Then why the pretense with me?" Color flooded her face. "What kind of game is he playing?"

"He's terribly anxious for the movie contract to come through—and terrified the word will get around that he's gay. It would destroy his image as the new Young Lover. But I couldn't let you believe that he was straight—"

"I was a prop." She was stunned. "How could I have been so stupid? He was charming, amusing—and it was pleasant to have dinner with him." Her eyes met his now. "There was never anything else. I mean," she stammered, "nothing romantic about our relationship."

"I felt you should know. Helen—" He paused. "You're special. I couldn't bear to see you hurt."

"Rod will have to find another prop." She lifted her head defiantly. "I knew I shouldn't be seeing him. I don't know why I did. It's just that he was so persuasive—and I suppose I was flattered that a Broadway leading man would spend time with me."

"A lot of men would like to spend time with you," he began.

All at once the moment was supercharged. Their eyes were saying what neither allowed to be said in words. But the moment was broken by the shrill ring of the phone. Helen reached out to pick up.

"Adam Fremont, Public Relations," she said with her usual cordiality and listened for a moment. "Who's calling please?"

Why is she looking like that?

"Please hold." She handed the receiver to Adam. Her face showing her anxiety. "It's Eric's school."

Alarm tightening his throat, he reached for the receiver. "Hello?"

"Mr Fremont, this is Dean Andrews. I'm sorry to be the bearer of bad news. Eric and a friend went out this morning to jog before

244

class. He was hit by a car that skidded on the ice. He's in the hospital emergency room. We couldn't reach his mother so—"

"What hospital is he in?" Adam demanded, his heart pounding.

"Our local hospital. It's—"

"I'll be up there on the next flight." Adam felt encased in ice. "What's the address of the hospital?" He scrawled down the address Dean Andrews gave him. "Tell Eric I'm coming!" He slammed the phone down.

"What's happened?" Helen asked, her face drained of color.

"Eric was hit by a car—he's in the hospital? Check with the airlines—find out the next flight to Boston that I can make."

"With this weather some flights might be canceled," she warned. "What about the train?"

"Too slow. Call the airlines. If the flights are on schedule, book me for—" He checked his watch. "Book me on a flight between ten thirty and eleven—I can make that. I'll drive to the airport, leave the car there."

While Helen focused on making a reservation, Adam scribbled notes for her. She'd have to cancel a lunch appointment, a 3 p.m. meeting with a TV producer, a five o'clock cocktail appointment. He'd phone from Boston about his tomorrow's appointments.

He remembered the packed valise he kept at the office for emergency trips. Take it with him. He'd have to be up there at least overnight. He wouldn't allow himself to think beyond that.

A few minutes later Helen hurried into the office. "You have a ten forty flight to Boston. The car service will be waiting downstairs in five minutes."

"Great." *She worries about my driving in this weather.* "Eric's going to be fine," she comforted.

"I can't believe this is happening." He checked his wallet, his credit card case. "I'll call you," he promised. "You've been wonderful."

Knowing Adam's pain, Helen stood at her office window and stared below as he entered the waiting car. Snow pelted the ground. Driving would be treacherous. Flying conditions bad. Would his flight be delayed? Or worse yet, canceled?

Adam was so frightened—the way she'd been frightened whenever Deedee and Zach had been hurt. He said, "I'll call you." He said, "You've been wonderful." But he was just referring to her efficiency as his assistant, she rebuked herself. Yet once again she couldn't erase from her mind what she'd read in his eyes.

Oh, why doesn't he say something? Why is he

so afraid to become emotionally involved? Can there be a second chance for us? I'd be willing to gamble.

But immediately she was attacked by guilt. She wasn't clear to start a new life. She had two children whose lives were unsettled. That's where her responsibilities lay. And in truth Adam was in thralldom to his ex-wife. Only in fairytales did people such as she and Adam have second chances.

Adam's trip from the office to LaGuardia was a nightmare. He fretted each time the car sat idle in traffic. He arrived just in time to make his flight, to learn that there was a forty-minute delay. His mind in chaos, he sought out a public telephone, called the hospital—in an outlying Boston suburb—to enquire about Eric's condition. There was no report available as yet.

Taking a seat again in the waiting area, he blamed himself for the accident. If he'd fought for Eric, had placed him in school in Manhattan, this wouldn't have happened. Where the hell was Zoe? Why was she always missing in moments of crisis?

Fifty minutes after his arrival at the airport, Adam was boarding his flight. A pair of passengers boarding just ahead of him were expressing anxiety about flying in such conditions. The plane had to make it to Boston. Eric needed him.

The brief flight was uneventful except for turbulence. Despite the traffic conditions he arrived at the hospital with little delay. After an interminable wait he was able to speak with the attending doctor.

"He'll be fine," the doctor advised him with a confident smile. "He's one lucky kid. A slight concussion and a sprained wrist. We'll hold him overnight just for observation. He'll be released in the morning."

"When can I see him?" Adam was conscious of the pounding of his heart—but it was from relief, he told himself. Eric was all right.

"In a few minutes. A nurse will tell you."

Adam sat at the edge of a chair and waited to be summoned. Eric was due for a week of winter vacation shortly. He was scheduled to go to Zoe. He'd insist that Eric come to him.

He leapt to his feet as a nurse approached him. Eric was in a private room, she explained—the school had insisted on this. "He's fine," she said, sensing his alarm. "He knows you're here."

He walked into Eric's room with a determined smile. "Hey, you scared me there for a while—" He leaned over the bed to kiss his son. "You're leaving this joint tomorrow morning." Deliberately flippant.

"I have to go back to school. We're having exams." Eric was anxious.

"Would you rather come home with me for a few days?" Adam asked. It seemed heartless to send him back to school after such an experience. The school would permit this.

Eric hesitated. "I think I have to go back to school." He was thoughtful. "I mean, I was jogging with Jesse—and he must be scared about what happened. But can I come home to you for the winter week off?" he asked eagerly.

"Sure thing," Adam promised. He'd have this out with Zoe. "Was Jesse hurt, too?"

"No. I saw the car skidding—and I pushed him out of the way—but I need to go back to school to talk to him about it." He gestured appealingly.

"I'll stay here with you." Adam managed a casual smile. "I'll go with you to the school in the morning. And then you'll come to me for the winter week off."

No matter what was required to accomplish this, he would do it.

Twenty-Five

Each time the phone rang, Helen hoped it would be Adam with news about Eric. She was about to have a very late lunch at her desk when he called.

"Eric's okay. A slight concussion and a sprained wrist. The left wrist," he added. "I'll be here overnight—" He gave her the phone number of his hotel. "They'll throw me out of the hospital at 8 p.m. Give me time to get to the hotel, then call me. You'll be free to do that?" he asked with an air of apology.

"Oh yes," she reassured him. "It's great to know Eric's okay."

They spoke a few minutes longer, discussed activities at the office, then Adam was off the phone. Helen reached for her sandwich, ate without tasting. She was relieved that Eric was in no danger. And from what the dean had told Adam, he was something of a hero for having pushed his friend out of the path of the car. Adam must be so proud of him.

Her thoughts turned again to Rod. She

would never see him again except here in the office. How humiliating to have been taken in that way. She was furious that Rod had made such a pretense of being infatuated. If he had been honest, explained that he needed to present himself as being attracted to a woman, she would have gone along with that. But he'd lied to her—and that hurt.

She'd take the coward's way out, she told herself. She'd write a note, explaining that she was resuming an earlier relationship and wouldn't be free to see him anymore. Nothing nasty—after all, she'd be seeing him here in the office. But no more Monday dinners. No more being a prop.

Gerry had known, she realized now—and was trying to build up the courage to tell her. Well, that wasn't necessary any longer. It must have been rough for Adam to tell her—it could have cost him a client if Rod found out. But he'd put her first, she thought in gratitude. She'd tell Adam how she was handling it. There'd be no repercussions.

Thank God, she'd never mentioned Rod to Deedee or Zach. They were having enough to deal with as it was. Both were upset about the divorce. Of course, Deedee was a grown woman—she had to make her own decisions. But it was painful for a mother to watch a child make a bad decision—and she was certain Todd was bad for Deedee.

Now Zach was trying to convince her he should take a year off from school after this year—work to save for tuition. Damn it, she never expected to have to worry about seeing Zach through school. If he took a year off, there was a strong chance he'd never go back to school—in an era when a college degree was essential.

Did life ever get easier—or was it always an obstacle course?

Adam remained in the Boston suburb for a day after Eric's release from the hospital. Eric was to spend an additional twenty-four hours in the school infirmary. Adam commuted between his hotel room—where he was in constant touch with the office—and the infirmary. Thank God, he told himself, for Helen's people skills. She held the office together in his absence.

"I'm coming to you for the winter week 'break,'" Eric reminded when Adam prepared to leave for his flight back to New York. His eyes pleaded for reassurance.

"Absolutely." Adam felt a surge of love for his son. If Zoe tried to pull anything, he'd threaten to hold up her alimony check. Yet—with a wariness born of experience—he remembered her earlier threat to have him charged with kidnaping if he ever took Eric without her permission. Would she?

Before boarding his midafternoon flight home, he phoned the office.

"I should be there by six o'clock," he told Helen. "If I'm a little late, could you wait?"

"Of course, I'll wait." Her voice held a note of relief that they were about to return to normal.

"Better still," he said on impulse, "why don't we have dinner together? Unless you have other arrangements—"

"Dinner would be fine," she said softly. "You'll pick me up at the office? I mean, rush-hour traffic can be heavy even coming into the city. You may be delayed—"

"I'll pick you up at the office," he promised.

Helen struggled to convince herself this was a business dinner. Adam was hungry—and in no mood for ordered-in food. *That's all his invitation means. Stop doing it again. Reading in what I want to believe.*

It was almost six forty when Adam arrived at the office.

"Traffic was a bitch," he apologized. "You're probably starving—"

"I had a late lunch." Trite words meant to conceal the silent conversation between them. "I was so relieved to hear that Eric's all right."

"He had me going there for a while." Adam's sigh of relief was eloquent. "I made a reservation for us for seven," he said, glancing at his watch. "When I saw the traffic I knew we'd never make it earlier than that. Let's take off."

"I'll get my notes," Helen said while Adam reached for her coat, held it for her.

For an electric moment—while she slid her arms into the sleeves—she felt as though he was about to embrace her. And then the moment was gone.

In the quiet, side-street restaurant that Helen knew was Adam's favorite they were led to a corner table. Here the tables were far enough apart to provide privacy. The fresh flowers a pleasant touch. Involuntarily she remembered the column item about Adam and Kelly. They'd dined in a celebrity studded restaurant—inviting columnist interest, Helen thought. That's all it had been.

"Tell me about Eric," she urged, disconcerted by the intensity of Adam's gaze.

"I wanted to bring him home with me, but he said he had to go back to school—an exam was coming up." His face reflected the depth of his love. "He's such a conscientious kid. But I promised to bring him home for their so called 'winter week.' " Adam paused, all at once apprehensive. "Zoe will put up a battle."

"Why?" Helen asked. "She never seems to be around when he needs her."

"She uses Eric as a pawn to keep me in line. She knows how important he is to me."

"But you control the alimony checks," she began and stopped dead in confusion. "I mean, Liz told me you're very generous to her."

"She knows I don't want any ugliness— that would be bad for Eric. So I play along." He gestured his feeling of futility. "But I promised Eric he'd come home to me for that week later this month."

Their waiter arrived. They focused on ordering. When they were alone again, Adam began to question her about office activities in his absence. Helen understood; the private moments were over.

When he loved Eric so much, why hadn't he fought for joint custody? Men did that these days. For all his show of deep attachment to Eric, did Adam put career ahead of his son?

Helen had geared herself for an encounter with Rod, still she was uptight when she heard his voice in the reception area a few days later.

"I miss you." Rod hovered in the doorway to her office with the charismatic smile that would be winning over movie fans in months ahead. "I envy the lucky guy."

"Hi, Rod. Congratulations on the new contract." Adam had told her Rod would be heading for Hollywood in six weeks. She vowed to be cordial to him, though she was still angry that he had played such a stupid game with her.

"Linda says the boss is out. Any idea when he'll be back? I need some help." He leaned forward, a hand on her desk. "I don't suppose you'd have lunch with me and let me cry on your shoulder?"

"Have a tissue." With a seemingly amused smile she extended the tissue container on her desk. "Why don't you buzz Adam around five? He'll be here then."

He sighed elaborately. "Will do. But I miss our Monday evening dinners."

She'd told Gerry and Sheila she wasn't seeing Rod anymore. "It was amusing for a bit—did great things for my ego. Then I got the message—I was his cover of the moment." She'd sensed their relief that she wasn't buying his amorous pursuit.

Adam returned to the office shortly past four. As usual she joined him in his private office to report on happenings in his absence.

"Oh, Eric's coming to me for the 'winter week,'" he told her when she'd finished her report. "It was a tough battle—but I won."

"Great."

"Have dinner with us while he's here," Adam invited and seemed disconcerted for a moment. "Eric's so fond of you."

256

"Thank you, I'd like that." *Was that an impulsive invitation—and now he's sorry he's invited me?* "If something else comes up, I'll understand," she said awkwardly.

"Nothing comes up when Eric's involved. We'll have dinner on—" He thought for a moment. "On Thursday evening?"

"Thursday will be fine."

"You still have that list of vegetarian restaurants?" But—again—his eyes were carrying on a different—more personal conversation.

"I have it." These moments when Adam seemed to be saying so much were unnerving. *He's terrified of becoming emotionally involved with a woman. Because of his ex-wife? Not every woman is like Zoe.* "I'm so glad you were able to work it out for Eric to come to you."

"It cost me." His smile was ironic. "I'm paying for a vacation in Bermuda. For two." He paused a moment. "Eric wants to finish out the school year—then come and live with me."

"That would be great for both of you," she said softly.

"Zoe won't allow it." He slammed a fist on his desk in frustration. "She uses the same threat—she'll have me arrested for kidnaping if I take him without her permission."

Helen debated inwardly. *I shouldn't be interfering.* "Have you considered going back into court to fight for custody?"

"I'm not sure I can handle that." He was somber now. "You know my crazy working hours."

"Eric would be in school till three o'clock five days a week. You could arrange for a housekeeper to be there when he comes home, supervise. She could prepare dinner, serve it, and leave. I think Eric would love to know that he could sit down to dinner every evening with his father." Something Deedee and Zach rarely did, she remembered. "And then you'd have your weekends with him. I know," she sympathized. "Your working hours are long—but you could reschedule your evenings. Make time for what's important—" For Paul career took precedence over everything. Even family. Only now was she becoming aware of how deeply Deedee and Zach had resented this. *I should have seen this.*

"You make it sound so tempting." But his eyes were pained. "It would be a futile battle. Zoe's the mother—the mother always wins out in court."

"Not these days," she refuted. Again, she debated about speaking her mind. "It would probably not be difficult to prove that you are the more fit parent." Her eyes were eloquent. She couldn't put into words her sense—from what Liz had told her and Adam intimated—that Zoe was far from a fit mother.

"No." All at once Adam was brusque. "It would be an ugly court battle. I can't put Eric through that. It's out of the question."

Twenty-Six

Deedee expected Todd to be asleep by the time she arrived home from the office. She knew he'd left with one of the big wheels late in the afternoon. She'd been stuck until past 2 a.m. But emerging from the car provided by the company's service, she saw lights on in the living room.

Unlocking the apartment door she heard the sound of the TV.

"Hi." Clad only in pajama pants, Todd was stretched out on the sofa and watching *Moneyline* on CNN.

"What are you doing up?" It was an unwritten rule that neither waited up for the other past midnight. Sleep was a precious commodity in their schedules.

"Big news," he drawled while she tossed aside her coat and kicked off her shoes. "I'm being sent to Tokyo for four months." He grinned at her open-mouthed astonishment, hit the "mute" on the TV remote.

"I'm to be part of the team to set up our offices there. It's been top-secret until today."

"But you knew about it?" *And he didn't tell me.*

"Well, yeah," he conceded. "But I was sworn to secrecy." Now he seemed defensive.

Why didn't he tell me? This must have been going on for months. "It'll be exciting," she conceded. *How could all this have been going on and he not tell me?*

"It guarantees I'm on the way up." His smile was smug.

"And I'm on the way out." All at once she knew—she'd had it with this crazy rat-race.

"What do you mean?" he demanded. "What happened?"

"Nothing happened yet." She settled herself at the corner of the sofa. "But I'm quitting. There has to be a job in the field that doesn't keep me working eighty hours a week."

"But what'll it pay?"

He's staring at me as though I said I was going to live in a mud hut in the Congo. "Enough for me to live on." She stared back defiantly.

"Shitty living." He flinched in distaste. "You'll never afford a great car—or a great condo."

"Maybe I don't need that." *I'm burnt out.*

Mom's right—I need a life. To have time for what's important. Todd's a carbon copy of Dad.

"You'd be out of your mind to quit! I thought you had a brain in your head!"

"Because I have a brain I want out of this rat-race." She was fighting to stay cool.

"I thought I knew you." His tone was contemptuous. "I don't know you at all."

"I didn't decide this on the spur of the moment. I've been thinking about it for weeks."

"I can't believe you could be so stupid. I was sure we thought alike. I don't know you."

"Okay. So this is the end of the road for us."

"Yeah. I sure as hell don't want to live in your world."

"And I've had too much of yours." *Why do I feel relieved? Maybe I knew all along that Todd was wrong for me. He just happened to be there.*

"I'm leaving in a week." He seemed to be in some inner debate. "I won't have any trouble subletting the apartment for four months—though the time is short."

"I'm sure you won't." *What do I do now? Sleep on the sofa in my old apartment? I can't put Mom out.*

"If you want to sublet, you can have the apartment for the regular rent—I won't ask for more because it's furnished."

261

"I can handle that." *How weird to be talking with Todd this way!* "Shall I just send the rent in a check to the management office each month?"

He thought about this for a moment. "No, FedEx the checks to me—I'll handle it from there."

"It's a deal." *This is unreal.*

"I won't be going in to the office in the morning—I'm taking the day off to take care of the passport situation, all that shit." *He's staring at me as though I was a total stranger.* "Then I'm heading to see my mother before I leave. I'll pop in some time during the week to pack." He reached for the remote. "I want to catch the rest of *Moneyline*."

Helen was surprised when Liz called her at home the Friday before Eric was scheduled to arrive for his "winter week" school vacation.

"I talked with Adam a little while ago," Liz said after preliminary conversation about happenings at the office. "I'm just furious the way he allows Zoe to lead him around like a forlorn puppy."

"What do you mean?" Helen was startled.

"Did he tell you how he arranged to have Eric next week—when it was supposedly Zoe's turn?"

"No." Instinct told her to deny this close-

262

ness with Adam. "I know he's been uptight," Helen conceded.

"Oh, when isn't Adam uptight?" Liz sighed. "But he's pleased with the way you've taken over." She paused. "He's very fond of you." The implication was unnerving.

"Everybody in the office is fond of Adam." Helen strived to sound casual. "But what about his arrangements to have Eric next week?" Pretend ignorance, she ordered herself.

"He paid for a week's vacation for Zoe and her live-in lover—down in Cancun. Isn't that sick?"

"He wanted to be sure there'd be no ugly battle," Helen interpreted. "He was thinking of Eric."

"Such a sweet kid. Adam promised to bring him over to see me while he's in town."

"How's your mother?" Helen asked sympathetically.

"It's a downhill battle—but I'll keep her with me as long as I can. I have someone come in to be with her for a couple of hours each day so I can go out and shop for groceries and pick up her prescriptions— things like that. I have to watch that she doesn't wander away. It's tough," Liz admitted. "But she was a single mother from the time I was seven. I have to be here for her."

"You're a good daughter," Helen approved. She thought about her own mother. Always dissatisfied with life, always certain others were out to take advantage of her. What an unhappy way to live. "You should find deep satisfaction in that."

She didn't want to think about the time when Liz would be forced to put her mother into a home. Liz would come back to the office—and she'd be out.

On a dismal Wednesday afternoon that reflected his mood, Zach sprawled on the foot of his bed in his dorm room while Doug paced.

"What's so terrible about dropping out of school after two years?" Doug challenged. "To listen to my folks it's like saying I'm going to open a falafel stand in Spanish Harlem. Hell, look at Bill Gates! He cut out—and now he's the richest man in the world!"

"Maybe we're jumping too fast—" Zach cringed at the prospect of telling his mother what he and Doug were plotting to do. She wasn't into the dot-com scene—she'd freak out. She was still shocked about their short run at day-trading. "Maybe we ought to cool it until the end of school."

"Are you kidding? When this scene is so hot? You've got some great ideas—and Chuck is dying to team up with us. He'll have his engineering degree the end of May. He's what we need!"

"Maybe we should wait till the end of the school year," Zach repeated.

Doug stopped pacing, hovered over Zach. "There's all that venture capital out there, just dying to find a home. What's to worry about?"

"We're supposed to talk to those guys down on Wall Street," Zach reminded. "You know, about the computer technician jobs." He and Doug had both been into computers since they were twelve. They'd been approached at a techie convention about summer jobs. Jobs, they said, that could become full time. They could be earning as much as Deedee. "They're talking about $50 an hour—and plenty of hours begging us to show up."

"That's small stuff," Doug said derisively. "We're looking at millions in the next couple of years."

"Right now the $400 we had to pay to be at that forum on Saturday—so Chuck can make our pitch—puts us on a starvation track for a month. And all we get is eight minutes to sell our deal."

"It's a hot dot-com market, Zach. We've got to be prepared to jump."

"They're going to look at us and think: Why should we put up two million— or three or four—to three college kids with

265

no experience?"

"They all want to get in early on something that's going to hit big. The guys who got in early on America Online are billionaires!" Doug was pacing again. "Your ideas about packaging are terrific. Look at the guy who made the styrofoam containers for the Big Macs—he made hundreds of millions."

"The container was dumped," Zach pointed out. "I think for some environmental reason."

"But not before the guy made hundreds of millions," Doug reminded. "We go with Chuck on Saturday. We let him do his pitch—and then we talk to people. Chuck's worked out all the details of manufacturing our packaging. He's worked out financial details, and—"

"Then why does he need us?" Zach countered, full of misgivings now.

"He needs your ideas and my management skills." Doug was emphatic. "We've all three worked our asses off on the presentation. It's professional. Chuck will make a sound case. Hey, by tomorrow night this time we may be talking about a $5,000,000 investment in DCZ Packaging."

"Let's go eat." Zach swung to his feet. "It may be the last decent meal we can afford." He paused in thought. "You don't think I'm off the wall in my idea to replace toothpaste tubes with push-button plastic bottles in jewel tones—and all the other angles?"

Helen glanced at her watch. Just past 6 p.m. The others were leaving for the day. The plan was for Adam and Eric—now in New York—to come to the office to pick her up for dinner. She'd seen little of Adam so far this week, she thought wistfully. He was making a point of spending every possible moment with Eric.

She heard voices in the reception area. Linda was leaving—Adam and Eric arriving. Oh, it would be good to spend some time with them. Adam was trying so hard to make this a special time for Eric. But why did Adam allow Zoe to take such advantage of him?

Eric charged into Helen's office. His face aglow. "We went to the Hayden Planetarium—it's different than what it was when I went there when I was a little kid. And before that we went on the Staten Island ferry. Wow, the water was rough!"

Adam strolled into view. "A few minutes ago, Eric, you said you were starving. So let's get this show on the road."

In a festive mood they left the office and took a taxi to Eric's favorite vegetarian restaurant. Helen was disconcerted when the waitress assumed that she was Eric's mother.

Eric grinned. "She's my adopted mother,"

he told the waitress. "And she's real cool."

They lingered over dinner. Eric seemed happy, Helen thought tenderly. Adam radiated love for his son. Why didn't he fight for custody?

"You had a big day," Adam told Eric, who was fighting yawns now. "You'll hit the sack early tonight."

"It isn't even nine o'clock," Eric protested.

"We've got plans for tomorrow," Adam reminded. "You still haven't been to the top of the Empire State building—and you said you wanted to go down to the South Street Seaport."

"Okay," Eric agreed reluctantly. His face brightened. "You said I could fly back to school instead of taking the train. Airports are cool places."

Adam exchanged an indulgent glance with Helen. She'd supplied him with a list of Zach's favorite "places to go" when he was fourteen.

"All right, let's hit the road."

Helen arrived home to find a message from Gerry on her machine.

"The weather people promise a great weekend. Almost spring-like. Let's hope they're right. The people we're buying the house from want to sell us some of the furnishings they'd originally planned to take with them. They're letting us spend the coming weekend out at the house to decide if we want to buy the stuff. We'll drive up tomorrow night. Would you like to go with us?"

Helen glanced at the clock. No, it wasn't too late to call Gerry. Oh, it would be nice to spend a weekend at Montauk!

Helen had just walked into the office when Adam called.

"Thanks for last evening," he said warmly. "Thanks for all the tips. Eric's in a terrific mood." He paused. "He'll be in a less terrific mood when I put him on the plane on Sunday—"

"Will he be in to say good-bye?" *Why doesn't Adam do something about gaining custody?*

"Sure thing," Adam promised. "Eric's mad about you."

What about Eric's father? How does he feel about me?

Twenty-Seven

Helen was relieved that she was able to leave the office shortly after 6 p.m. on Friday. Gerry and Sheila would pick her up at her apartment at 7 p.m.—barring unexpected tie-ups at their respective offices. They'd take their car from the garage in their building, fill up the gas tank and drive over.

"Don't bother about dinner," Gerry had blithely ordered. "We'll pick up sandwiches at the deli, bring along a thermos of coffee, and eat on the road. We'll have dessert and more coffee when we arrive at the house."

Adam said—when he brought Eric in to say good-bye—that the two of them would have a lazy Saturday and Sunday. "Eric says it'll be okay just to hang-out over the weekend."

At the apartment Helen packed the few items she'd need. She'd called Deedee at the office—still self-conscious about phoning her at Todd's apartment—to say she was going out to Montauk for the weekend with Gerry and Sheila. She'd left a message on Zach's machine.

Rather than wait for the doorman to buzz

her, she went downstairs with her week-ender a few minutes before 7 p.m. She was exhausted, she admitted. This had been a week that required decisions on her part in Adam's absence. She felt relieved that everything had moved along smoothly—but it had been a stressful week. How nice that Gerry and Sheila had the use of the house this weekend.

She saw Gerry double-park in front of the building, hurried out to the car.

"I think we're missing the rush-hour traffic," Sheila said with a complacent smile while Helen settled herself on the back seat. "There should be no tie-ups on the road."

"It's not exactly high season." Gerry chuckled. "It'll be a different story three months from now. We'll be looking for back roads to avoid the traffic."

The car was toasty warm. A Cole Porter medley filtered in from the radio. Helen was conscious of a rare serenity. This weekend, she promised herself, would be an escape from the world.

"You'll love the house," Sheila said. "It cost more than we'd planned on spending, but we couldn't resist it."

"I feel guilty about buying it." Gerry was all at once somber. "But then if we hadn't, somebody else would have bought it. Thank God, I had money from the divorce settlement and Sheila had savings, so we could handle the down-payment. And we can manage the monthly mortgage payments."

"Why do you feel guilty?" Helen was baffled.

"Because so many young people—who were born and raised here—have to move away because they can't handle the fancy Hampton prices. Not with the low-salaried jobs available. And many of them seasonal at that."

In a corner of her mind Helen remembered the houses she and Paul had bought through the years that they really couldn't afford—but Paul was always sure of a big deal coming up. She'd loathed being caught up in huge mortgage payments. So now, she mocked herself, she was caught up in—considering her salary—huge rent payments.

What would happen if Deedee broke up with Todd and needed the apartment? She prayed that Deedee would see the absurdity of living with Todd—yet where would *she* go in this era of rental insanity? And what if Liz's mother had to be placed in a nursing home sooner than anticipated? She'd be out of a job.

Don't think about such problems for this weekend. Try to unwind. Like Gerry always said, live one day at a time.

As Gerry had anticipated, traffic on the Long Island Expressway was moving well— despite the endless construction sites. There was a festive air in the car as they ate their deli sandwiches and sipped at hot coffee. The moon was an enticing yellow ball in the sky. Stars twinkled in glorious abandon. A perfect night, Helen thought. *What are Adam and Eric doing tonight?*

"We're making good time," Gerry said as they left the LIE at Exit 70 and headed across to Route 27, the final stretch through the Hamptons.

"We'll sleep tonight with the sound of the ocean as our lullaby." Sheila sighed with blissful anticipation. "After a frantic week in the city, a couple of days in Montauk will be lifesaving."

"Let's remember to stop by Claudia's Carriage House," Gerry said. "I have to shop for birthday presents for my kids. Claudia comes up with the greatest gift items."

Roughly one and a half hours later they were driving down Main Street—still Route 27—in Montauk. Like the other Hampton towns they'd passed through—Bridgehampton, East Hampton, Amagansett—Montauk wore its winter garb. Little signs of life other than a few cars parked at the curb before Shagwong, the popular local restaurant and bar.

Gerry swung off Main Street. "We're three minutes from the house. Just up the hill ahead and around the bend and we'll be home."

The house they were buying was a charming terracotta cedar that sat atop a slight incline, with a wraparound deck and seemingly endless glass sliders.

"Hear the water?" Gerry emerged from behind the wheel to stand beside the car in rapt attention. "We'll sleep well tonight."

"I think we've had enough television for the night," Adam told Eric, fighting yawns now. "Let's hit the sack."

"It's early," Eric protested as usual. "A little past nine."

"You've had a busy day." Adam's eyes were indulgent.

"What are we going to do tomorrow?" Eric asked.

"I hadn't thought about it much," Adam admitted. Eric had said, "It'll be okay just to hang out over the weekend." But Adam suspected Eric was conscious now that the week was drawing to its end. He didn't want to go back to school. How to divert him? "What about our running out to Montauk?" he asked on impulse. "Providing we can get accommodations."

Eric's face lighted. "Cool!"

"Let me call Gurney's—see if they have a unit for us. If they have, we'll drive right out tonight." *There'll be little traffic—we can be there by midnight.*

* * *

274

Like yesterday morning, Helen awoke early. Birds were singing in the trees. Daylight filtered between the drapes. A sybaritic warmth suffused her bedroom—lending an "all's right with the world" atmosphere. If she hurried, she could be on the beach in time to see the sunrise, she decided with pleasurable anticipation.

She washed her face, rushed into clothes, applied a minimum of make-up. She'd shower later, have breakfast with Gerry and Sheila when she returned from the beach. By then, she thought affectionately, they'd probably be awake.

It would be cold on the beach, she reminded herself. She reached in her valise for the wool cap and gloves she'd packed. She hadn't worn her L. L. Bean ski jacket since the four-day winter weekend she'd spent with the kids at Killington. That had been one of many trips where Paul had pulled out at the last moment because of "business." Weird, how she had never suspected his philandering.

In their beachfront "Forward Watch" unit at Gurney's, Adam reached into the closet for his ski jacket, pulled it on. He glanced at Eric, sprawled in slumber. He felt a surge of serenity. He was glad they'd been able to get this unit on such short notice. Only because it was off-season. Being out here was a slice of heaven—a cherished escape from reality.

What was Helen doing this weekend? She was wrapped up in her two kids, the way he was with Eric. Now a somberness rolled over him. Helen thought he ought to fight for full custody of Eric, didn't she? He saw it in her eyes—always so expressive, so revealing of her inner thoughts.

Was he wrong in believing she felt something special for him—as he did for her? But hell, he was forty-eight, set in his ways. He had a demanding business. They'd both love to turn back the clock twenty years, he thought wryly—but life wasn't like that.

Okay, go walk on the beach, welcome the sunrise. This was a million miles away from Manhattan. Cherish every minute. He glanced again at Eric. Leave a note on the night table—not that Eric was apt to wake up before he returned. He'd have a brisk walk, come back, and they'd go upstairs to the dining room for one of Gurney's fabulous breakfasts.

He walked out of their unit, across the deck onto the beach. The water was gray and rough, pounding the shore like an impatient lover. In minutes, he thought, the sun would rise over the horizon in one of those magnificent moments that were bestowed on an often unobservant world.

The beach was deserted except for the seagulls. A cluster of gulls rode the choppy waves. The sand was untrampled. Not one pair of footprints, no dog paw imprints on display, he thought whimsically—relishing this solitude.

He walked briskly, enjoying the cold, crisp air. It would have been good, he thought, to have brought along a thermos of coffee. His eyes were drawn to the horizon—waiting for the dramatic moment when the orange-red ball began its ascent.

Staring towards the horizon, he became aware of a moving form far down the beach. Human or four-legged? Minutes later he realized the sole beach walker other than himself was a person. And all at once he felt a flicker of excitement. No, his imagination was working overtime. The person walking towards him couldn't be Helen.

Involuntarily he swiftened his pace to just short of a jog. In a corner of his mind he remembered hearing Helen speak with deep affection of a trip to Montauk years ago. *Was* that Helen—in a bright red ski jacket— walking towards him? Incredible!

"Hi!" she called out, faintly breathless. "I can't believe this!"

"Fate bringing us together," he said, his smile dazzling. "I decided last evening that Eric and I would come out here if we could get a reservation." They paused, both caught up in this miracle meeting.

"Gerry and Sheila are buying a house out

here." Adam knew both women. "They came out to do an inventory on the furniture—or some such deal—and invited me to come along."

"We're at Gurney's. I left Eric asleep in our unit," he explained. "I wanted to come out here and see the sunrise."

"My thought exactly." Helen swung about to face the horizon. "In truth, I should have been walking in the other direction. I kept turning around to see if the sun was sneaking through yet."

"Let's walk in that direction now." His eyes speaking from the heart, he reached for her hand. "This is fate, you know."

"Something like that," she conceded.

"I realize you're working through an ugly divorce," he said quietly. "But I want you to know that you're very special to me. I won't rush you," he promised, "but I'd like to believe there can be a future for us—together."

"I'd like that, too." It was an ardent whisper.

He reached to pull her into his arms on the empty beach while the ascending sun bathed them in color. "I'm angry at all the precious years we've missed."

"Let's be grateful for the ones ahead. But let's not rush. Let's be sure this time." Her laughter was shaky. "How many people get a second chance?"

He kissed her with the passion of twenty,

rejoiced in the knowledge that she responded in the same vein.

"I wish we could make love this minute—right on the empty beach." His mouth at her ear, his body swaying with hers.

"I'm afraid that'll have to wait." A hint of fresh laughter in her voice. But he knew she yearned for this as much as he. "Remember the life expectancy these days. We've got a lot of years ahead."

"I'll be jealous of every day without you," he warned. "But I understand," he added quickly. "We're not to rush. Because this will be for the rest of our lives."

Yet he asked himself if they were playing a dangerous game. *Are we too old—too tied down with obligations—to make a whole new life for ourselves? Will we wake up tomorrow morning with the realization that we're playing a fool's game?*

Zach focused on appearing laid-back, but his body was tense with excitement. A lot of young faces, he noted, gazing about the huge room where the Saturday conference was being held.

Doug was listening to the current speaker as though he was understudy to God, Zach thought. He was conscious of sweating, though the room was comfortable. Still, Chuck would do great in his presentation. Shit, he'd rehearsed a hundred times.

"It's us next," Doug whispered. "Cross your fingers. Cross your toes. Cross everything."

The last presenter was leaving the platform. Chuck was heading there. The whole scene was being handled with terrific efficiency, Zach thought. Every presenter knew his stuff, handled himself well. Everyone knew what was at stake. All that venture capital just dying to be spent.

Do we have a chance with all these others who're so smooth?

Chuck took his place. He was in his element, Zach thought in relief after the first few moments. He exchanged a triumphant glance with Doug as Chuck approached the end of his pitch:

"We need $4,000,000 investment capital to set up our factory and promote. We're already in contact with three prospective markets—"

Zach glanced around. These characters— the venture capitalists—were real interested. They remembered the guy who'd made a hundred million packaging for McDonald's. They were already counting up the profits.

"We're going to get nibbles," Doug whispered. "We'll walk away with half a dozen appointments."

Chuck ran over his time, but nobody complained. The atmosphere was overwhelmingly tense. Everybody here knew DCZ Inc.

was on the right track. Of course, they weren't actually incorporated yet—but Chuck's brother was fresh out of law school—he'd handle this for them.

Zach nudged Doug with an elbow. A guy in a $2,000 suit was making a beeline for Chuck as he walked away from the platform. The $400 they'd spent to be here was the best investment they'd ever made.

Twenty-Eight

Helen knew it would be difficult to hide their changing relationship from the others in the office. Still they must make a valiant effort. In an odd way she was relieved when Adam had commitments for their first three evenings back in the city—even while she ached to be with him.

"Dinner tonight?" he asked on a phone call before he came into the office on Thursday. "I wish it could be out in Montauk—but I'll settle for whatever is available."

"I can't tonight. I'm having dinner with Deedee." It had astonished her that Deedee had called early this morning to suggest dinner tonight. Was Deedee feeling guilty that they hadn't seen each other for a while? She understood Deedee's time was tightly scheduled. "But what about tomorrow night?" she asked and then dismissed this. "No, you have a meeting with those West Coast people." A prospective major new client.

"Saturday," he said triumphantly. "The whole day—the whole weekend—will belong to us. Oh damn," he broke in. "I have another call coming in."

This Saturday Adam wouldn't be going up to Boston to see Eric, she remembered. As he'd said, she recalled with joyous anticipation, the whole weekend would belong to them. How would they spend it? The divorce might not be officially final—but she was free.

Adam talked about a future together for them. He hadn't put it into words—but he meant marriage, didn't he? Was she being naive to think that? Did it matter? It would be enough to know that Adam loved her, that they could be together whenever his insane schedule permitted. That would be enough—wouldn't it? They were two mature people.

She'd spent all her life striving to please others. First her mother—which was her responsibility. Then Paul—which he didn't deserve. Then the children, the most precious gift of her life. But they were both grown now. It was her time to please herself. And it would please her to be with Adam at every possible moment.

In the privacy of Adam's office—though they knew that a brief knock would be all the warning before one of the staff entered —they managed a few moments together. Not quite enough, Helen acknowledged to herself—and she saw the hunger in Adam's eyes. But the weekend would be theirs.

As arranged, she checked with Deedee to report that she would be free shortly past 6 p.m. For once, she thought, Deedee seemed all clear at a normal hour. By six thirty she was hurrying into North West, the charming, oak paneled restaurant at 79th and Columbus. Deedee was already seated at her favorite table.

"It's good to see you out of the office at a decent hour." Helen slid into the chair opposite Deedee. Her eyes searched Deedee's now with a flicker of concern. Deedee appeared so tense. "Are you okay?"

"Yeah." Deedee's smile seemed forced. "Todd and I had a big blow-up a few days ago. I realized he was a big mistake. Oh, I'll be staying on in his apartment for the next four months. He's been sent over to Japan to help set up the firm's new office over there." She paused, took a deep breath. "And I'm quitting my job. I agreed to stay on for another three weeks—but then I'm moving on."

"You want a life." Helen's smile was reassuring. "You'll find something less insane."

"I already have three offers," Deedee admitted. "Considerably less money—but I can live on it. And like you said, I'll have a life."

Helen hesitated. Maybe she was butting in, but this was her baby. "Cliff will finish his residency in July," she said softly. "He'll be off his insane schedule. Maybe the two of you could pick up again." She knew Deedee felt something for Cliff. Something warm and loving, she thought, remembering little things.

"He's probably furious at me." Deedee's eyes were wistful. "He sent me those beautiful forget-me-nots on Thanksgiving—and I didn't even send a thank-you note."

"You could send him a bunch of forget-me-nots—with your new phone number," Helen said. "I'll bet he'll call you."

"That seems so crass." Deedee seemed ambivalent.

"Think about it," Helen urged. Sometimes one simple little move could be so important.

"I'll think about it," Deedee hedged and smiled at the waiter who hovered at the table now.

Along with Doug and Chuck, Zach listened

attentively to the man who sat at the impressive huge desk in the private suite of the venture capitalist group that seemed their most likely partners.

"I've told you what we can do for you," the VC emphasized. "You know the percentage we expect before we take you public. You're young and inexperienced—but we'll help you with your start-up and management. And we'll all make a bundle of money," he predicted.

Like his partners in the start-up venture, Zach was dazed as they left the VC's offices and waited for an elevator to take them out into the world. Wordless, they rode down from the fortieth-floor offices to the lobby in silence, strode out onto Madison Avenue.

"Wow!" Doug let out an extravagant sigh. "Did you ever think we'd be in business so fast?"

"My old man will bust a gut when he finds out DCZ will be going public. He's been trying to do that for a dozen years." Chuck shook his head in disbelief. "And wait'll he hears about our capitalization."

Zach was silent. He worried about how they were going to be able to operate and still remain in school. He didn't want to think what Mom would say if they had to drop out before the end of the school year. But when she saw the scope of DCZ, she'd understand they couldn't stay on the traditional path. These were special times.

There was no way this could blow up in their faces. Was there? He felt a tightness in his throat as he considered dropping out of Columbia and then having the corporation collapse.

Chuck took off for a late class. Zach and Doug rushed to their copy center jobs. As of this week they were working at the same store, same hours.

"We'll have to tell John we won't be able to stay with him," Doug said uneasily.

"Hunh?" Zach was startled.

"How can we work for him when we're moving like a Gatling gun on DCZ?" Doug pantomimed reproach. "Be practical. It's going to be a bitch to stay in school and handle the business. How the hell can we spend three days a week at a copy machine?"

"Yeah." But Zach was apprehensive. Without the job he couldn't give Mom the weekly payments he'd promised until he'd paid off the thousand he'd borrowed on her Mastercard. "We'll have to give John two weeks' notice—"

Doug considered this. "We'll tell him our problem. If he can replace us earlier, then we'll be off the hook earlier."

"Yeah." But Zach wasn't happy.

In a lull at the copy center Zach prodded

himself to call Deedee. Shit, she ought to understand what was happening to DCZ! He was offering her a great business deal. A percentage of his share of the company for $1,000.

He'd have to call Mom for Deedee's phone number, he recalled, and reached for the phone.

Deedee paced about the living room. She was crazy to have sent Cliff the forget-me-nots and her new phone number. He was pissed at her—and could she blame him? She'd checked with the florist—the delivery was made last night, just an hour after she'd been in the shop.

She started at the shrill ring of the phone, lunged to pick up. Her heart pounding.

"Hello—"

"Hi, Deedee—" The familiar warm voice. "It's me. Cliff."

"I miss you," she said. "I've made a terrible mistake—you'll probably hate me for it—"

"I could never hate you," he chided. "I'll love you until the day I die." He paused a moment. "I gather you've moved—"

"I'm in a sublet for four months." *It's going to be awful to explain about Todd.*

"I just came off a double shift and found your flowers sitting down in the package room. Could I come over now?"

"You must be exhausted." She remembered other double shifts.

He chuckled. "Not that exhausted. Honey, I have such a hunger to see you."

"May I come over there instead?" She didn't want to see him in the apartment she'd shared with Todd.

"Sure." His voice electric.

"Leave the door unlocked in case you fall asleep," she joshed.

"A bottle of Valium couldn't put me to sleep now. Hurry, baby. Hurry!"

In a flurry of anticipation she pulled a coat from the closet, reached for purse and gloves. The phone rang again. She hesitated. No, let the machine pick up. She had fences to mend. As she slid the key into the lock, she heard Zach's voice. All right, she'd call him later.

A taxi was pulling up before the building to disgorge a passenger. She waited for the woman to emerge, then jumped into the taxi. Cliff's apartment was just eleven short blocks north—but she was too impatient to walk. It was as though she was coming home after a painful exile.

The night doorman at Cliff's building called up. Smiling broadly, he nodded her on. Hurrying from the elevator, she heard the sound of Gershwin's *Rhapsody in Blue* filtering into the hall. Their music.

The apartment door was ajar. Deedee

walked inside. Cliff stood there—barefoot and in his favorite terrycloth robe. He held out his arms to her.

"You've come home, baby. Welcome."

"Cliff, I've been such an idiot." She wallowed in the pleasure of being in his arms. For the moment it was enough just to be close this way. "I've quit my job," she said with an air of defiance. "I wanted my life back."

"I've missed you so damn much." A hand fondled her rump. "You left such a hole in my life. I warn you—I won't let you get away again."

"I have to tell you about these last months," she began. "You may not want me back."

"I want you back," he insisted, his mouth reaching for hers. A hand made its way beneath her sweater.

"I was living with somebody else," she said breathlessly when their mouths parted. Her eyes pleading for forgiveness. "A dumb thing to do."

"You'll have to pay a penalty," he said with mock ferocity. "Make love with me until we both fall asleep."

"What a wonderful way to fall asleep," she murmured while he pulled her sweater above her head and tossed it aside. With a gamine smile she released the sash of his robe. The robe parted. Oh, he wasn't about to fall asleep.

He allowed his robe to fall to the floor, lifted her into his arms and carried her into the bedroom. With a murmur of pleasure she felt the firm queen-size mattress beneath her—and then the warmth of him probing.

"Cliff, I was so stupid," she murmured. And then there was no time for talk—only to share the tumultuous passion that blended them into exquisite satisfaction.

Later—much later—she remembered that Zach had called. Cliff was asleep. He'd probably sleep for hours. She tossed one leg across his, pulled the covers over the two of them. She'd call Zach in the morning—

Twenty-Nine

Helen awoke with an instant realization that she was to meet Adam for breakfast—and then they'd plan their day. A whole day that would belong to them alone, she rejoiced. She glanced at the clock on her night table. It was just seven thirty—stay in bed another half hour. She wasn't meeting Adam until ten.

It was so luxurious, she thought, to lie in

bed with no demands on her time. What was it like outdoors? She remembered last night's weather report. Today would be cold and raw with the possibility of snow flurries. What did it matter? She'd be with Adam.

He said he knew of a restaurant where they could have breakfast before an open fireplace. He'd never admit to being a romantic—but he was. How would they spend the rest of the day? But she knew the finale, she thought with tender anticipation. So strange to feel this way about Adam, when she'd been so sure such feelings belonged in the long past young days. Strange and wonderful.

She arose at eight, lingered in the shower, made dressing a pleasurable rite. When the phone rang at shortly past nine, she guessed it was Adam.

"Hello—" A warm, sensuous greeting.

"Helen?" For a moment she didn't recognize the voice at the other end. Jeff Madison.

"Yes. Good morning, Jeff." *Why is he calling me? All the papers for the divorce have been signed.*

"I'm sorry to bother you, but something's come up." He cleared his throat, as though gearing himself to deliver an unpleasant message. "Paul just called from California. He—he'd like you to approve a Mexican divorce."

Helen was startled. "Why this sudden rush?"

"Uh—Paul has a—a problem." Jeff was searching for words. "He's been living with a young woman since he went out to Silicon Valley—"

"That doesn't surprise me." What is he trying to tell me?

"She's pregnant," Jeff said in a rush, seeming relieved to have delivered this message.

"And he wants to do 'the right thing,'" Helen drawled. A change of pace for him. "But are Mexican divorces recognized in this country?" Hadn't she heard stories about problems?

"Mexican divorces are legal unless they're contested by the defendant. You won't be contesting, so there'll be no problem." But he sounded nervous. Does he think I'll fight it?

"I won't contest it," she agreed. "And what's this person's name?" Why do I care?

"Stephanie," Jeff said, somewhat startled. Is he afraid I'll go after her with an axe? "I've prepared papers that require your signature," he pursued. "Necessary if the divorce is to go through without a hitch."

"Mail them and I'll sign them," Helen said with distaste. Her mind chaotic. A little sister or brother for Deedee and Zach. How will they take this?

"They must be signed and notarized. I'm a notary. I know it's an imposition, but

292

could you possibly drive out some time this afternoon? I'm not free to drive into town—I have to stand by for an important phone call. But I can arrange to be at my local office whenever it'll be convenient for you."

"I have plans for today." Today belonged to Adam and her. "Why can't I have the papers notarized here in New York?"

"Paul's made arrangements to go to Mexico on Wednesday morning. He was able to get time off from the office for the rest of the week. You realize he's in a new job—he can't be demanding. He—"

"Why does he have to be there in Mexico?" Helen broke in. "I thought these things could be handled through the mail—or faxes."

"Stephanie's very nervous—he promised he'd fly down to make sure there are no mistakes." *He's nervous—I'll bet he wishes he'd never taken this on.* "Can you make it Monday? I can FedEx the papers to Paul and—"

"I'll be working Monday," she began, but her mind was charging ahead. She and Adam could drive up to Westchester, have lunch up there—and play it by ear after that. "All right," she agreed. "We'll do it today. I can be at your Westchester office around two thirty. Will that be okay?"

"That'll be fine." He sounded relieved. He'd expected to be paid his agreed upon fee for the divorce, she assumed—to be handled by Paul—but with less work entailed. "See you at two thirty."

She braced for Adam's disappointment when she phoned to report on this new problem.

"We'll deal," he soothed. "Let's push up breakfast a half-hour, have a leisurely drive up to Westchester, stop off at this charming old bookstore I discovered years ago, then look for a good place to have lunch."

"There's talk of snow," she warned. But Westchester was beautiful when it snowed.

"A little snow isn't going to frighten us away," he scoffed. "And pack an overnight bag," he added, his voice deepening with promise. "We'll find a place to stay two nights—drive in to work Monday morning." He chuckled. "We'll be a commuting couple for the day."

"I'll bet Paul's girlfriend made a major effort to get pregnant," Helen said with biting humor. "Just to make sure she becomes Paul's trophy wife." *She'll be Deedee and Zach's stepmother.*

"Does this upset you?" Adam was solicitous.

"No," she said after a moment of consideration. "Only that I suspect the kids will be upset—and that annoys me."

The ringing of the phone was a raucous intrusion in Zach's dorm room. He grimaced, without opening his eyes reached to pick up the receiver.

"Avery Morgue." He managed to open one eye, squinted at the clock. Shit, it was only 10 a.m. He hadn't gotten to bed until almost five. "Who's calling at this ungodly hour?"

"Your sister," Deedee shot back. "And what's ungodly about 10 a.m.?"

"What do you want?" he demanded.

"You called me," she reminded—in the familiar adversarial mode. "What do you want?"

"Oh, yeah—" All at once he was fully awake. This was going to require a sales pitch. "Well, yesterday I went with Doug and Chuck—my two partners in this project—to a venture capital forum—"

"What for?" She was astonished.

"We're in business." He felt a surge of triumph. "Doug and me—and Chuck. With four million in capitalization."

"What are you on?" She sounded alarmed.

"Euphoria," he gloated. "It's going to be hell to stay in school till the end of the year and carry on business," he conceded, "but Mom'll freak out if I quit school mid-term."

"Who gave you kids four million in capitalization?" Now she was skeptical.

"Lothrop Enterprises," he said. She was in investment banking—she'd know who they were.

"They're a start-up company themselves!"

"Haven't you heard?" he drawled. "Start-up companies have become venture capitalists. Anyhow, I was telling the guys we ought to invite you to be on our Board."

"Why?"

"Well, you know the business—we're just feeling our way. Anyhow, I have a problem. I borrowed $1,000 from Mom and—"

"You borrowed from Mom?" Deedee was outraged.

"Not exactly. I used the Mastercard she gave me on my last trip to get a cash advance. I promised to pay her back each week—you know I'm working three days a week at a copy center." Upped from the weekend to include Friday. "But now—with DCZ in work—"

"What DCZ?" she interrupted.

"Our corporation. Doug-Chuck-Zach. Lothrop expects us to be on the ball and—"

"Wait a minute—what does DCZ do?"

"We're into packaging. I'm the idea man —packaging to fill an important need can earn millions. Doug is strong on management—and Chuck will have his engineering degree in May. He's already designed the equipment for our first packaging deal. Anyhow—since you're my sister—I'm willing to give you five per cent of my share of the corporation for $1,000. To get me off the hook with Mom," he admitted. "In time you might earn a million."

"And my $1,000 might go down the drain with you." She was silent for a painful moment. "I'm probably out of my mind— but okay, have your lawyer draw up the papers. You do have a lawyer?"

"Sure, he's already got the incorporation papers in work." He took a deep breath. "Could I have the money first thing tomorrow morning?"

Snow flurries began to hit the ground as Helen and Adam headed up the West Side Highway. Helen sat with her head resting against Adam's shoulder, their thighs touching. Heat provided sybaritic comfort. She listened while he talked about the years with Zoe—as though, she thought tenderly, he felt a compulsion to share his past life with her.

"I'm boring the hell out of you," he apologized.

"No!" She was emphatic. "I want to hear everything."

"I never expected to have a whole life after the ugliness with Zoe. I thought I'd misspent the young—the passionate—years, and there could never be a second chance." One hand left the wheel to caress her knee. "I didn't think there could be anything in my life except for work and Eric."

"I thought my life would revolve totally around the kids. I thought what I feel now," she said with candor, "belonged to the young Helen." Yet while she moved through each day with a sense of wonder that Adam and she could feel this way, she was conscious of disturbing doubts. Would she wake up tomorrow and find this was a brief dream? "Tell me what you were like as a little boy," she prodded. "I'll bet you were very like Eric—"

All at once she was conscious of a painful tension in him. He seemed in some inner struggle. *What did I say to upset him this way?*

"I'm going to tell you something I've never told a living soul." His knuckles were white as he gripped the wheel. "I love him deeply—but he's not my son."

"Adam, that's ridiculous," Helen rejected.

"I thought Eric was a 'preemie,' " he said. He'd told her just today how Zoe had pushed him into marriage with the report that she was pregnant. "He was full term—though he was barely six pounds. Zoe told me she was pregnant by a man she knew before we began an affair. That doesn't change the way I feel about Eric—but he's not my son." Pain seeped into his voice now.

"Adam, I don't believe that," Helen protested. "He's the image of you!"

"He's fair-haired and blue-eyed. My hair is dark brown and my eyes are hazel."

"So he has Zoe's coloring. Every feature is yours. Anyone looking at the two of you would know you're father and son!"

"You're saying Zoe lied to me—"

"Of course, she lied. Nobody in their right mind would believe otherwise. He has all your little mannerisms. The way you put your head to one side when you're thinking—the way you twist a strand of hair when you're feeling relaxed—which isn't often, I admit," she said with a hint of laughter. "The way you hunch your shoulders when you're tired. Adam, I will never believe that Eric isn't your son. No one who knows the two of you would." She hesitated. "And there are ways to make sure if you need that—" DNA tests were accurate.

"I'm reeling from what you said." His voice was an awed whisper. "All these years I believed Zoe—"

"Look in a mirror," Helen urged. "Not now," she conceded, "but when we're on stable ground. Look in the mirror and see Eric."

Thirty

The road was white with snow by the time Helen and Adam pulled up before the bookstore he'd mentioned—in a village close to their destination. The owner had known Adam for years, greeted them warmly.

"How's Eric?" he asked. "He must be a big boy now. I haven't seen him in half a dozen years." His eyes were appraising her, Helen realized. He was approving. Had he known Zoe?

"I had a house near here for a while," Adam told Helen. "A sort of escape hatch. Eric would come out to spend some weekends with me." His face tightened. "Before Zoe started trekking across the country. Once Eric couldn't come out for weekends, I sold."

"We were almost neighbors," Helen realized in astonishment, then made mental calculations. "You probably left soon after we moved out here—" How strange to think that they might have passed each other at a shopping mall, eaten in the same restaurant.

They browsed a bit until Adam made his selections.

"This could develop into a real snow," the bookstore owner warned as he rang up the sale. "There've been bulletins out in the last hour. The weathercasters expect four to six inches."

"It'll be beautiful," Helen predicted. "I've always loved snow—outside of the city," she amended.

"We'll linger to enjoy it," Adam promised. And Helen saw the way the bookstore owner gazed from Adam to her with pleased comprehension. "We've got an appointment about fifteen miles up. We'd better get cracking."

They stopped for lunch at a white colonial converted to a restaurant that Helen had always liked. She glowed when he admired the charming dining room, the perfect service, the excellent food. Paul had preferred glitzy restaurants.

"Another cup of this perfect coffee and we'll be on our way," Adam decided. His eyes searched hers. "You're not upset about this change to a 'quickie' divorce?" he asked again. "In a way, it's great."

"I'm not upset." Her smile was meant to be reassuring.

What does he mean?—"It's great." Her heart began to pound. *Does he mean that it'll clear the path for us? He's never once mentioned marriage. He said he wanted us to share our future. Couples live together these days without marriage. The word is "companion"—not just for gay and lesbian couples. Would the kids be upset if I moved in with Adam? It would solve the apartment problem.*

They drove in comfortable silence to Jeff Madison's local office, in a pleasant low building in the center of the village. He was going to be surprised to see her with Adam, she guessed. She relished Adam's protective air as she introduced him to Jeff.

"This won't take long," Jeff assured them. "Please sit down." He was pulling papers from a folder. "You just have to sign these, Helen—and I'll notarize them."

She was amazed by the questions she read in Jeff's eyes. Had people out here expected her to fall apart when Paul walked out on her? She felt reborn. But why did doubts tug at her at unwary moments? She was distrustful of something so wonderful, she mocked herself. Was this all an illusion that would disappear without warning?

Adam seemed pensive when they returned to the car.

"Show me the house where you lived?" A doubt in his voice that she would comply.

"If you really want to see it," she agreed after a startled moment.

"I'm jealous of all the years we've missed."

"It's just three miles from the village," she told him. "Make a right at the next corner."

She tried to gear herself to drive by the

302

house where she'd lived with Paul.

"Up the hill," she instructed Adam. In truth, she didn't want to see the house again. She wanted to push it out of her memory. A few minutes later, she pointed to the weather-shingled colonial cape that sat above a terraced acre. "There she is—"

Adam slowed to a crawl. "That's yesterday," he said quietly. "Another world." He stared hard at the house for another moment, then accelerated. "We don't want to go back to the city in this snow, do we?"

"I packed for a weekend out of the city," she reminded. Was this really she, Helen Avery, going to a motel with a man? A man she loved more than she'd thought humanly possible. "You wouldn't disappoint me, would you?"

"Let's find a place we like and check in." All at once, he, too, seemed self-conscious. *We're two sophisticated people—why should we feel this way?*

"If we get back on the highway, we'll see the usual chains—" The weathercasters hadn't been wrong—the snow was coming down steadily. The area had become a winter wonderland.

"You didn't pack boots," he accused and sighed. "Neither did I. Okay, first stop, the neighborhood shopping mall. Two pairs of boots coming up." He was making it sound like an adventure, Helen thought tenderly.

Paul would have yelled at her for not remembering to pack boots for both of them.

At the shopping mall, they located a shoe store that carried boots for both men and women. The sales clerk thought they were a married couple, she guessed.

"We need warm socks," Adam decided after he'd paid for their boots and herded her in the proper direction.

Adam was in such a jubilant mood, she thought while he debated about what color socks they should choose. She'd never seen him in such high spirits. They must have more weekends like this, she promised herself. It was good for both of them. But now—belatedly—she worried that Deedee or Zach would call and be upset that she wasn't home.

How could I tell them I was running off for a weekend with Adam? It wasn't what they'd expect of their mother. If they call, they'll leave a message. I'll check with the answering machine.

Deedee had been living with a man she'd never met. She doubted that Zach was virginal. Their father was shacked up with some young slut he'd just got pregnant. Why should she feel guilty at spending a weekend with the man she hoped would share the rest of her life?

Adam's words tickertaped across her brain: *"I won't rush you, but I'd like to believe there can be a future for us—together.*" He'd kissed her with the passion of twenty—and she'd responded in the same fashion. Yet it all seemed unreal.

"Can you believe it's way past five?" Adam —consolidating their parcels into one— punctured her introspection. "This day is running away. We have to find a place to light for the night." His free arm settled about her waist as they headed for the car.

"There's a lovely inn about four miles north," Helen remembered now. "Not that I've ever stayed there," she added with a quick laugh. They wouldn't run into any of her old neighbors, would they? Suddenly she was self-conscious. And what if they did?

In the car—with much laughter—they changed into warm socks and boots. He reached to pull her close for a moment.

"I hope there's a terrific snowstorm during the night—and we're snowed in. Oh, we'll be able to send out for food. But for a little while we'll be able to shut out the rest of the world."

Helen directed him to the inn. They left the car and walked together into the office. It was absurd, she scolded herself, but she leaned over his shoulder to see how he signed the register. "Adam and Helen Smith." It was natural not to sign his real name, she considered. Only married people did that.

They found their way to their room. Adam unlocked the door, threw it wide—then with startling suddenness swept her off her feet and, carried her across the threshold.

"We're home," he murmured in satisfaction and gently deposited her on the king-sized bed.

"I suppose we should start thinking about dinner—" Her heart was pounding. Incredible she could feel this way!

"Later," he soothed, dropping to the side of the bed to remove his new boots. "I have another destination in mind right now."

"I suppose that could be allowed," she flipped, but her body was saying, "Make love to me, Adam. Make love to me!"

Now he reached to pull off her boots. "Do I have to do all the work around here?"

"I'll help," she promised. They were both all at once shy in this situation, she realized.

"I've waited so long for you," he murmured. "I was afraid it would never happen."

"It's happening," she said in glorious abandon. "Oh, Adam, I never thought I could ever feel this way again..."

They lay exhausted in each other's arms while twilight settled about the outdoors and the wind howled.

"I suppose we should go out and find a

place for dinner," Adam said at last, a teasing glint in his eyes. "Have to rebuild my strength."

"I know the perfect restaurant. It'll probably be empty tonight—considering the weather. They have this huge fireplace—"

"Like where we had breakfast? Was that just this morning?" he asked with an air of disbelief.

"An even bigger fireplace," she recalled. "And the seafood is superb. You do like seafood?" There was so much she had to learn about him.

"I'm allergic," he said and chuckled at her air of concern. "Kidding," he soothed. "I love seafood. But not lobster," he admitted. "Not since I took Eric out for a lobster dinner when he was about nine—and he was so upset when he saw how they were cooked. We both swore off lobsters for life."

"That's Zach, too," she recalled. "And you know," she said with an air of astonishment, "I'm hungry."

They dressed, left for the restaurant. There wouldn't be anybody there she knew, Helen surmised. Not in this weather. And suppose there was? She was as good as divorced. Still, she was relieved when they walked into the charming restaurant to find only a handful of diners—none of whom she knew.

They made a production of ordering, invited the advice of their waiter.

"He wondered how I managed to snare a beautiful younger woman like you," Adam whispered, his foot finding hers beneath the table. "He's envious of me."

"Flattery will get you everywhere," she promised. *I feel young with Adam. I don't feel like a woman staring at fifty. Well, it's a long stare.*

"You look at me like that, and I'll insist we skip dinner and rush back to the inn," he warned.

"We'll settle for one cup of coffee after dessert. Oh, desserts here are fabulous," she recalled. She'd brought the kids here on very special occasions—which too often Paul missed.

They ate dinner in an aura of euphoria. By the time they left the restaurant, the roads were being cleared by snow plows. They'd have no trouble driving back into the city, Helen told herself.

"We won't be able to pick up Sunday's *Times* to read tonight," Adam reminded. A Saturday night ritual in Manhattan. "But I don't think we'll mind that tonight."

"I think we'll survive."

Back at the inn Helen debated about calling and checking with her answering machine.

"I know it's absurd," she admitted, reaching for the phone. "But the kids don't know

308

where I am. I just want to check to see if either of them tried to reach me." She punched in her number, waited for the message, then punched in the code that would bring up messages. Only the discordant sound of somebody calling and not leaving a message. Another telecommunications person. "No calls," she reported.

"You dedicated mothers," he teased, then reached for the phone. "I might as well call my machine—not that I expect any calls. We get so geared to doing this," he grumbled.

Helen tensed as she saw him stiffen as though in shock at what was being relayed from his answering machine.

"What the hell!" He charged to the chair where his ski jacket lay, reached into a pocket, then another.

"Adam, what happened?" A coldness closed in about her.

"That was a message from the school." His voice was uneven. "Dean Andrews thought I ought to know. Zoe arrived this morning. She took Eric with her. She told Dean Andrews that she was going to Europe for a year."

Thirty-One

Helen struggled for calm. "She can't do that! According to the court decision you have Eric on alternate holidays. He can't commute from Europe."

"Zoe doesn't believe in rules." His face was taut. "I'll call my lawyer, ask him to get an injunction. If she tries to leave the country, she'll be stopped at Customs." His words were positive, yet Helen felt his panic. "I'll call Mark at home—he'll understand this is an emergency." Again, he reached for his telephone book.

Helen sat by while Adam tried to reach his attorney. He wasn't at his Manhattan apartment. After another search in his phone book, Adam located the attorney's ski lodge in upstate New York. She listened intently while he explained the situation.

"Sure, she's not supposed to take him out of the country—" Impatiently Adam brushed this aside. "But you know Zoe—she makes her own rules." He listened for a few moments now. "Okay, phone Zoe out in California—if she's back there by now. Oh

God, maybe she wasn't going back to California! Maybe they're headed already for wherever in Europe she plans to settle!" Again, Adam was listening. "Yeah, get out the injunction. Let's make sure she doesn't skip the country!"

Helen's mind was in high gear now. Maybe this was the moment for Adam to try for full custody.

"Adam," she began slowly—as though speaking with a distraught small child, "would you want full custody of Eric?"

"I'd give ten years of my life for that. Until you set me straight, I didn't think I deserved it—I was terrified that Eric would learn I wasn't his father. But Zoe won't let me have custody. And what chance would I have in court?"

"You said she uses Eric as a pawn," Helen continued. Adam nodded. "Suppose she didn't need him as a pawn? You said she's living with some man twenty years younger than she—but she won't marry him because she'd lose her alimony checks—"

"I'm not following you—"

"What if you offered her a large settlement in lieu of alimony—but to be paid out on the same schedule as the alimony checks—provided she relinquishes custody of Eric." She saw Adam's face light up. He was following her thinking. "That would free her to marry without losing her income.

311

And as a safety precaution, there could be a stipulation that if she should die before the settlement was paid out, the balance would go to Eric."

"Eric has always been a threat to her image," Adam conceded. "When he was a toddler, she loved playing the adoring mother—though nannies were raising him. But now a teenage son doesn't fit the picture she wants to create for herself—"

"Have your attorney make that offer to her," Helen prodded. "It won't be more of a financial hardship than paying alimony—and it could buy you custody of Eric."

"Knowing Zoe, I suspect she worries that her young lover might walk. She'd feel more secure if they were married. And the older Eric gets, the more the threat to her cherished image. She wants to be eternally young." Adam frowned in thought. "I can figure a settlement based on actuarial charts. Her monthly alimony times life expectancy. Her actual age," he said with a touch of humor. "Not what's for public consumption. It might work."

"Call Mark back," Helen urged. "Have him contact Zoe—make the offer. She won't need Eric as a pawn."

"I'm his father," Adam said with fresh confidence. "I won't have an ocean separating us." His face softened. "How could I have been so stupid as to believe Zoe when she said I wasn't Eric's father? You woke me up, my love. You gave me my son."

Helen understood Adam was anxious to return to the city—where Zoe would know where to contact him. Where Eric might conceivably try to phone him. They checked out of the inn just past 9 a.m. Adam had tried to reach Mark, first at his ski lodge, then on his cell phone—with no luck.

"There's no connection points wherever Mark is," he explained. "I'll have to wait until he's back in New York to badger him."

"You said he knows Zoe," Helen encouraged. "He'll know how to deal with her." But she knew Adam couldn't relax when he was aware that Eric might be slipping from his grasp.

"The road has been sanded again," Adam noted with relief as they settled themselves in the car. "We'll be in town in an hour—an hour and a half at the most. If Zoe is still in California, with the time difference she'll still be asleep."

"Don't try to contact her yourself," Helen warned. Mark had told him earlier to stay out of negotiations.

"Eric must be so upset. First Zoe dumps him in boarding school, then she yanks him out with some story about spending a year in Europe." His hands tightened on the wheel.

"This might be the best thing that could

happen for you and Eric," Helen said gently. "Zoe will have financial security without having to worry about losing her alimony. She's sharp enough to realize that one day you might track her down, discover a way to eliminate the alimony."

"I want Eric with me. I have the right to have him with me." One hand left the wheel to reach for hers. "We'll make up for cutting this weekend short," he promised.

Traffic was light. They debated for a moment about stopping along the road for breakfast, dismissed this.

"We'll have breakfast at the apartment," Adam stipulated. "Is that okay?"

"Sure." She was conscious of a faint stir of pleasure at the prospect of breakfast in Adam's apartment.

They were in Manhattan shortly past 10 a.m., drove directly to Adam's apartment building. The doorman greeted him warmly. Helen saw quiet approval in the doorman's eyes as they rested for an instant on her. She sensed it was rare for Adam to bring a woman here.

In the elevator—occupied only by them—Adam reached to pull her close.

"It's so good to be with you," he said. "You have a beautiful serenity that reaches out to calm me."

"A sort of non-addictive Valium." He couldn't know that calm was only on the surface.

"Oh, most addictive," he countered. "I need you in my life to survive."

The elevator slid to a stop on the twentieth floor. Adam prodded her into the elegant, carpeted hall and to the right. She'd never been here, Helen realized. She was entering an unknown segment of Adam's life.

She waited while he unlocked his apartment door. It was as though with this gesture Adam was taking her more deeply into his life. Yet she was uncertain about their destination. What commitment did he have in mind?

Adam flung the door wide. "I'll try Mark again," he began and paused. "I've been living here for not quite four years," he said gently. *He is reading my mind: did he live here with Zoe?* "It still needs some finishing touches."

"It looks charming—" She gazed about the large foyer, the beautifully furnished living room beyond while he charged towards the phone.

His answering machine was flickering. He pushed the message button. Eric's voice filtered into the room.

"Dad, I don't want to go to Europe! Zoe says we're flying to New York day after tomorrow." Three years ago his mother had taught him to call her Zoe. "Then we'll make a connecting flight to Paris. I don't

315

want to go!"

"Call Mark," Helen urged. "He can use that information."

While Adam—struggling for calm—spoke with Mark on the phone, Helen explored the kitchen. She opened the refrigerator, noted its sparse supplies. But there were eggs and butter, coffee beans, orange juice. She checked the freezer, found frozen bagels. They'd have breakfast.

The shriek of the coffee-grinder filled the air for a few moments, blocked the sound of Adam's exasperated voice. He wasn't happy about progress on Mark's part, she surmised.

"I like mine scrambled dry," he said, hovering at the kitchen door. Straining to hide his frustration in the current impasse.

She glanced up with a smile. "There'll be a short wait for breakfast. What did Mark have to say?"

"He's sure Zoe hasn't left California. The phone's still on. She wouldn't be leaving for a year without a disconnect. Not even Zoe," he said drily.

"Perhaps she's away for the weekend," Helen soothed.

"First thing in the morning he'll get an injunction to stop Zoe from taking Eric out of the country. Right now he's arranging for an attorney out there to try to go to her and make the new offer. But it's scary. If they leave the country, what chance would I have of tracking them down?"

Thirty-Two

Zoe lounged on a chaise on the deck of the Malibu beach house she'd rented for a long weekend from a long-faded and impecunious movie star. She inspected one long thigh with merciless candor. The last cellulite session wasn't as effective as she would have liked.

Damn, the plastic surgeons grew more greedy each year. Just about everything that could be lifted on her almost-anorexic body had been lifted—but she envisioned further efforts. With the cost of living jumping up the way it was, Adam ought to increase her alimony checks.

She heard the faint swoosh of a slider opening onto the deck.

"Here's your drink, sweetie." But Zoe was conscious of an undertone of reproach in Tim's voice.

"How does it feel—sleeping in an ex-movie star's bed?" She tried for flipness. Her eyes resting on his sleek, trunk-clad body that had been at her disposal for almost a year now.

"We'll be out of here in the morning," he reminded, lowering himself onto the adjoining chaise. "Where did you get this crazy notion about living in Europe for a while?"

"It'll be exciting," she soothed. He was pissed because he couldn't be chasing down possible bit parts in some new movie. He was great-looking, sure—but he'd never be another Heath Ledger, whom of course he detested. Heath was making it into the million-dollar-a-film category. He was lucky to get a two-line part—usually in the briefest of swimming trunks.

"I'll hate it," he sulked. But he'd stay with her because otherwise he'd be sleeping on the street somewhere. "What'll you do with Eric?" he asked curiously.

"He'll go into boarding school. I've already got one lined up. The old school is already sending on his records." She'd told Tim that she'd been raped by Adam when she was fourteen. He'd married her to keep out of prison—and the alimony was to keep her quiet. "We'll be free as a pair of birds," she cooed.

"I'll hate it," he warned.

"You'll love it," she insisted. He was annoyed, she understood, that she refused to marry him. Then he would have felt secure. But to marry meant to sacrifice her alimony. What would they live on? Tim's unemployment checks? In the back of his mind Tim realized that—but he wasn't happy about it.

"Zoe—" Eric came trudging up from the beach. "When are we going home? I mean, back to the apartment—"

"In the morning. I thought you loved the beach," she reproached.

"Yeah, I do." He hesitated. "When are we flying to New York?"

"Day after tomorrow—and then it's Paris, here we come," she bubbled. "I told you— I've found the greatest boarding school for you. And yes," she said yet again. "They speak English there."

Helen returned to her apartment a little past 8 p.m. She had tried hard to alleviate Adam's anxiety—though she, too, was upset. How awful of Adam's ex-wife to put Eric through such trauma.

She knew Adam had hoped she would remain at the apartment with him. But suppose Deedee or Zach tried to reach her and she was unavailable? They'd be so worried. How could she leave a message on their answering machines that said, "Darling, don't worry about me—I'm at Adam Fremont's apartment."

She was on the point of calling Adam when the phone rang.

"Hello—" She half-expected the caller to

be Adam. He was so distraught at the prospect of Eric's being swept off to Europe.

"Mom, can I come up for a while? I'm right near you—" An anxiety in Zach's voice triggered alarm in her.

"Of course you can," she said instantly. Thank goodness, she'd come home. "Have you had dinner yet?"

"Yeah, I'm not hungry. I'll be up in five minutes."

Helen was at the door as soon as she heard the elevator open. The doorman didn't bother to announce Zach—they all knew that wasn't necessary.

"Hi, Mom—" Zach kissed her, pulled off his jacket and tossed it towards the sofa —just missing—then sauntered into the kitchen.

"Would you like something to eat?" she asked solicitously as he pulled open the refrigerator door.

He grinned. "I'm just checking up." Now he reached to open the freezer door, chortled in approval. "Mama, we share the same addiction," he reminded and pulled out the container of Chocolate Cherry Garcia she always kept on tap—for both of their pleasure.

"How's the job," she asked while he scooped out a portion of frozen yogurt. "You're managing all right?" He said he was working close to thirty hours a week. Was that interfering with his class work?

"I—uh...quit." He walked back into the living room, dropped into a corner of the sofa. "I'm kind of affluent right now." He put down the dish of frozen yogurt and fished in a shirt pocket. "I can pay you back the grand."

She stared in shock. "Zach, where did you get that kind of money?" Horrible possibilities—selling drugs, fleecing the elderly out of their life-savings—darted across her mind. "What have you been doing?"

"Don't look as though you think I robbed a bank," Zach scolded good-humoredly. "Mom, we're living in a wild world. I'm in business—on the net." She looked blank. "On the Internet, Mom. You know about that," he teased.

"I know about the Internet." She was grim. "I know how all you young people are terrified of dehydration—or why else would you all walk around clutching your bottles of water? I know how you all cling to your cell phones—as though it's a fate worse than death not to be always available. But what's this about your being in business?" What kind of business would give a college student a thousand dollars just out of the blue?

"Sit down, Mom. I've got a story to tell you. And don't look so scared—it's legitimate. Honest," he emphasized and began to explain the workings of DCZ Corporation. "Right at this moment we're the three luckiest guys in the world. We know what we're doing—and we've got terrific help from our venture capitalists—"

"You're warning me you're dropping out of school," she said, feeling herself a failure as a mother. *I've put too much pressure on Zach. A nineteen-year-old shouldn't have the worries I've thrust on him.*

"We'll try hard to finish out this year," Zach soothed. "And if—if things don't work out, we can pick up fifty bucks an hour as computer consultants. I'll go back to school if this doesn't work out," he vowed. "But we'll work our butts off to make it." His eyes were zealous. "Sure, a lot of the dot-coms will drop by the wayside—but we're going to make it. Mom, it's what I want to do. Hey, Bill Gates's mother didn't have a heart attack when he dropped out of college—"

"I won't have a heart attack," she promised. "But I worry about you."

"And about that grand I just gave you—" His smile was sheepish. "I didn't take that from the business. I sold Deedee a part of my share of the corporation. Look, she's in the field—she knew it was a good bet." He hesitated. "I won't be like Dad—always looking for something bigger. And I'll know when to jump off the bandwagon if things go bad. And you know," he joshed, "you're partially responsible for our getting into the business. The way you complain about the ugly toothpaste tubes. The other packages you make noises about. So I figured out ways to make them better—and our venture capitalists are sure we have something great going. And when you think about it, we're getting a graduate-level business education in this deal. Wow, would Dad be surprised!"

"If he ever finds out, don't let him muscle in," Helen ordered. Later she'd talk to Deedee about this. Right now her head was whirling with all that Zach had told her. Deedee had her feet on the ground business-wise. But Deedee had already invested in Zach's corporation. And this would never have happened if Paul hadn't walked out on his family.

Helen started when the phone rang. She reached to pick up. "Hello—"

"Hi. I miss you already," Adam said. "How long has it been? Close to an hour."

"About that," she said, oddly uncomfortable in talking with Adam in Zach's presence. *What am I to tell the kids about Adam?*

"Mom, I'm cutting out," Zach whispered. "I'll talk to you later."

"Adam, could you hold it a moment? Zach's here—he's about to leave—"

"Don't worry about me," Zach urged. "I'm going to be fine." He leaned over to kiss her, picked up his jacket and headed for the door.

"Adam, I just have to lock the door." She hurried after Zach. "I'm proud of you," she told him. "My nineteen-year-old entrepreneur."

Back on the phone she talked with Adam until he had another call coming in.

"I'll call you right back," he promised, excitement in his voice— anticipating a call from Mark. "Keep your fingers crossed—"

Helen paced about the small living room —anxious for Adam to call back. The phone rang. She picked up instantly.

"Hello—"

"Mark's been talking with his attorney contact out there. Neighbors told the guy that Zoe was away for the weekend—and that her apartment would be available for rental at the end of the month. I gather she made arrangements with moving people to store her furniture once she left." Adam took a deep breath. "Mark pulled strings— an hour ago he acquired an injunction to prevent her from leaving the country. He's already shipped it out by World Courier." That meant a person was boarding a plane to deliver the injunction in person, Helen realized. "Mark understood I wasn't concerned about the expense. His lawyer contact will serve it in the morning."

"Thank heaven for that." Helen felt a surge of relief. At the very least, they knew

Zoe wasn't taking Eric out of the country in the immediate future.

"At the same time," Adam pursued, "Mark's lawyer contact will approach her about the lump sum settlement." He sighed. "Knowing Zoe, she'll make it difficult. She'll have to discuss the arrangement with her lawyers. She'll try for a better deal. But with a little luck the deal will go through— and Eric will come to live with me."

"Hold on to that thought," Helen said tenderly.

"Of course, crazy things can happen," he conceded. "But I'll do whatever it takes to get custody of Eric. Unfortunately," he added wryly, "Zoe will be quick to realize that."

Earlier than normal Helen prepared for bed. It had been an exhausting day. But all at once she realized she'd said nothing to Zach when he was here about Paul's request for a "quickie" divorce—and imminent fatherhood. She'd been too startled by Zach's report about his business venture. Wow, wouldn't that rock his father! Nor had she said anything to Deedee, she remembered.

She glanced at the clock on her night table. Call Deedee now. She punched in Deedee's number, waited. Deedee wasn't picking up—the answering machine was spewing out its message. How could she tell an answering machine what she had to say?

"This is Mom," she recorded. "Call me when you get a chance."

Ten minutes later the phone rang. Helen reached to respond.

"Hello—"

"What's up, Mom?" Deedee asked.

"It's been a crazy weekend—" Helen sought for words. "I had a phone call yesterday morning from Jeff Madison. The lawyer who's handling the divorce," she explained.

"What did he want?" Caution lurked in Deedee's voice.

"He's been in communication with your father. Instead of waiting the long period before a New York divorce becomes final, your father wants a Mexican divorce—which he'd handle."

"Meaning he's the one who's suing?" Deedee demanded.

"I don't care about that," Helen dismissed this.

"Why the sudden rush?" Now Deedee was suspicious. "He's found a rich divorcée who's panting to pay his bills?"

"Not exactly," Helen explained. "His live-in companion—her name is Stephanie—just discovered she's pregnant."

"Oh my God! That means Zach and I will have a half-sister!"

"Or half-brother," Helen pointed out.

"That's gross!" A word Deedee hadn't used since she was fifteen.

"I told Jeff I'd agree. Not for your father or his pregnant girlfriend," Helen said with an ironic chuckle. "For the sake of the baby. Of course, I know—there are millions of single mothers in the world today. But let your father assume one responsibility for a change."

"Did you tell Zach?"

"Not yet." Helen recognized Deedee's outrage. Zach would feel the same way. Still, the new baby would be Zach and Deedee's half-sister or half-brother.

Why does this make me suddenly feel so old?

Thirty-Three

Helen had suspected the coming days would be tension-ridden. But by Tuesday of the second week she was exhausted. Adam walked about in a daze. Faxes were flying back and forth between Mark and Zoe's team of lawyers.

Adam stalked into Helen's office and closed the door. "She's crazy! Read her newest demands!" He threw the latest fax onto her desk.

"What does Mark say?"

"He thinks she's bluffing. Who does she think I am? Bill Gates? I can't pay that kind of money." He sighed. "I suppose I'll have to ante up more up front—"

"Adam, listen to Mark," Helen urged. "He knows how to deal in situations like this."

"What am I to say to Eric? He knows what's going on." Adam shook his head in frustration. "He called me again last night—the third time this week. He calls me when he's alone in the apartment. He wants to come to me."

"Zoe will retreat when she knows you won't go further." Helen strived for calm. "You're the only game in town, Adam."

"Suppose she just decides to resume everything the way it was—stay in California because she can't legally leave—and send Eric back to boarding school?"

"Adam, she wants to marry that boy she's living with. Give her a little more time—" He mustn't allow Zoe to bleed him dry.

"I'll tell Mark to keep negotiating," Adam said after a moment. "But if there's no breakthrough by the middle of next week, I'll have to cave—"

"Mark will make her see the light," Helen predicted. "Just give him a little more time."

"Have dinner with me tonight?" he urged. "The evening's clear—no business."

"I'd like that."

"Dinner at the apartment? We'll send out—"

"Perfect," she agreed.

"Stay over?" His eyes were an ardent plea.

She hesitated a moment. No need for her to sit at home and wait for phone calls, she derided. "I think that can be arranged."

"In the middle of all this craziness," he murmured, "I just want to hold you in my arms."

"I'll run home from the office to pick up a few things, then come over," she promised. She'd leave a message on Zach's answering machine and on Deedee's—"just touching base"—say that she would be out for the evening. Later she'd check to see if they'd left any messages.

"I can't wait," he whispered, his face suddenly seeming less tired.

"Sorry, but I'm afraid you'll have to." Her smile was luminous. "No playing during business hours."

The hours till she could leave the office dragged. Adam was trying so hard to conduct business with his usual high-powered skill, she thought with compassion. He probably hadn't had a decent night's sleep in days. But tonight, she promised herself, he would sleep well.

Adam left for an obligatory cocktail party at shortly before 5 p.m.

"I'll cut out no later than six," he told her.

"I'll be home by six thirty. We'll order in when you arrive."

Today Helen contrived to close the office only minutes after the others left. She decided to be a spendthrift, took a cab home. The flickering red light on her answering machine captured her immediate attention. The caller was Jeff Madison.

"I just heard from Paul. He's back in Silicon Valley. The divorce has gone through. You'll receive final papers in about three weeks. He said to tell you he's grateful you agreed to his going down to Mexico. He wishes you luck."

Oh, yes, he wishes me luck, she thought in derision. Almost twenty-five years of marriage, and now it was history. But she ought to be glad—she was free to spend her life as she wished. *I've been given a second chance.*

Adam knew about the Mexico divorce, she taunted herself. He said nothing about their marrying. Of course, they'd known each other such a little while. Was he content to let things ride as they were?

Why is it so difficult for me to accept this? We're into the twenty-first century—even celebrities publicly admit to living with lovers. But how will Deedee and Zach feel if—when— they find out?

Now Helen made her brief calls—neither Deedee nor Zach was home. How was Zach doing with his business? It all seemed so incredible at his age. She mustn't let him know how anxious she was. And what was happening with Deedee and Cliff? She mustn't be a nosey mother. Still, she worried. She'd always worry about the kids, wouldn't she? Even if she was ancient and they were senior citizens. It came with motherhood.

Packing an overnight bag with a blend of anticipation and guilt, she reminded herself that—once this business with Zoe was finalized—she must start thinking about how to locate another apartment. Deedee said she'd be in Todd's apartment for four months—but time had a way of speeding past. And the rental situation in the city was bizarre.

She brushed aside truant images of moving in with Adam. He hadn't suggested it, she rebuked herself. And she wasn't sure she was ready for that.

She arrived at Adam's apartment moments before he appeared. She was standing at the door waiting for him when an elevator opened on the floor and Adam strode towards her.

"I should give you a key," he apologized. "You had no trouble coming up?"

"The doorman seemed to remember me—he didn't ask questions." The doorman suspected they were having an affair, she thought with a flicker of amusement. Some-

331

thing Paul would never suspect. But the woman who was married to Paul wasn't the woman who was having an affair with Adam. They lived in different worlds. "How was the party?"

"The usual." He shrugged. "Everybody there had an axe to grind." He chuckled. "Including me." He unlocked the door, thrust it wide. "And what would you like for dinner? Seafood, something French, Italian?"

"What would you like?"

"Now don't play that game," he scolded. "You choose."

Instinctively Adam inspected his answering machine. No calls. Now he reached for the phone with one hand, picked up a handful of leaflets with the other. "Here're our choices. Pick, my love."

They contrived to brush aside all anxieties over dinner—eaten to a background of first Beethoven and Bach, then George Gershwin.

"I think Gershwin must have been a very passionate man," Adam said while they lingered over the fabulous tiramisu that had been briefly stored in the refrigerator. "How else could he have composed such passionate music?"

"I gave all my CDs—including a huge collection of Gershwin—to the Friends of the Library thrift shop," Helen recalled.

"Stupid of me—"

"We have my collection," he murmured. "I must send Liz a wild bonus check—for bringing you to me. How did I exist without you?"

"You were a workaholic—"

"I suppose I should put up coffee—" But his eyes sent a different message.

"Coffee can wait."

His hand reached across the table for hers. "I'll go out of my mind if I don't make love to you this minute—"

"We can't have that—now can we?" Her smile was dazzling.

Helen awoke first. Adam was asleep—one arm across her waist. It amazed her that she could feel so euphoric. The past twenty-five years—well, closer to twenty, she amended —had been a wasteland. She'd been sleep-walking all those years. Only half alive. But passionate love wasn't only for the very young.

She was conscious that Adam was stirring. He opened his eyes, smiled, reached for her.

"I think I've died and gone to heaven," he murmured.

"I should get up and dress," she said after a moment. "This is a working day—"

"In time," he said, pulling her close. "We have to make up for a lot of years."

It astonished her that she could feel such

passion in the morning. With Paul love-making had been a nocturnal affair, quick and silent. At times she'd felt like a prostitute he'd picked up on the street. Adam made her feel as though she was the favorite concubine of a mighty ruler of ancient times —who'd decided to make her his queen, she thought whimsically.

"I wish we could be together like this forever," Adam said, moving with a sensuous slowness that elicited faint sounds of pleasure from her. Knowing his hands would arouse her to heights she'd never known.

And then they were both caught up in the need to reach the ultimate moment of their merging. How wonderful, she thought in a corner of her mind, to feel such exquisite satisfaction. To share this with a man she loved more than she'd ever thought possible.

They lay tangled together in the cozy warmth of Adam's bedroom—reluctant to abandon this special parcel of time. But in a little while they'd come down to earth, Helen warned herself. Adam would be imprisoned by anxiety, worried about the outcome of his latest battle with Zoe.

"I'll make breakfast for us." At last Adam succumbed to reality. "By the time you're out of the shower, I'll be ready to serve." Unexpectedly he chuckled. "I suppose we shouldn't arrive at the office together—"

"You always come in later," she reminded. "You make calls here from the apartment."

"I curse the difference in time between here and the Coast," he confessed. "I know Mark's attorney out there will be asleep for another three hours. That makes mornings the worst time of day—except this morning."

Adam managed an atmosphere of lightness over breakfast, yet Helen was aware of his inner tension. In a way it was Eric who had brought them together—but would it be his concern for Eric that would ultimately keep them apart? Was there room in his life for her on a full-time basis?

Is there room in my life for Adam on a full-time basis?

Deedee was fighting against wakefulness when she heard the sound of a key in the door. Instantly she was conscious that she was in Cliff's apartment, in his bed. He'd been summoned to the hospital moments after they'd fallen asleep. Some emergency.

"Don't move—" He hovered at the bedroom door—already shucking his clothes. "I want to go to sleep beside you." He grinned. "Okay, you can get up when I'm asleep."

"It's almost 8 a.m.—did they truly need you all these hours?" she protested. That after a twenty-hour shift.

"I was needed." He crossed to the bed, stretched out beside her. "In another four months I'll be out of there. I can't wait."

"You're still undecided about which route to take?" she asked. He was inclined to go against the trend—as she was. There had to be more to life than working seventy or eighty hours a week. There had to be a feeling of satisfaction beyond the prospect of soaring salaries and exorbitant bonuses. "Well?" she prodded because she knew he was being pursued to join a highly successful practice.

"I made up my mind last night," he admitted. "There in the emergency room while we fought to save this young guy's life. I don't want to practice in a situation where the first words a prospective patient hears is, 'And what medical insurance do you have?' "

"So what's it going to be?"

"That little town upstate I told you about," he said gently. "Where my parents have this 1837 farmhouse that they run to every chance they get."

"Yes?" Cliff loved going there, she recalled. He kept saying he wanted her to go up with him one of these days.

"They desperately need a doctor. The only doctor in town has been practicing there for fifty-two years—he's pushing eighty and worrying about who'll take over when he can't handle the practice. He's never made a lot of money—but he's earned a lot of love and respect. And he's not one of the 100 Most Needy," Cliff added defensively.

"You told him you'll join him in practice," Deedee guessed.

"I said I'd have to discuss it first with the woman I hope to marry—"

"And who might that be?" Deedee asked, her heart pounding.

"Hey, don't play coy with me," he scolded. "Do we accept that practice or not?"

"We accept," she said.

He allowed himself a wide yawn. "All right—now I can go to sleep in peace."

Helen was surprised when Deedee called her at the office. It was a first—she always called at the apartment.

"I've accepted a temporary job," Deedee reported. "But there's more. Could we meet for an early dinner?"

"Not quite an 'early bird' dinner," Helen said, chuckling. "But barring the unexpected, I can meet you around six thirty." *What does Deedee mean—"There's more"?* She'd planned on having dinner as usual with Adam—but he'd understand.

"Six thirty will be great. Will North West be okay?"

"I'll see you there. Oh, if something bizarre comes up and I'll be late, where can

I call you?"

"I'll be at the apartment," Deedee told her—and Helen caught a hint of excitement in her voice. About the new job? Or something else?

Adam was in and out during the course of the day. He was nursing Kelly through yet another crisis, he reported. She was scheduled to leave in three days for a concert in Los Angeles. *"I can't be there on time—all of a sudden I'm scared to death of flying. I'll never make it by train!"* But as Adam pointed out when he arrived close to the end of the day, Kelly paid him for "special care."

"I need my high-paying clients," he reminded. "What with the way Zoe's acting up." But Helen sensed that more than Zoe's latest crisis was upsetting him now.

"Any new bulletins?" She tried to hide her anxiety.

"Zoe said she's speaking with Dean Andrews about taking Eric back in the school. His tuition was paid for this term. Mark thinks it's just a scare tactic, but how do we know?" he said with an air of desperation.

"You're on good terms with Dean Andrews," Helen recalled. "And you had the impression she dislikes Zoe. Why else would she have called to tell you Zoe had taken Eric out of the school?"

"So?" He was puzzled.

"Call her and ask if Zoe's been in contact," Helen urged. "Find out for sure that Zoe's grandstanding."

"God, you are smart," he marveled. "I'll do that right now."

Five minutes later Adam returned to Helen's office. "Guess what?" he gloated. "Dean Andrews hasn't heard a word from Zoe." He paused. "She wouldn't lie to me, would she?"

Thirty-Four

Adam struggled to focus on the campaign for a new client he'd just acquired. Damn! It was hellish to be creative when his mind was swamped with questions about how to deal with Zoe. Some people could compartmentalize their lives. He couldn't.

His private phone line rang. He reached to pick up.

"Yes?"

"Hi." It was Mark. "I've been on a long call with Meadows." Their West Coast attorney. "The private investigator he hired has come up with some interesting data. Meadows thinks there's a good chance we can prove Zoe is an unfit mother."

"No!" Adam was terse.

"Just listen to the facts," Mark soothed. "The PI said neighbors reported that Eric has not been attending school. School authorities have been on Zoe's back. It was probably the same neighbors who've been bitching about the noisy parties. Even now," he emphasized, "with Eric there—there're wild parties. It seems that the boy toy is dying to be the next new young screen lover. The parties are supposed to provide contacts. I don't know that we can prove it," Mark acknowledged, "but there was talk of drugs."

"We can't do that," Adam objected. "The authorities will bring in Eric. Question him. He's been through enough already." But the mention of drugs was unnerving.

"Then let Meadows go to Zoe, tell her to accept the new deal or you're withdrawing it."

"Mark, you know Zoe." Adam clutched at a new approach. "You went through the shitty divorce with me. Will you go out to the Coast, talk with her? I know, it'll be a lot of billing hours—but I can handle that. Mark, please. Go deal with Zoe yourself." Adam clutched the phone while Mark deliberated.

"Okay," Mark agreed. "I'll fly out tomorrow morning."

Adam sat motionless at his desk—staring

into space. He'd thought Zoe was too sharp to get involved in the drug scene. Or was that her young lover's deal? But now Eric was there with them—and he was terrified.

At 6 p.m. sharp—moments after the others on staff left the office— Helen prepared to leave. The door to Adam's office was open. He sat slumped at his desk. His face mirrored his dejection.

"I have to run to meet Deedee for dinner," Helen reminded him. "She'll probably have plans for later. Will you be here or at the apartment?"

"Probably here—" He forced a smile. "I have to work on the campaign for the new account." A major account. "I can't let the business go to hell."

"Let me order dinner sent up." She felt guilty at leaving him alone.

"I'm not hungry. I'll call later," he added because of her reproachful cluck.

"Zoe's got to stop playing this game soon," she consoled.

"I just had another call from Mark—"

"What did he say?"

Adam repeated Mark's report. "Zoe figures she can hold me up for more money. Mark knows how far I'll go." He took a deep breath, exhaled. "The question is, will it be enough to satisfy Zoe."

"Adam—" Helen's mind was charging

ahead. "Is there something else—something besides an insane amount of money—that you could offer Zoe?"

He stared blankly for a moment. "Like what?"

"I'm fishing," she admitted. "You said the man she's living with is trying for a film career. Is there anything you can do to help?"

"She's a 44-year-old woman trying to hang on to a 24-year-old hunk. I might be able to wangle an introduction to somebody out there—but it'll amount to nothing. I gather this guy—Tim—is big on muscle but small in talent." Then all at once he froze. His eyes radiated new hope. "Helen, you may have hit on it! Zoe would love to be able to offer him some plum. Like having his photo in a syndicated column with some woman celebrity. Kelly!" He snapped his fingers in triumph. "I'll tell Mark that if she goes along with my new offer, I guarantee to have Tim photographed with Kelly on the night of her major concert out there. Zoe will be in heaven." He paused. "Now all I have to do is convince Kelly she can fly out there and do the concert as scheduled. But first I'll call Mark—"

Helen was surprised to find Deedee already at a table at North West. Usually Deedee would rush in at the last moment. But she wasn't at the old job, Helen remembered. When she gave notice, they'd dumped her immediately. And now, she said, she was scheduled for a temporary job. What had she meant when she said, "There's more"?

"Hi, Mom." Deedee was radiant. That, Helen told herself, was reassuring.

"Have you been waiting long?" She always felt guilty at keeping anyone waiting for her.

"I just got here." Deedee flipped open the menu. "I'm starving."

The waiter arrived to take their orders. They made their choices—with an almost festive air on Deedee's part.

"Tell me about the new job," Helen ordered with an optimistic smile, but her eyes were probing.

"It's just for three months," Deedee explained. "The salary's little more than half of what I've been seeing, but I can deal." She took a deep breath. "I'm seeing Cliff again."

"Great." Helen exuded approval. "He's special."

"It took me a while to realize that. He knows about Todd, of course—I couldn't lie about that. It doesn't bother him." Her eyes glowed. "He'll be going into private practice in this little upstate town." *He's leaving New York?* "He'll be a partner for a while, then he'll take over. His partner's about eighty— he's been practicing up there for fifty-two years," Deedee said indulgently. "Mom, we're getting married over the July 4th weekend." Her eyes begged for approval.

"Darling, that's wonderful!" *How far upstate?* "We'll have to start planning the wedding—"

"Just family," Deedee insisted. "Cliff feels the same way. So we've got plenty of time."

"I'm so happy for you." Her baby getting married!

"I warned Cliff—if he tries to divorce me in twenty or thirty years, I'll put arsenic in his coffee." Deedee's face tightened. "I'll never forgive Dad for what he did to you."

"I don't want you to feel that way," Helen insisted.

"I don't want my kids to grow up the way Zach and I did," Deedee began, then paused. "Mom, you were great," she said quickly because Helen's face betrayed her shock. "You were always there for us. But the family always came in second with Dad. The big thing in his life was the career."

"Maybe it was the times," Helen said uncertainly. "When you two were kids, parents thought it was urgent to fight for the material things. That was a sign that you cared about your kids—" But deep in her heart she, too, had rebelled. She hadn't realized that Deedee and Zach felt that way, too. Better a smaller house, a less expensive car, less fancy toys and a father who was present in their lives. Not a weekend fixture. "Maybe I should have fought with your father to give us more of himself. To be more of a presence in our lives."

"Nobody would win with Dad," Deedee derided. "I remember times when you argued with him about being at a birthday party or finding time to be at a school play or a soccer game. You didn't have a chance—"

"You've got your head on straight, my darling. You've learned the right values."

"Cliff feels that way, too," Deedee said with satisfaction. "Maybe I was chasing after the big money and the important title to show Dad I could do it," she admitted. "But that was crazy."

Should she tell Deedee about Adam? Would she be upset? It wouldn't change their relationship. "You might say your father did me an enormous favor in asking for a divorce." She was conscious of Deedee's shock at this assessment. "I told myself it was a good marriage. It stopped being that by the time you were four. I thought that's the way marriages were after the passage of time." She hesitated, prodded herself into pursuing this. "I'm seeing somebody, Deedee. A wonderful man."

For a moment Deedee gazed at her in amazement. "Mom, that's terrific!" Yet Helen sensed her ambivalence.

"He's been divorced for nine years. He has

a darling fourteen-year-old son."

"Is this serious?" Deedee asked after a moment—still encased in astonishment. *How will Zach take this?*

"Well, we've only known each other since just before Christmas," Helen hedged. *Adam talks about our spending the rest of our lives together—but does that include marriage?* "We're just—playing it by ear."

"Have fun," Deedee urged. "You deserve it."

"I'm absolutely stunned by this business of Zach's." Helen searched for safer ground. "I know so little about the Internet. And Zach's so young."

"I'm the older crowd now." Deedee giggled. "These kids are digging in so young! Of course—" she was all at once serious, "a lot of the dot-coms will fall by the wayside in six months or a year. But I can't get over it—my baby brother and his buddies raising four million in venture capital!" She paused, seeming all at once self-conscious. "There won't be many investment banking companies in that tiny town where Cliff and I will be living, so I might just do something on the Internet myself. Not with that kind of capitalization," she conceded. "Maybe selling from a website. Anyhow, it all sounds exciting."

"You said a town upstate. How far upstate?" Already Helen felt a sense of loss that Deedee would be out of the city. But these days—sadly—families were so often separated by long distances.

"It's just under two hundred miles," Deedee said gently. "On the Vermont border. We can drive it in four hours. We'll come down often—and you'll come up. And Zach will be chasing up for ski weekends," she guessed. "It's a short drive to the slopes." She paused, seeming in some inner debate. "We don't need to mention the wedding to Dad, do we?"

"We don't even have his address," Helen reminded. "And I gather he'll be otherwise occupied."

How strange to think of Paul with a young, pregnant wife. But that was part of yesterday. Still, the baby his wife was carrying was Deedee and Zach's sister or brother. Would they ever know their half-sister or half-brother? It was a disturbing thought.

Helen glanced at her watch after seeing Deedee off to meet Cliff. It was minutes before 8 p.m. Call Adam. See if he's had dinner yet.

She looked about for a public telephone. Sooner or later she'd succumb to a cell phone, she admitted to herself. There, across the street were a pair of public phones.

Adam answered on the first ring. "Hello."

347

An urgency in his voice.

"Have you had dinner yet?" Helen asked.

"I've been too busy. Where are you?"

"On the West Side. I'll hop in a cab and come over. Would you like Italian or Chinese?"

"Surprise me—"

"You're taking your life in your hands," she warned.

"I've never had it so good," he murmured. "In some ways—"

"You talked to Mark?" Again she felt his anxiety.

"Yes. Now I'm trying to get hold of Kelly. She's got this habit of not answering the phone even when she's home if she's in a rotten mood. And she turns off the answering machine."

"Let me get your dinner. I should be there in fifteen minutes. It's well past the rush hour."

Adam was on the phone when she arrived at the office. He pantomimed that Mark was on the line. While he talked, she brought out a plate and flatware from the small supply Adam kept in the office. How like Adam to provide this amenity, she thought while she removed the gourmet ravioli and the salad from paper containers.

"I'm working on it, Mark," Adam emphasized. "I think I can get Kelly there for the concert—and arrange for Zoe's boy toy to be her escort at the after-concert party. Kelly owes me," he said with an edge of desperation. "And it might just be the catnip to put this deal across. I want Eric here with me," he stressed. "He needs to be with me. Mark, don't fail me!"

Thirty-Five

In Kelly's starkly modern penthouse living room Adam sat on a corner of her oversized white leather sofa and made a pretense of listening to her melodramatic explanation about why she couldn't keep her concert engagement in Los Angeles. Mark's voice echoed in his mind:

"Adam, that was a brainstorm—offering to get the creep's photo in a syndicated newspaper column with a quote about his being Kelly's new love interest." He hadn't promised the "love interest" quote, but Kelly would go along with that.

"You'll make them understand," Kelly declared with outstretched arms. "I can't possibly climb aboard a plane the way I feel about flying!"

"Kelly, they won't understand." His voice was calm, as always in these scenes with her.

How many times had he battled with her to fill contractual obligations? But this time was different. He had a personal stake in this concert. "Still, if you feel that it's time to move out of the spotlight, give up your career, then what can I say? I want you to be happy, Kelly." A touch of paternal affection in his voice now.

"What do you mean?" All at once she was defensive. "Why would I give up my career?"

"Because if word gets around that you've walked out on a sold-out concert, nobody will touch you again." Her agent had thrown up his hands and tossed the problem into his hands. How many times had they gone through this same routine? Dear God, let it work again. "You might still be able to pick up a TV commercial somewhere along the line—but nobody will want to take a chance on you again." His eyes held hers. "And that makes me sad, Kelly—because you could have a marvelous career ahead of you. But if you can't deal with it emotionally—" He gestured eloquently.

"I have my recording contract!" She clutched at this.

"The big boys will find a way out of it. Kelly, you can't walk out on a concert and survive. Do you know how many great careers have been aborted because of something like that?"

"But I can't fly," she whimpered. "I just can't."

"You can," he insisted. "You've got that emergency phone number for your shrink," he reminded. "Call him." Even though it was close to 10 p.m. "Tell him you must see him tonight. He has to help you through this fear." Kelly wasn't afraid of flying—she was shrieking for attention. In the four years that he'd been her public relations man he'd learned this—and catered to her needs. "Kelly, call Dr Ross!"

"Will you fly out with me?" She was at the pouting stage now—that battle was half-won.

"I have to stay here and set up coverage for the concert—I have to be in New York to work for you," he emphasized. "And while you're out there, I have a small assignment as a special favor to me. There's this gorgeous hunk who's mad about you—"

Kelly listened avidly to his build up. She had a weakness for "gorgeous hunks." Barring a slip-up, Adam soothed himself, he could deliver what Mark was promising Zoe. Now get the hell out of here and back to his office. Helen was waiting there in the event Mark called.

Ignoring the drink in his hand, Mark sat across the table from Zoe and Tim on the terrace of her rented guest cottage in

351

exclusive Bel Air and waited for his words to sink in. For an instant he caught a glimpse of Eric at the slider. Eric was bright—he knew this meeting concerned him. Then Eric was gone—back to the computer in his tiny bedroom, Mark surmised. It was always the kids who suffered the most in divorce cases, he thought compassionately.

Zoe sucked noisily on her frozen Margarita while she pondered over Adam's addition to his offer. Tim stared in abject wonder. This was a dream situation. A bit player hitting the columns with a bigtime vocalist.

"How will Tim get in to the concert?" Zoe broke the heavy silence with an air of disbelief. "It's sold out! Who's going to pay for his date with Kelly Olson?"

"I'll pick up a pair of house seats, always held for Kelly." Zoe lifted an eyebrow in momentary amusement. So she could attend with Tim? "I'll arrange for Tim to meet Kelly before the concert, to pick her up afterwards. She'll sign any tabs. She'll even take you home in her limo," he told Tim.

"Why is Adam willing to do this?" Zoe shook her head in disbelief. "I don't buy it, Mark."

"He knows it'll be important to you." Mark decided on bluntness. "And he wants Eric—in a deal that he can handle." Meaning, don't expect the money to rise—but here was a choice deal-sweetener.

"Baby, me on the town with Kelly Olson!" Tim exuded pleasurable anticipation. "My name in the columns—you know how important that could be to my career!"

"I don't trust Adam." Zoe remained suspicious.

"Zoe!" Tim was growing apoplectic.

"Mark, you tell Adam I'll sign the agreement provided Eric will come to me for the week after Christmas, the Easter weekend, and a month in the summer. *And* if you add this business about the 'public relations' deal for Tim. Plus he agrees to a $50,000 penalty if Tim doesn't make the columns with Kelly Olson and I have full custody of Eric."

Mark debated for only a moment. Why not agree to the visits? A hundred to one she'd be otherwise occupied. And in a little over three years Eric would be eighteen. A free man. No doubt in his mind that Kelly would fulfill her obligation. "We've got a deal, Zoe."

Helen and Adam heard the shrill ring of his phone as he slid the key into the apartment door lock.

"It's Mark," Adam guessed—clumsy in his rush. It was just 8 p.m. on the Coast.

"He'll hang on," Helen soothed. "Relax."

353

Adam was so on edge, exhausted from the strain of these last days. Each time Eric managed a furtive phone call, Adam died a little.

By the time they charged into the apartment, the ringing had stopped. They heard the message Mark was recording. Adam had a deal with Zoe. In forty-eight hours Eric could be on a New York-bound plane.

"Oh Adam, this is wonderful!" Helen glowed.

"Just a simple little thing like the date with Kelly—and I'm getting Eric," Adam marveled. Now he forced himself to be realistic. "I'm getting Eric provided everything goes on schedule."

"It will. Kelly's not going to back out on the publicity stunt you set up. And you said her devious little mind loves the thought that you'll be beholden to her."

"There's so much to do!" Adam sighed, stared into space as though grappling with disaster. "Eric will have to be registered at school here in the city. How will I get him into a private school in mid-term? I remember what I went through to get him into nursery school. I'll—"

"Cool it," Helen ordered. "There may have been dropouts. Families who've moved away from the city. I'll get a list of all schools, make calls. Somehow, you'll get him registered."

Adam reached to pull her close, as though to seek strength from her. "You've been through this business of raising kids. You know what I have to do. And Eric's room," he pinpointed. "I must refurnish it. It was just a guest room before—now it'll be Eric's room. A room that says, 'a teenaged boy lives here.' Helen, you'll have to help me. I can't mess up on this."

"I'll help you," she promised.

Long after he and Helen had made love, Adam lay awake. She was being so wonderful about Eric, he told himself—but was he setting himself up to lose her? She'd raised her kids. Would she be willing to accept a package deal: Eric and himself?

He'd promised her he wouldn't rush her. He knew what trauma she'd been through with her divorce. But they both knew they'd found something very special.

I don't want to lose her. But I have obligations to Eric. The moment Zoe told me she was putting Eric in boarding school, I sensed trouble ahead. He was so unhappy there.

Through the years Eric has given wistful— plaintive—hints that he wanted to spend more time with me. I agonized over this. I didn't dare to try for full custody. I was convinced if I did, Zoe would go into court and say that he wasn't my son—I had no right to him. I couldn't bear to have Eric know that he wasn't mine.

355

How strange—and wonderful—that it was Helen who made me understand that Zoe had been lying to me all these years. Eric's my child. She lied for power over me because she knew how much I loved him. I don't need to try for a DNA test—I know Eric's mine. And I owe that to Helen.

But once I understood, knew that I have a right to fight for full custody, I put my future with Helen in jeopardy. She's so warm and loving with Eric—but will she take on the package of me plus Eric?

Thirty-Six

Helen knew the next forty-eight hours would be traumatic. She hadn't known how traumatic. She was relieved that—at her urging—Adam had spoken to the semi-retired housekeeper who came to his apartment twice a week to clean, do the laundry, pick up dry cleaning and handle other small tasks. She was delighted to expand her schedule to five afternoons a week and to remain to cook and serve dinner.

"I know it's going to be rough to clear my schedule," Adam had said determinedly, "but Eric and I will sit down to dinner together every night. Like a real family." She'd felt a sudden wall coming up between Adam and her. "And you'll dine with us often—"

There was little time to consider what Eric's arrival would mean to her relationship with Adam. Now she was pursuing the one open place in a private school on Eric's behalf. Frenziedly Adam was calling friends who might be helpful. All this, she thought, to get a fourteen-year-old boy into a good school.

She and Adam were searching furniture stores where floor samples—suitable for Eric's room—were available for immediate delivery.

"He'll have to have a computer," Adam realized. "Why didn't I think of that?"

"It's on order," Helen told him. "You said, 'get whatever a fourteen-year-old would want in his bedroom.' So I thought of Zach at fourteen and knew a computer was a 'must.'"

On the day of the concert—moments after she arrived in the office— Helen received a phone call from Liz. She wasn't surprised— she knew Adam was keeping Liz apprised of the situation with Zoe.

"We're keeping our fingers crossed," she told Liz, and explained the deal about to be consummated.

"And Adam's a nervous wreck," Liz guessed. "Scared to death something will go awry."

"How's your mother?" Helen asked, always sympathetic.

There was a faint pause. "I dread the thought—" Liz's voice was suddenly anguished. "But she's reaching the point where she needs around-the-clock supervision. The doctor told me yesterday—it's a matter of weeks before she'll have to go into a nursing home."

Helen focused on consoling words, but she was falling apart inside. When Liz's mother went into a nursing home, then Liz would expect to return to her job. *But I won't think about that now.*

She was glad that business calls required close attention. The others arrived. Linda brought her coffee. She was caught up in office routine. Adam phoned in just before 10 a.m.

"I'll be in around noon," he reported. "I'm at the Plaza—I'm having a business breakfast." Helen understood it had to do with publicity about Kelly's concert. "If something urgent comes up, call me on the cell phone."

"Right."

Off the phone she remembered a message on her answering machine yesterday. Zach had acquired a cell phone—he wanted to give her the number. Was Zach becoming one of those people who rushed down the street with a cell phone clutched to his ear? It was startling sometimes to hear the intimate details of a stranger's life.

Deedee had told her that her cleaning woman had a cell phone. She'd thought this was the newest toy of the affluent.

"The poor use it because they have no credit and can't put down a big chunk of money for a deposit with a phone company," Deedee explained. "And then, my cleaning woman told me, she got her first bill and nearly had a heart attack at the size of it. She hadn't stopped to figure out the costs. Still," Deedee had commiserated, "she's keeping it for emergencies—and trying to convince her kids it's for super-emergencies."

At noon Adam arrived, settled in Helen's office—the door closed.

"Everything seems under control," he reported, striving for optimism. "But with Zoe—and with Kelly—anything can happen." He shook his head as though exhausted. "This whole scene seems unreal. But if Eric comes to me, it's worth whatever it costs in time, effort, and money."

She hadn't told Adam about Liz's call this morning, Helen thought guiltily. But he had enough on his mind now. Would he be happy at the realization that Liz might be ready to return to the office in a few weeks? Life seemed painfully complicated. If Liz returned, would there be a place for her in the office? Again she asked herself, will there be room in Adam's life for me once Eric is here?

A few minutes later Helen was startled by the knock at her door. Normally, Linda or the others would knock and immediately enter. No more. They sensed there was something more than business between Adam and her, she suspected—and they approved.

"Yeah—"

Linda opened the door and came into the office, handed Adam several letters to be signed, smiled saucily at Helen.

"Get them out today." Adam was terse. Self-conscious because, he, too, knew the others suspected a romantic connection between the two of them.

"Mail always goes out the same day." Linda was reproachful, yet Helen sensed she was not truly annoyed. "I think it's great about Eric coming to live with you. We all do."

"Thank you—" Adam smiled. "And if I'm bitchy these days, you should understand," he added with mock gruffness.

"Sure thing, Boss."

Tonight Helen made a point of stalling over

dinner in Adam's favorite neighborhood restaurant. The three hours difference in time meant Kelly's concert wouldn't begin for another three hours. Earlier Adam had talked with her agent.

"Everything's on schedule, everybody in place," he'd reported. "And that's a small miracle."

"Let's go home," Adam said at last. Helen smiled. *He makes it sound as though it's our home.* "I know—it's morbid to think Kelly might pull some last minute craziness," he conceded. "Still, I want to be reachable."

"Everything is in place, you said," Helen reminded. "Zoe has the tickets for the concert. Tim has talked with Kelly's assistant about where he's to pick Kelly up for their 'date.' The reservations have been made for the post-concert party."

"I'm sweating out that photo of Kelly and Tim," Adam admitted, signaling their waiter for the check. "There'll be a couple of lines about her 'new romance' in the newspaper column. Everything looks right—"

"A very brief romance." *Is that all I'm to have with Adam?*

Unexpectedly Adam chuckled. "Wouldn't it be a wild joke on Zoe if it wasn't a 'brief romance.'"

The night air hinted of spring, lent an atmosphere of change. The driver's radio played a medley of Cole Porter songs as they seated themselves.

"I don't know how I would have survived these days without you." Adam reached for her hand.

"The worst is over," she comforted. "With any luck at all, Zoe will put Eric on a plane some time tomorrow or the next day." Was that her place in Adam's life? To see Adam through the bad days? Was she still on the old track of trying to be helpful? Was she—and Adam—mistaking gratitude for love?

It was going to be a rough evening, she warned herself when they arrived at the apartment. In truth, not until the morning newspapers came out—with the column item Adam was committed to arrange—would they know that Eric would soon be New York-bound.

"I'll put up coffee." Adam rose to his feet.

"I'll do it," Helen said and smiled wryly. "We don't have to worry about being kept awake tonight."

"You don't have to stay up with me—you can nap."

"I'm staying up." She trailed off into the kitchen. How many pots of coffee had she put up through the years in moments of stress?

She found a minor comfort in grinding beans, taking the routine steps before switching on the coffee-maker. She glanced up to see Adam beside her. She knew so well that amorous glow in his eyes.

"The coffee'll be ready in a few minutes—"

"To devil with it." He reached for her. "I have another—a very special—hunger."

"I'll turn off the coffee," she whispered.

How will I survive if Liz returns to the office and I have to leave? And so much of Adam's life will be tied up with Eric now. What room will he have in his life for me?

"Helen?" Solicitude in Adam's voice as they walked together to the bedroom. "Are you all right?"

"I'm fine," she declared.

Don't worry now—when tomorrow comes I'll deal.

Thirty-Seven

Dozing on the sofa, Helen stirred, became aware that Adam was speaking with someone. She forced her eyes open, saw him talking into the living room phone. Instantly she was wide awake.

"Thanks for calling," Adam wound up in an aura of relief and put down the phone. "Wow!"

"Mark?" Helen asked, on her feet now.

"Mark's on a plane bound for New York." Adam chuckled. "That was Claudia, Kelly's assistant. The concert was a huge success. Kelly's en route to the post-concert party— with Tim. And tomorrow there should be several photos—not just the one I expected. Kelly was playing it big—all over Zoe's hunk. It's over—the damn nightmare is over. I'm getting Eric."

Helen glowed. "That's wonderful!"

"None of this would have happened without you—" He reached to draw her close.

"Call Zoe in the morning. Morning California time," she amended. *Is it love or gratitude Adam feels for me? Will I ever know for sure?* "Tell her to schedule Eric's flight, and let you know when to pick him up at the airport."

Adam glanced at his watch. "We'd better hit the sack. Tomorrow's a business day."

"I napped," she pointed out. "Sleep late in the morning. You're all clear until lunch time," she recalled. "You're having lunch at the Four Seasons."

Late in the afternoon Linda reported there was a call for Adam from his ex-wife.

"Shall I give her his cell phone number?"

"No," Helen said, per Adam's instructions. He wanted to avoid a direct communication with Zoe. "I'll take the call."

"Hello, Adam is out on an appointment."

She struggled to sound impersonal. "He suggested you leave a message with me."

"You're not Liz," Zoe said warily.

"Liz is on leave," Helen explained. "I'm her replacement." Now there was silence on the other end. "If you're calling regarding Eric's plane flight, I'll make sure Adam receives the information."

"I suppose that'll be all right." Zoe was cold. "Here's his flight number and arrival time—"

Helen realized she was trembling when she got off the phone with Zoe. This was the woman who'd caused Adam so many years of anguish. She'd wanted to lash out at her. But as Adam had said, the nightmare was over. Tomorrow at this time Adam would be driving out to JFK to collect his son. The following day Adam would take Eric to the private school where he was to be enrolled.

Over a late dinner Adam was consumed by anxiety. "Do you think I should take a week off from the office?" His eyes searched Helen's. "It seems so callous just to dump him at the school—and not see him until dinner. He doesn't know his way around Manhattan," he added in fresh apprehension.

"The school is a simple, five-minute walk to your apartment," she soothed, as she might a small child. "Eric is almost fifteen—you don't need to be there to hold his hand.

He'll come to the apartment, and Mrs Mc-Ardle will be there." The warm, motherly housekeeper. "She'll give him milk and a piece of fruit. Occasionally," she added with a chuckle, "she'll give him a cookie." Mrs McArdle made it clear that she agreed with her dentist that "cookies are bad for the teeth."

"Will you have dinner with us tomorrow night?"

"No," she rejected. "Not his first night home. Not until Saturday," she stipulated. "He'll need you all to himself for a couple of days. It won't be easy for him to settle into this new life—no matter how much he wants it. A new school, new friends, a new home—"

Adam nodded. "As usual, you're right."

Adam left the office shortly before 3 p.m. to drive out to JFK to collect Eric. His appointments for the afternoon had been rescheduled. Helen was conscious of a disconcerting sense of loss. She wouldn't be seeing Adam this evening. She hadn't realized how her waking hours revolved around him.

Later in the afternoon she remembered to call Liz and tell her Eric was in New York. Adam had taken a moment at the airport to "check the office" and tell her Eric's flight had been on schedule. She dreaded talking with Liz—because she knew that soon Liz would report that her mother had been moved to the nursing home. *And where does that leave me?*

Her life was beginning to fall apart again, she told herself in the following few days. At any time Liz would announce her return to the office. Adam was devoting himself to getting Eric settled in. He brought Eric to the office for a brief visit. It was clear Eric was the center of his life. And it should be that way, Helen told herself defensively. This was his son. But what lay ahead for Adam and her—if anything?

She had dinner with Deedee and Cliff on Friday evening. Both insisted that arranging wedding plans could be put off for weeks. They were more concerned about driving up this weekend to the small town where they were to live and to look around for a house to buy.

"My folks will make the down-payment," Cliff explained. "That's their wedding present. And we expect you to buy us our coffee-maker." Helen understood—he didn't want her to worry because she couldn't be as generous as his parents. What a sweet young man.

The following evening—Saturday—she was to have dinner with Adam and Eric.

"Eric says we don't have to go to a vegetarian restaurant," Adam had reported in high spirits. "He says he can order vege-tarian at a 'regular restaurant.' "

Saturday each hour seemed endless. Gerry and Sheila had driven out to Montauk for the weekend. Deedee and Cliff were driving upstate. Around noon she phoned Zach—just to hear his voice. He wasn't at the dorm. She was recurrently uneasy about his business dealings. Four young kids handling all that money!

She decided to run out for a quick lunch—just to get out of the apartment for a little while. Adam and Eric wouldn't be picking her up until 6 p.m. Thank God, Eric seemed happy with his new living arrange-ments.

Over a Western omelet and decaf, she fought off yawns. Maybe she should have had regular coffee, she thought with a flicker of amusement. What Zach called "the real thing." She glanced at her watch. Adam and Eric wouldn't be over for hours. Take a short nap when she returned to the apart-ment.

A sharp wind was blowing by the time she left the coffee shop. The temperature was dropping. In the apartment she went around closing the windows that she had opened earlier because the day had begun almost springlike. In the bedroom the calen-dar lay on the floor. She bent to pick it up.

Staring at the date, she frowned. All at

once she realized she was ten days late—
that never happened. Was she going menopausal? Women her age did go into the
menopause—it wasn't shockingly early. But
she'd figured that was still several years
away.

All right, forget about that for now—
stretch out and nap. But a startling possibility edged into her thoughts. No, she
couldn't be pregnant—that was absurd. At
forty-six? So she and Adam had been careless—they assumed there was no need to
take precautions at her age. Was there?

She kicked off her shoes, lay down on the
bed. She was menopausal—so what? It was
part of the process of growing older. It
wasn't a tragedy.

But despite her drowsiness she lay awake.
Her mind overactive. All right, stop this
nonsense, she ordered herself. Go down to
the drugstore, buy one of those pregnancy
tests. *There's no way I can be pregnant!*

Fighting self-consciousness, she went out
again, searched on the drugstore shelves for
her quarry. This was stupid, a waste of
money, she chastised herself. A woman in
the aisle saw her linger before the packaged
tests, smiled. *She probably thinks I'm worrying about a teenaged daughter who might be
pregnant.*

Twenty minutes later she stood in the
bathroom in shock. The test was positive. It

said she was pregnant. But tests were notoriously wrong on occasion. She wavered for a few moments, then decided to go down and buy another test. Put her mind at rest.

Go to another drugstore. Maybe there was a rash of inaccurate tests in the first drugstore—a whole batch that was bad. And yet she remembered the avid discussion she'd heard between two women on the bus yesterday morning—about a romance writer who'd had a child at fifty-two. She remembered the movie star who'd had a baby at fifty-two.

Her heart pounding, she repeated the test. Dizzy with shock, she checked the results. Positive. Her mind shot back through the years—when she was pregnant with Deedee, then with Zach. She'd remembered the drowsiness in the very early weeks. Like now.

I'm pregnant. I'm not menopausal. I'm pregnant.

Thirty-Eight

At a few minutes before 6 p.m. Adam and Eric arrived.

"We're starving," Adam announced. "We slept late, had a light breakfast at the apartment, and we've been traipsing around the South Street Seaport ever since."

"It was cool," Eric approved.

"Then let's go eat," Helen said, on impulse reaching to hug Eric. He sopped up affection like the proverbial sponge, she thought tenderly. "Just let me get my coat."

In an atmosphere of conviviality they left the apartment and headed for the restaurant Adam had chosen. Eric was spilling over with talk about school. For all his shyness, Helen thought with relief, he was fitting in. Adam's life would settle into a comfortable pattern, she told herself—and then reality took over.

He would be horrified when she told him she was pregnant. That was the way Zoe had hooked him into marriage. But she'd make it clear she wasn't trapping him. They'd handle the situation like two mature people.

But this would remove her forever from Adam's life, she thought in anguish.

She was grateful that Eric was so talkative over dinner. Little in the way of conversation was required of her. And Adam glowed. He was going to be devastated when she told him she was pregnant. He'd blame himself for being careless.

Still, she had to tell him. He had to know that this could happen. But she'd make him understand that she realized they could handle the situation. She remembered that Liz said he'd helped Kelly through two abortions. *"Kelly has a talent for getting involved with the wrong men."* So this time it would be on a personal level.

But dizzying possibilities crept into her thoughts as they lingered over dessert and coffee. *I want this baby. It's part of Adam and me—all I'll ever have of him. He'll have Eric—and I'll have our baby.*

Already she felt a towering love for this baby they'd created. So she'd be a single mother. Other such women managed. She refused to confront the problems that lay ahead. As Gerry always said, "Live one day at a time."

"Let's pick up the Sunday *Times* and go home and read," Adam suggested when they'd left the restaurant. "I admit it—I just want to sit down again. My feet are killing me."

"I won't stay long," Helen warned. "I woke up so early this morning. Some garbage truck was grinding away right beneath my window," she fabricated. "I'll be falling on my face by nine thirty."

But for a little while she wallowed in the pleasure of sprawling with Adam on his sofa while they pretended to fight over sections of the *Times*. Eric was at the computer in his bedroom. Adam seemed so content, she thought. But he didn't know about the bombshell she would drop at his feet.

When would she tell Adam? Monday at the office, she decreed—when the others were gone. He'd have no responsibilities. Somehow, she'd manage. She banished from her mind—with uncharacteristic impracticality—the financial problems that lay ahead.

Fleetingly she wavered when she considered the reactions of Deedee and Zach. They'd be sure she'd lost her mind. Perhaps that this was in retaliation to Paul for his becoming a father again. It wasn't like that. *This is Adam's baby and mine. I won't be losing Adam totally—I'll have our baby.*

At moments past nine thirty—stifling yawns— Helen announced it was time for her to leave.

"I'll drive you home." Adam rose to his feet.

"I can take a taxi," she brushed this aside.

"No, you can't take a taxi," he insisted. "I'm driving you home."

Helen said a warm good-night to Eric, went with Adam to the basement garage where he kept his black Mercedes. In the darkness of the car he reached to kiss her.

"Eric thinks you're the greatest thing since he discovered computers," he told her.

Despite her sleepiness, she lay awake until dawn. Again, she asked herself if both pregnancy tests were wrong. Was this all a stupid nightmare? Then reason intervened. She was pregnant. And she was going to have this baby to see her through the years ahead. Adam's life would revolve around Eric. Her life would revolve around their baby.

She was at a solitary breakfast when Adam called.

"Hi. I wish it was Monday already, and we'd be together at the office. I miss you—"

"I miss you, too." But by Monday evening he would feel differently. He had gone through such hell with Zoe—and here was the same situation again. Only she had no intention of dragging him into an unwanted marriage. He'd said so often that he wished them to spend the rest of their lives together. He'd never said, "Let's get married." And now he had Eric—and he needed nothing else.

"Dinner this evening?" His eyes hopeful.

"No," she rejected, but her tone was gentle. "The weekend belongs to Eric."

She spent the remainder of the day taking care of mundane needs—cleaning the apartment, doing laundry, running down to the produce place to shop. But her mind was haunted by the anticipation of a confrontation with Adam.

She had health insurance from the office, would be able to continue to hold it for eighteen months—so her medical bills would be covered. The current job market was so great she'd be able to find another job—though probably with a steep drop in salary, work till close to delivery time. Women did that these days.

All right—she couldn't afford to stay in the apartment. Unless she took in a roommate. With the insane rents people doubled up these days. Two strangers were sharing studios. *Play it by ear. I can handle this situation.*

So her precious baby would never know his father. How much did Decdee and Zach see of Paul through their growing up years? She would be mother and father—and part of Adam would be with her.

Her head was in such a whirl. Nothing she said made real sense, she scolded herself. But she couldn't put Adam through a repetition of his marriage to Zoe. He'd grow to hate her. She couldn't bear that.

He had Eric now. He realized that Eric was his child. How could he have thought otherwise? His life would be full. Without her. Without their child. Liz said it was a matter of weeks before she'd have to put her mother in a nursing home. Liz would be back in the office. She would move out of Adam's life. They would have been two ships that passed in the night.

Helen awoke after a night of broken slumber. She had to go into the office today and pretend nothing had changed. She must gear herself to put Adam at a distance. Before she began to show, she must be out of the office. Adam was all wrapped up in Eric—he'd barely notice at first that they were moving apart.

Again, she tried to envision Deedee and Zach's reaction. They'd be upset—but they'd understand. They'd be with her. She'd refuse to tell them who was the father. They'd respect that. Gerry and Sheila would be with her. They might suspect Adam—but they wouldn't pry.

Battling tiredness, she prepared for the day. Adam understood they couldn't be together every evening—not now, with Eric in the apartment. Not with Eric in his life full time. Oh, she would miss the closeness they'd shared these last weeks!

She arrived at the office at her usual hour,

settled at her desk to check Adam's schedule. He'd be making phone calls from home in the morning, call her to see what was happening at the office. Then he was scheduled for lunch at Michael's with Kelly's record people. Despite all the talk about the very short business lunches these days, he'd be with Kelly's people for a solid two hours. It would be close to three before he came to the office.

Linda sauntered in a few minutes before ten.

"Coffee?" she asked and Helen nodded. "You had a good weekend," Linda said and giggled. "You've got a special glow about you this morning."

Helen was startled. Her mind darted back through the years, to that special period when she'd just discovered she was pregnant for the first time. A neighbor had said, "You've got a special glow about you this morning," and then had asked with pleased suspicion, "Are you pregnant?"

"I got a good night's sleep," she fabricated. "The garbage truck didn't wake me before 5 a.m."

"I bitch about the subway ride from Queens," Linda admitted. "But I get to live in a private house with trees and grass and quiet." Now she giggled. "And the rent I pay my folks would just about cover my Con Ed bill if I had my own apartment in

Manhattan."

"Did I hear you say something about coffee?"

"Coming right up," Linda chirped.

As Helen had anticipated, Adam called in at eleven—on his private line, which meant they could talk in privacy.

"Hi, honey—" A lilt in his voice that said "all's right with the world." "Anything I need to know?"

Helen briefed him on activities in the office. She struggled to sound as though this was just another day in their lives.

"Eric told me at breakfast that he's joining some after-class activities at the school. I guess that means he's settling in."

"It does," she agreed, aware that her heart was pounding. "He'll tell you about it at dinner tonight. It's great that you're determined to keep the evenings clear—that you'll be sitting down to dinner with him every night." That had rarely happened with Paul, she remembered. How many commuting fathers sat down to dinner with their kids?

"I want so much to be a good father." He paused for a moment. "Zoe used to taunt me, tell me I wasn't capable of giving her a child. And all those years I believed her. I was convinced I was sterile."

"No!" Helen rejected in fresh rage. "That's not true!"

"Anyhow, I managed to produce Eric—"

"Adam, I'm pregnant—"

She froze in shock. How had that slipped out? *I'm out of my mind!*

Thirty-Nine

Pale with shock, Helen clung to the phone. The moment before Adam spoke seemed a century.

"Cancel my lunch date," he ordered. "I'll be right there."

She winced as he slammed down the phone. He was stunned. His mind must be racing back in time—reliving the shock of learning that Zoe was pregnant. Remembering all the painful years. *How could I have been so stupid as to tell him?*

Oh, she must cancel Adam's twelve thirty lunch date. Her mind sought for an alibi for this last-minute switch in plans. She fought for poise as she handled this, sighed in relief when the call was over. She could just walk out now, she told herself in one tumultuous moment. No, she couldn't leave Adam hanging that way.

I'll say I'm going to have an abortion. Gerry will set it up for me. No obligations on Adam's

*part. I'll remind him that Liz will be coming
back into the office in weeks. It'll be time for me
to move on.*

She clung to this as she waited for Adam
to arrive. He had his son—that's all he
needed to complete his life. If they married,
he'd come to hate her. For the second time
he was being forced into a marriage.

She started when Bill charged into her
office. "Helen, I don't know how it happened!" he stammered. "This was supposed to
go out yesterday. Linda says it's urgent!"

She ordered herself to listen to him, deal
with his problem. He couldn't know her life
was in chaos.

"Okay, Bill, send the packet FedEx," she
told him. "It'll arrive in time. It's okay," she
soothed again.

She closed her office door, began to pace.
She didn't want to have to face Adam just
yet. She was doing everything wrong. That's
what Paul used to say when he was frus-
trated. Gerry said he used her as a whipping
post.

She stiffened at attention. Adam was in
the reception area—talking with Linda. She
clenched her hands at her side. Her throat
tightened. This wasn't playing out the way
she'd planned. How could she have allowed
herself to tell Adam?

Adam charged into the office, closing the
door behind him.

"Helen—" His voice was calm, but she sensed his inner tension. "Was I hallucinating—or did you tell me you're pregnant?"

"It'll be all right, Adam—" Her words were tumbling over one another. "I'll arrange for an abortion. Gerry will help. And Liz will be coming back in a few weeks. Everything will go back to normal—" *Why is he looking at me that way? With such horror.*

"Helen, you can't do that to me. It's our baby, created with love. Our second chance at life—"

"I thought you'd be upset," she whispered. "I didn't think you'd want the baby. I mean," she stammered, "I remember how Zoe tricked you into marrying her—" But he hadn't said, "We'll be married—"

"How could you think of having an abortion?" he scolded. "This is our baby—" Awe in his eyes now. "I was afraid to rush you— afraid you wouldn't want to marry me now that I'm a package deal—that you wouldn't want to take on Eric and me. I stalled because I was afraid you'd turn me down. But now you can't," he said urgently. "You can't refuse to marry me now—"

"I never planned to have an abortion," she confessed while he drew her into his arms. "I was going to raise the baby—somehow— on my own."

"And deny me my child?" he scolded. "Deny Eric a little sister or brother? We'll be a family, my love."

"You'll be a real father." Her face was luminous. "There for all the important little moments. Zach and Deedee never had that—" She shook her head in disbelief. "I can't believe this is happening. At our age."

"Haven't you read the statistics lately?" he clucked. "We have half our lives ahead of us. Let's use those years well."

"Deedee and Zach won't believe this," she warned. "Gerry and Sheila won't believe it."

"Well, let them know they're to be part of a wedding party. I think," he mused, "that we should be married on the beach at Montauk. I'll put in an order for a bright, beautiful day."

"Even if it rains, it'll be beautiful."

"Remember that poem by—was it Keats? 'Grow old along with me, the best is yet to be—'"

"It was Robert Browning," she said tenderly. "And it's a promise."